U0112288

China's Robots

Wang Hongpeng & Ma Na

图书在版编目（ＣＩＰ）数据

中国机器人：英文 / 王鸿鹏，马娜著；悦享怡然文化译 .
-- 北京：五洲传播出版社，2019.1
（创新中国）
ISBN 978-7-5085-4009-2

Ⅰ . ①中… Ⅱ . ①王… ②马… ③悦… Ⅲ . ①报告文学—中国—当代—英文 Ⅳ . ① I25

中国版本图书馆 CIP 数据核字 (2018) 第 188775 号

© 辽宁人民出版社，2017

作　　者：王鸿鹏　马娜
译　　者：悦享怡然文化
出 版 人：荆孝敏
责任编辑：姜珊
助理编辑：宋歌
装帧设计：北京牧涵文化传媒有限公司

中国机器人（英文）

出版发行：五洲传播出版社
地　　址：北京市海淀区北三环中路 31 号生产力大楼 B 座 6 层
邮　　编：100088
电　　话：010-82005927，82007837
网　　址：www.cicc.org.cn，www.thatsbook.com
印　　刷：北京画中画印刷有限公司
版　　次：2019 年 1 月第 1 版第 1 次印刷
开　　本：710×1000　　1/16
印　　张：23.25
定　　价：128.00 元

Preface

Prelude: Where are China's robots?

In 1920, Karel Čapek, a Czech writer, wrote a sci-fi stage play called *Rossum's Universal Robots*. It tells the story of robot workers or *robota* (meaning forced labour in Czech) produced by the eponymous company in the title. The machines, with a human appearance and physique but without their own mind and thoughts, repeat their arduous manual work, day in, day out. Later, with the help of humans, *robota* start to develop emotions and even independent thinking, while remaining under the control of their human masters. As the story evolves, *robota*, having been oppressed for so long, rebel and seek to destroy all human beings and eventually rule the world.

Thus, Čapek was not only the first person to conceptualize machines that could both help and attack people.

Returning to the play, it is a relief, at least at first, that *robota* cannot reproduce. However, amid the desperation in the closing moments, two *robota* fall in love with the help of a human sympathizer. In turn, they become a machine version of Adam and Eve, who sustain the existence of their fellow beings by creating a "new version of human".

This bizarre stage play was a sensation when it was first staged in Prague in 1920, before going onto capture the imagination of the entire Western world. Why did it have such an impact?

For all the progress made in terms of productivity, the Second Industrial Revolution turned laborers into living machines or slaves serving as machines. Broadcast in China at the end of the 1970s, *Modern Times*, starring Charlie Chaplin, satirized the miserable existence of industrial workers in large factories. In the same vein, Čapek anticipated the use of employing robota to free humans from monotonous jobs, thus striking a chord with industrial workers who aspired to free themselves from the shackles of "industrial slavery" and rebel against mass production. Simply put, robota was a product of its time.

The word *robota* was translated into robot in English and, since its introduction into the language, it has denoted a human-like machine. From the moment that robots were conceived, albeit only in literary form, they have been synonymous with cruelty, violence, uncontrollability and rebellion against human dominance leading to their eventual disruption of the whole world.

Bringing these lawless machines under control did not occur until Isaac Asimov, a Russian American sci-fi writer, well known in the US, established three regulations for these beings.

In his 1941 short story *Reason*, he proposed the "three laws of robotics". First, a robot may not injure a human being or, through inaction, allow a human being to come to any harm. Second, a robot must obey orders given to it by human beings except where such orders would conflict with the first law. Third, a robot must protect its own existence as long as such protection does not conflict with the first or second law.

These three laws, according to Professor Qu Daokui, should also be observed by the US and Japan, which are currently involved in fierce competition in robotics.

Asimov's series of sci-fi novels based on these three laws contributed to his reputation and popularity in the US. Some of his works were even adapted into Hollywood films, which envisioned a future characterized by both conflict and peaceful coexistence between human and robots. Idealistic as they are, the three laws are still regarded as the "cornerstone of modern robotics" and acknowledged in the research and development of robots in the science world. For this reason, Asimov is respectfully known as the "father of robots".

It defied Asimov's expectation that he would witness the imagined kingdom of robots being turned into a reality. But it truly happened.

In 1954, American scientists invented the first programmable robot that could replace humans in carrying out arduous and dangerous tasks. It gained great popularity in the US and marked a new start for the era of robots. Indeed, the robot was one of the greatest inventions of the 20th century.

In that sense, imagination is the prelude to any great human endeavour, while literature is the cradle of scientific breakthroughs.

In fact, humans showed considerable ambition thousands of years ago with their invention of tools. By inventing, we show our desire to reshape our existence, know ourselves better and realize accomplishments beyond our capabilities. That is how robots came into being.

Ancient China witnessed many machines designed with human or animal features by scientists, inventors and craftsmen; these were the "ancestors" of modern robots. According to historical records, almost 3,000 years ago in the Zhou Dynasty, a skilful craftsman called Yanshi created a painted human-shaped machine, which could sing and dance, out of leather, wood and resin. More than 2,500 years ago in the Spring and Autumn Period, Lu Ban, a famous carpenter made a wooden bird that "could fly for multiple days in a row". Over 1,800 years ago, in the Three Kingdoms Period, Zhuge Liang invented a handcart to transport military supplies. Epitomizing the wisdom of Chinese people, these inventions represented the precursors to modern robots.

The 21st century has ushered in a new era for scientific and technological development. Robotics, 3D printing, cloud technologies, brain cognition, quantum computing, big data, nanomaterials and graphene have all witnessed rapid progress, pushing human society ever closer towards comprehensive usage of artificial intelligence (AI) at an increasing pace. Undoubtedly, AI, which involves the deployment of robots, will become an essential platform and offer devices for the smart society of the future. At the same time, AI technology is gradually shaping the way in which we work and live. A new wave of technological revolution is around the corner.

Contents

Contents

Contents

Contents

Chapter I
Robots: Another
Chinese Dream

A Chinese vision: as scientific development gains momentum, a new chapter in our history starts with the fulfilment of a new dream.

I. Laying the foundations with an ambition

In 2000, the name of a new company, set up by the Shenyang Institute of Automation (SIA) of the Chinese Academy of Sciences (CAS), prompted heated discussions among science professionals. Should the name be in Chinese or English? Conventional or trendy? Or a mixture? It was hard to decide.

Two smart people, despite their age gap, turned on the "search engine" in their head and tried to think of a name that suited the vast virtual world, but with no luck. Time was up. They had to come up with something.

The older scientist fixed his gaze on one of the pictures he saw while casting his eyes over the bookshelves behind his office desk.

It was a photo he had taken with some of the world's best scientists who had visited China several years before. Suddenly struck with an idea, he turned to the younger scientist and said, "Hey, why don't we name the company after your professor, Xinsong?"

The elder scientist was Wang Tianran. Born in Hailun, Heilongjiang Province, in 1943, he is now both the director of the SIA and the director of the National Engineering Research Centre on Robotics, as well an academician with the Chinese Academy of Engineering. The younger scientist was Dr Qu Daokui. Born in Qingzhou, Shandong Province, in 1961, he is now both the deputy director of the National Engineering Research Centre on Robotics and the director of the Department of Engineering Research and the Development of Robotics at the SIA. Back in 2000, however, they were building China's first robotics company.

Wang Tianran said, "On the one hand, we should commemorate Jiang Xinsong, the former director of our institute, an expert in automation and a founding exponent of China's robotic cause. On the other, the name also passes on the history of our institute. His pursuit to develop China's robotics should be inherited by later generations as a tribute to this groundbreaker."

"Good. We will lay the foundation of the company with this

pursuit." Qu Daokui agreed.

That is how the company SIASUN Robot & Automation Co., Ltd., got its Chinese name "Xinsong" (新松). Naming a company after a person is less common in China than abroad. Indeed, it may even be the first example of its kind among the state-owned enterprises of China.

"What Mr Jiang Xinsong left us was not only a considerable amount of high-technology assets, but also his mind. Incorporated into the business culture, his legacy has influenced generation after generation at SIASUN. Now everyone remembers Jiang Xinsong because our company is thriving and impressive. I am so happy that we have lived up to Mr Jiang's expectations. If he were here to see this, he would also take pride in our company." As he spoke, Qu Daokui had some tears in his eyes, thinking of his teacher, who passed away three years previously. His mind was then cast back to the past three decades or so.

II. The first student

Brimming with vitality and dreams, the cool early summer of 1983 was heated up by the eagerness of young people.

A group of students from Changchun Institute Geology (now part of Jilin University) was about to complete their college years and thinking about their future.

They were a blessed generation as they had been able to enrol into universities thanks to China's reform and opening-up policy. Therefore, they shouldered the expectations and future responsibilities of this new era characterized by the when they stepped outside the campus and into the society. Excited about their future, the students sat together, sharing their plans and hopes.

One young man, with a square face and bright eyes, was rather silent when asked about what job he would like to be assigned after graduation. Waving a copy of *Overseas Automation*, which he had been given by the college information office in the air, he said with great determination, "I will apply for postgraduate programmes in robotics".

Robotics?! That answer stunned his peers. Robots was still a concept that only existed in the fictional world, if not unheard of. How could there be any postgraduate programmes like that? Aren't you crazy? This passionate young man was Qu Daokui, then a graduate of the Department of Electronic Equipment.

Smiling, Qu Daokui showed an article in the magazine to his friends. He said proudly, "We should pursue the new disciplines and lay our hands on something new. Robotics must be a lot of fun."

When graduation was drawing to a close, the students started to imagine what their future would be like. Back then, employment was taken care of by the country, so everyone had such modest hopes about having a decent and well-paid job. There were only very limited quotas for postgraduate students and very few applicants for the programmes. But Qu Daokui was part of the minority who wanted to further his study.

Thinking of the past, Qu Daokui said, "I never ran out of curiosity as I was always intrigued by new stuff. I spent a lot of time in the library and reading room in search of research directions and subjects. Because of an accidental encounter with an article introducing robots, I decided to apply for a postgraduate programme in robotics."

So, which article and by whom was powerful enough to change the life course of this person? 'An Observation Report of Robots and AI' by Jiang Xinsong.

Qu Daokui was intrigued by robots after reading the article because it was claimed that machines could replace human labour. Although keen on thinking, Qu is not the type of person who wants to get his hands dirty. In that sense, at the time of reading this article, he found robots to be nothing but relevant. Drawn to their magic, he instantly had an interest in these new creations. Luckily, Jiang Xinsong was assigned by the CAS, which had a quota of only one postgraduate place in robotics that year. Qu Daokui took that opportunity and submitted an application.

Robotics thrilled Qu, as it has always has had for almost every boy. Like an X-ray, it can reach you deep inside once the discipline touches you.

With a strong desire to approach and explore the unknown and other mysteries, Qu saw robot research as his dream. The passion was translated into a driving force. Once the goal was set, he became a totally different person as he put in every effort in preparing for the postgraduate school entrance examination. The next two and a half months were devoted to the revision of multiple subjects and the self-teaching of modern control theories. It was truly the most stressful but fulfilling time of Qu's college years.

In July 1983, having been offered a place at the postgraduate school, Qu Daokui finally became Jiang Xinsong's first student in robotics. He could not wait to meet his future tutor in person when he went to pick up the offer from the SIA. To his dismay, Mr Jiang was on a business trip.

Instead, Qu Daokui spent two days in Shenyang in the company of a college friend who lived in Tiexi District, Shenyang. His hometown was distinguished by tall chimneys and closely arranged factories with rumbling machines and splattering water, a huge population and busy traffic. This scene of large-scale industrial production impressed Qu, who, for the first time, personally witnessed the importance and magnificence of this industrial hub in the north-east of China.

Tiexi District in Shenyang was indeed extraordinary at that time. Shenyang itself, an industrial city reliant on equipment manufacturing, represented the cradle for the industrial development of the new China, stretching across Liaoning Province and the rest of the north-eastern industrial base. Qu's student friend could not hide the sense of pride about Tiexi when talking about his hometown.

The impressive scene of production throughout the city inevitably amazed Qu Daokui. He exclaimed, "Goodness! The expanse of factories in such large numbers makes this district equivalent to a city!" His friend was both jealous and confounded by Qu's decision to continue with postgraduate programmes. He asked, "Look, this place is never short of machines and workers. Where is the place for robots?"

Suddenly, one sentence from Jiang Xinsong's article dawned on Qu Daokui. "Robots are humanized and intelligence-enhanced machines." What would this place be like when machines took on human features? Qu was lost in the imagined version of what he was seeing.

"Hey! Snap out of it!" Qu's friend called out to him when his mind seemed to wander. Qu smiled and answered, "You've made your point. It is so tiring to work all day long around machines.

Would it be perfect to replace human laborers with machines? I made the right choice in terms of both the research subject and the location!"

A decade later, in this city, the first industrial robot resembling a human worker was developed and put into use by Qu Daokui and his colleagues.

Qu Daokui still remembers the first time he met Jiang Xinsong in his office when the semester began.

"Why do you want to learn about robotics?" Jiang Xinsong found his smiling student to be spirited and affable. A person's attitude is manifested in his/her appearance.

"I read your article and I loved it."

"Good. Interest is the best teacher. Besides that, you should study hard to be the best student."

His serious look was like a ray of microparticles. Still an unsophisticated young man, Qu Daokui withdrew his smile under his tutor's gaze. Meanwhile, his pride as a young person pushed him to confront authority innately as he did in college. Sitting up straight, Qu responded to his tutor, "Where there is a good teacher, there is a good student. I will work hard, please have faith in me."

There was an undetectable surprise in the tutor's eyes. The

unusual answer from his student amazed him. He appreciated the straightforward young man, who reminded him of his younger self.

Feeling excited, the professor started to teach his first lesson. "Do you know that robotics is not a discipline like any other. It represents the most advanced science and technology in the world. It can lead to a wide application of robots and intelligent industries in the future. Developed countries, including the US, Germany and Japan, are the frontrunners in this field. The country that commands the best technologies in robotics dominates advanced technologies around the whole world. China has been left far behind! We need to start running now to catch up with them. That is where the hope of our country lies."

III. Bringing ideas back to Beijing

Qu Daokui soon became disappointed. He did not expect that there would no teaching materials or laboratory available when he studied robots in the SIA. There were only a few references, most of which had been published one year earlier. Some books and journals have been published two or three years before, thus lagging behind the times. Before long, Qu Daokui had read through all the materials he could find. He felt that what his teachers were teaching was novel, but he was able to quickly digest the knowledge he was given. Qu Daokui's "hunger for new knowledge" grew more and more intense. Jiang Xinsong sensed his student's potential for learning.

In 1984, Jiang Xinsong was hired as a part-time professor

by Tsinghua University. Meanwhile, he has become friends with a professor from the Mathematics and Mechanics Department of Peking University, so Jiang invited Qu Daokui to study at both Peking University and Tsinghua University. Tsinghua University had an open and vibrant academic atmosphere as well as offered many exchange opportunities with universities abroad. Jiang Xinsong often took Qu Daokui to attend domestic and international academic conferences, where they collected substantial materials for further research and were informed about front-end theories, techniques and development trends, as well as tendencies in the robot industry.

Afterwards, Jiang Xinsong was hired as a part-time professor by Shanghai Jiaotong University, the University of Science and Technology of China, Xi'an Jiaotong University and many other universities. He was also the deputy chairman of the Chinese Association of Automation, the Chinese Association of Robots and the Chinese Association for AI, and a member of the expert committee at the International Federation of Automatic Control. With the development of robots in China, Jiang Xinsong often gave lectures and reports all over the country. He also went abroad to carry out investigations and busily promote China's research and development in the robot industry. In addition, he had a temporary residence in the Beijing Friendship Hotel. Upon his return from his trips, Qu Daokui would go there and talk about his learning process and listen to Jiang's lectures.

"He gave lessons unlike ordinary teachers. He never taught you concrete methods, which should be learned by yourself through reading books. He talked more about global development tendencies and the latest development directions. What he talked about was not confined to the robot industry; every field he knew was included. With a husky voice, he taught in a vivid, attractive and fascinating manner." As Qu Daokui recalled, "One thing impressed me the most. When he came back from abroad, he described with gestures and spoke with passion: 'In the future, Chinese robots must be like their counterparts in the USA and the Soviet Union, and fly and dive; they must be like their counterparts in Japan and Germany, and run in the factories.' At that time, listening to his lectures widened my horizons, in an enjoyable way. It all felt fresh, as if the spring breeze was caressing my cheeks. It was like a spiritual deep breath, as well as a nutritional food in the form of academic theory."

Were the lectures of Jiang Xinsong the most charming on earth? Well, Wang Yuechao only had to listen to one report given by Jiang to become deeply obsessed with his personality and his study of robots. After that, Wang registered for the examination to become Jiang's postgraduate student.

"I was a postgraduate at the institute at that time, mainly focused on the study of robot control. Being Professor Jiang's student was my life's ambition." Wang Yuechao always had a lot to say when he recalled that period, which influenced him a great deal...

Wang Yuechao was born in Shenyang in 1960 and graduated with a major in automation from Jinzhou Engineering College in 1982. As a local of Shenyang, he was allocated to the Liaoning Machinery Research Institute. He wanted to be scientist even when he was a student. Wang Yuechao was so obsessed with Jiang's personal charm that he was determined to become his postgraduate student. Luckily, he realized his dream and became fellow apprentices with Qu Daokui.

As Qu returned after finishing his studies in Beijing, Wang went to Beijing to study fundamental theories. Although they did not learn together, they shared the same learning pattern. In most cases, they attended lectures at universities or academic conferences in order to gather new materials for further research. Conference papers were usually highly sought-after. Qu and Wang bought whatever they could afford and borrowed copies of what they could not. Sometimes,

Jiang brought them the latest materials and essays from conferences at home and abroad, which they guarded like treasure.

"Our living and studying conditions were arduous over a period of more than six months in Beijing. There was one sentence popular at that time: 'Poor students go to Tsinghua University. Rich students go to Peking University. The students who are not afraid of arduous work go to the University of Science and Technology of China.' However, we have benefited a lot." Qu Daokui recalled with emotion, "Through systemic study and research, we had a thorough knowledge of the frontier theories in the robot industry on the one hand, while sorting out the development timeline for robot techniques on the other, in turn laying the theoretical foundations for further study. In other words, we did all the preparation work in a down-to-earth manner. Our professor gave us a great deal to think about. He used his own shoulders to support us, so to speak."

One time, Jiang Xinsong came back to Beijing after researching in the US and gave lectures at the Beijing Friendship Hotel, where he was living, introducing new techniques and achievements from overseas in the robot field. After his lectures, discussions began. Qu Daokui put forward one unexpected question: "Professor Jiang, how did you get around to studying robots?"

Jiang Xinsong hesitated for a few seconds, stood up and walked to the window. He looked out onto the Beijing night, preoccupied and solemn. Then, he turned around and told his followers his life experience and why it was closely connected with robots.

IV. This is how one giant grew up

History always leaves deep footprints because of its heavy footsteps.

On 3rd August 1931, Jiang Xinsong was born to an ordinary family in the north of Chengbei County, Jiangyin Municipality, Jiangsu Province. His father, Jiang Zhenting, worked far away from home to earn a living for the family. As a result, the job of raising and educating the children fell on the shoulders of his mother, Lu Suwen. Lu was brought up in a well-educated family, knowledgeable and gentle. She named her eldest son Jiang Xinsong because she hoped he would grow like the "song" (pine tree in English), which was able to weather wind and rain and had grown to become the country's backbone. Everyone's life choice could find some trace in his/her childhood. The first word that Lu Suwen taught Jiang Xinsong was "guo" (country in English), while the second was "jia" (family in English). She told Jiang that "guo" and "jia" were closely intertwined. There was no "jia" without "guo".

The two words, "guo jia", were deeply imprinted on Jiang's mind when he was a child.

Meanwhile, in 1937, the War of Resistance Against Japan broke out. Both the country and every family suffered. Jiang Xinsong and his family had to take refuge in Yangzhou County. Jiang's childhood was spent in a period of war and turmoil. In the spring of 1938, Jiang's family returned to Jiangyin from Yangzhou. The first thing that Lu Suwen did upon returning home was to arrange for her children to go back to school as soon as possible. Jiang Xinsong was talented and hardworking, always coming top in his class. He graduated from primary school at 10 years of age because he continuously skipped grades. One day, Jiang Xingsong came to the banks of the Yangtze River, watching the surging water and flying seagulls and realizing that his own life goal had also spread its wings to fly high in the sky. He could not help taking the slightly enlarged graduation photo from his schoolbag and writing one sentence on the back, in a high-spirited fashion: "One giant is growing up."

In 1942, Jiang Xinsong realized his dream and entered the best middle school in the local area, Nan Jing Middle School. He was keen on mathematics, physics, chemistry and literature, especially domestic and foreign scientists' autobiographies. As he once wrote, "My ambition is to become a scientist or inventor like Isaac Newton, Thomas Edison, Nicolaus Copernicus and Albert Einstein when I grow up, becoming the nation's backbone."

This was Jiang's ambition when he was a child, realizing his dream of becoming a "giant".

However, Jiangyin's economy was in depression before the foundation of the People's Republic of China (PRC), with people living in dire poverty. Jiang Xinsong, at the age of 15, who had not finished classes in first year of senior high school, had to give up studying and start working to earn a crust for his family because of economic hardship.

In 1949, when the PRC was founded, Jiang went back to Nan Jing Middle School with his mother's support and graduated with excellent grades. In 1951, he was admitted to the Department of Electrical Engineering at Shanghai Jiaotong University, a prestigious university. It was at this moment that Jiang left his home and embarked on the journey of becoming a "giant"...

In 1952, Jiang Xinsong finished his freshman year. The university made an exception and recommended him to sit the unified examination in East China that prepared students for studying in the Soviet Union. Jiang Xinsong's name was on the list of successful candidates. His excellence derived from his hard work and talents. A beautiful and bright prospect was unfolding in front of him. He could not restrain the excitement in his heart and immediately wrote to his mother to tell her the good news.

His mother replied: "Xinsong, you have not let me down. The whole family is happy because of your achievements. The construction of the newly founded PRC requires a large amount of talents. Cherish the opportunity and do not be proud. Learn the knowledge well and make a contribution to our nation. You still have a long way to go. Whatever conditions you encounter, persevere and never give up. As long as you persist, you can succeed."

Unexpectedly, when he advanced smoothly along the path to success, destiny gave him a fatal blow without mercy. When Jiang Xinsong arrived at the Beijing Preparatory Department with delight and completed the short Russian training course, preparing him for study in the Soviet Union, he was diagnosed with tuberculosis during the physical examination! This sudden strike made him dispirited. He felt dazed and had to go back to university with disappointment.

At this time, his mother came to him, offering him comfort and encouragement with tenderness as warm as sunshine. With his mother's concern and care, Jiang Xinsong restored his health on the one hand and devoted himself to studying on the other. When he worked as an intern at Jinan Machine Tool Works, his graduation design, "Multi-tool Automatic Lathe Machine-driven System", was recognized for its excellence. He received the graduation certificate for his automation major in industrial enterprise and gradually recovered physically. Jiang Xinsong made the decision to realize his ambition of becoming a scientist. The boat of dreams set sail once again.

In the summer of 1956, Jiang Xinsong graduated from the Department of Electrical Engineering at Shanghai Jiaotong University. As he had wished, he was allocated to the Automatic Control and Remote Control Institute of the CAS and went to work in Beijing. Although the dream of studying in the Soviet Union was shattered, the major he would work on was what he had always desired. Jiang Xinsong was assigned to the team led by scientist Tu Shancheng and focused on studying digital computer storage. The new work greatly engrossed Jiang Xinsong who embarked on the road to fight for his dream.

Tu Shancheng was a famous expert in automatic control in China and one of the founders of the Chinese Association of Automation. He was born in Jiaxing, Zhejiang, in 1923. In February 1948, he went to the USA to study. After receiving his doctoral degree from Cornell University five years later, he stayed in the USA to teach. In 1956, with the belief that science could contribute to the nation, he came back to his motherland to participate in the construction of socialism and become a pioneer of Chinese artificial satellite projects. He made a huge contribution to space technology, satellite control systems and related aspects. Tu Shancheng's patriotism, strict discipline and dedication to science had exerted a subtle influence on Jiang Xinsong. Later, he recalled that, "Since I entered the door of the CAS, I combined my destiny with the nation's cause for the first time. Since then, working for the nation became my lifelong pursuit."

Jiang Xinsong's talents, hard work and studiousness soon made Tu Shancheng think highly of him. His outstanding work won not only Tu Shancheng's appreciation, but also his colleagues' respect. On the research team led by Tu Shancheng, Jian Xinsong stood out. Furthermore, he was part of a group known as the "Four Gifted

Youth", together with three other young people in the institute.

In October 1963, Jiang Xinsong was sent to Ansteel to conduct research on the automation of cold-rolled sheet. Thanks to the accumulation solid theory and rich practical experience, he soon came up with an international standard thesis in the automation field and recommended to participate in the first annual conference of the Chinese Association of Automation, winning the appreciation of Yang Jiachi, deputy director of the Institute of Automation and recognized nuclear bomb, missile and satellite scientist afterwards, who had just come back from the USA.

In 1965, on the recommendation of Yang Jiachi, Jiang Xinsong was invited to attend the General Conference of Weights and Measures, held in Sweden. Although Jiang Xinsong was not present because of exceptional cases, his thesis was well received at the conference.

V. Becoming attached to robots

Jiang Xinsong was not able to fly to Sweden and attend the international annual conference in person. However, his colleagues who did attend brought him back conference materials, which made Jiang Xinsong feel like he had been given treasure. He looked through these materials carefully and soon had a brilliant idea as if he had been struck by lightning. The virtual encounter between robots and this Chinese scientist happened accidentally!

Jiang Xinsong came across materials that introduced robot research taking place overseas, which included theoretical literature reviews, academic theses and other information, which greatly piqued his interest.

Ever since, Jiang Xinsong has been attached to robots, which have become his lifelong love.

In 1965, Jiang Xinsong was transferred from Beijing to the Liaoning Academy Automation Institute of the CAS. Being able to embrace the cause he loved, Jiang Xinsong came to the Chinese capital from Shenyang with delight. His excellent capacity for scientific research manifested at work made him the most outstanding figure in the institute.

In 1967, there was a cold-rolled sheet machine at Ansteel that could not brake accurately, so the employees turned to the Liaoning Academy Automation Institute for help. The academy formed a team to tackle the problem. Jiang Xinsong went to Ansteel as group leader of the research team and succeeded in solving the problem at the first attempt. Later, his work won the Major Scientific and Technological Achievements Award of the CAS, as well as the Major Achievement Award of the China Science Conference in 1978.

Soon, he found that, in some domestic scientific and technological information journals, robot was translated as "ji qi ren" ("machine man").

While some people talked about robots as they belonged in *The Arabian Nights*, Jiang Xinsong was busy studying robots, realizing, with the acute judgement of a scientist, their value and meaning in the future based on information from overseas and that China should get down to work!

With an acute eye and scientific wisdom, this scientist recognized that robots were ringing China's doorbell.

On 15th August 1972, Liaoning Academy Automation Institute of the CAS changed its name to SIA of the CAS. On becoming officially established, the institute had made their research field in automation explicit. In the same year, Wu Jixian, Jiang Xinsong and Tan Dalong jointly drafted a report for the CAS entitled *On AI and Robots*. This was the first time that Chinese scientists had put forward suggestions concerning robots and the first time that the idea of "robots" was published in an official Chinese document.

The report said that developing robots was in tune with the trend whereby the equipment manufacturing industry would realize total automation in the future, as well as an important symbol indicating that a country had a robust industrial capacity. As the US, Japan and some European countries had already entered the phase of industrial application, it was critical for China to take steps in this direction as early as possible. However, at that time, few people in China knew what a robot was, so the conditions were not right to conduct relevant work in this field.

Jiang Xinsong did not change his initial intention and persisted in researching in silence, never giving up. In 1977, as the representative of the SIA, Jiang Xinsong went to Beijing to draft a development plan for automation and prepared to organize and attend the National Natural Science Plan Conference, which would be held in 1978. As one of the major authors, Jiang Xinsong drew up the *Draft China Automation Development Plan* for the Beijing Institute of Automation and the SIA. He put forward the idea of developing robots once again.

Before the conference, he put up posters, hosted lectures and promoted the extensive application and value of robots. He went hither and thither and spared no effort in claiming that, "Robots will become the representative high technology when we enter the 21st century. If we lose scientific and technological advantage in one field, we may lose it for all time."

Although some people had their doubts, most scientists were in favour of Jiang's proposal. In particular, Tu Shancheng, Yang Jiachi, Wang Daheng and Song Jian, top experts in automation, showed their support without equivocation.

Thanks to Jiang Xinsong's efforts, the project of developing robots was officially listed in the *1978-1985 Automation Science*

Development Plan. Robots had been given the go-ahead in China. Moreover, Jiang Xinsong was appointed as the director of the Robot Department in the SIA.

The burden of robot development in China fell on the shoulders of the SIA as well as those of Jiang Xinsong. Although a robot was listed in the plan, nobody had seen what a robot looked like, let alone where to start. Everyone's mind drew a blank.

Apparently, there were no conditions in which Jiang Xinsong and his colleagues could pick up the subject of developing robots in the institute. He was destined to shoulder the responsibility and conquer this lone road amid boundless desert. This was a lonely, arduous and unknown task.

The development of Chinese robots saw a historic transition when the PRC began its reform and opening-up policy in 1978. Chinese intellectuals welcomed their spring! Modernization construction called for all scientific and technological personnel to try their best.

The CAS broke the rules and made a rapid adjustment to the leading group in the SIA, which made people feel that China was eagerly demanding a new era that would revitalize science.

On 10th January 1980, Jiang Xinsong was appointed the deputy director of the SIA by the CAS. In July, Jiang Xinsong was appointed the new director of the CAS (it should be noted that there had been no director in the SIA since its foundation more than 20 years ago). Jiang Xinsong clearly recognized that what he shouldered was not only responsibility as director, but also the responsibility and future of a nation.

VI. When Deng Xiaoping met "her"

In October 1978, Deng Xiaoping paid a visit to Japan as the Chinese leader, which represented the prelude to the reform and opening-up policy and the hallmark event indicating that China was entering a new era. This visit, for Deng, was part of his learning experience concerning the great strategy behind China's modernization process.

On the afternoon of 24th October, Deng paid a visit to the Nissan factory in Kanagawa. The robot assembly line had just been introduced into this factory, thus undoubtedly making it the automobile production factory with the highest degree of automation in the world.

During the visit, Deng stopped in front of a strange-shaped

machine to watch its automatic welding operation. The reason why "she" was strange was that this welding machine was like a clever and deft embroidery girl, wielding her nimble arm to combine operations. Furthermore, in the blink of an eye, she could assemble the frame of a vehicle in the right order. The accompanying staff told Deng that this was a robot. Deng smiled, "A robot?" Obviously, this sparked an interest in Deng.

Finally, a great Chinese statesman met a robot.

When Deng Xiaoping became aware that the staff in this factory could produce 94 vehicles per person each year, he said with deep feeling, "Oh, your robot is remarkable. The annual production per person of your factory is far more than that of the First Automobile Workshop in Changchun, by a margin of 93 vehicles."

What did this mean? That 94 vehicles could be produced each year by every employee in the Nissan factory, while only one could be produced each year by employees in China's most advanced factory at that time. That was 93 times more than ours! Compared to them, what else could we do apart from wiping away tears? They had no tears to wipe anyway. This is the magic of robots!

Deng expressed the situation with great wisdom and humour. Rather than simply state "94 times the production of the First

Automobile Workshop in Changchun", he referred to "a margin of 93 vehicles". The accompanying staff exhibited an understanding smile. Faced with a scene of an efficient operational robot assembly line, Deng said, "I know what modernization is from this Japanese visit".

Jiang Xinsong was full of excitement after reading this report. "I was thinking, at that time, that we can only step into prosperity if we squarely confront the deficiencies", Jiang said with great passion. Indeed, he was very fond of emphasizing his own country when talking: "We need to invent Chinese robots and Chinese unmanned factories. Let Chinese-made equipment gain an international reputation and step onto the world stage!"

It is easy to say something along those lines, but not that easy to fulfil. Robot technology was the world's cutting-edge technology. Without the technological capacity or the professionals, and with the blockade on technology imports to China imposed by foreign countries, how could they country develop in this field? Without practical measures, all that China could do was to make some attempts on its own with boldness.

Jiang once said that there was a special moment during Deng's Japanese visit that impressed him greatly.

During the Chinese leader's visit to Panasonic Co., Ltd., he was invited to visit the exhibition room where he was shown the company's latest products such as the microwave oven. The guide invited Deng to watch him heat some shumai dumplings in the microwave oven. Deng picked up one of them, looked at it and then promptly put it in his mouth, saying "yummy" while chewing it.

This moment exceeded the expectations of the Panasonic staff. It was never planned for Deng to eat that shumai. Everyone gasped with admiration at Deng's courageous spirit to try something new.

"Look at him. He not only points the way but sets an example." Jiang expressed his feelings without reservation. He talked to his students, "We can accept that, at the beginning of the reform and opening-up phase, Deng put forward the idea of 'trying boldly and adventuring boldly'. This specific point just gives us a mental inspiration, which, in the scientific field, means that we have to try and seek out adventure. Learn from Deng by eating shumai and making Chinese robots. The path only appears when people walk along it. If you want to ask me how I study robots, the answer is I just get on with it, try it and break it."

That night was a sleepless one for Qu Daokui. He was deeply impressed by his teacher's story and his exhortation. He thought that the title "first" was not as fun as he had thought.

After undergoing plenty of ups and downs, Jiang Xinsong was the first scientist engaged in robotics. He was also the first postgraduate major in robots in China, so what kind of future was waiting for him?

The field of robotics is related to China's modernization. Qu, as one of the first cohorts of postgraduate majors in robotics in China, shouldered the mission of realizing China's modernization in the 21st century. Since then, Qu has reached a self-subversion through the distillation of his study and research, evolving from a kind of hobby and interest to a sort of responsibility, which is characterized by the revitalization of the country and the prosperity of the nation. In turn, he strengthened his idea of "industry serving the country" after he established SIASUN Robot & Automatic Co., Ltd.

History will leave a magnificence behind "her" light-footed dancing.

In the autumn of 1985, Beijing held the China-Europe Academic Conference on Robotics at the invitation of the Chinese scientific community. During the conference, the nations in attendance selected several distinguished papers to be exchange through discussion. Qu Daokui, as the only Chinese student representative, was recommended to present his own paper at this high-level international forum.

Qu bought a suit on Wangfujing Street especially for that day.

He caught everyone's attention due to his youthful elegant manner. He talked about his paper, 'A New Way for Robot Self-adaption Control', in flowing English. Though his pronunciation was not that accurate, he was still in high spirits and spoke with fervour and assurance, just like a real scholar. His paper proposed a new theoretical research direction in the robot field. It was creative and cutting-edge, showing the world that China possessed great research potentiality and a promising future in this area, thus gaining the applause from the participating experts.

When G. Geralt, the director of CNRS in France, discovered that Qu was a student of Jiang Xinsong, he walked directly towards Jiang to shake his hands in a congratulatory manner. Geralt was also a member of PCF, which meant he was a friend of China as well as the Chinese people. Jiang had actually met him at an academic conference on robotics in Europe several years before and become great friends. During the conference, Jiang and Geralt effortlessly reached an agreement to exchange communications on robotics between China and France, resulting in the signing of a memorandum of understanding. Geralt also invited Qu to study in France.

Every time Qu recalled this memory, he could not hide his happiness. "I am very lucky to have met such a great mentor in my life. If I had met a mentor who was engaged primarily in theory, the future would have been very different. Jiang is very learned, with both a high theoretical proficiency and a strong practical ability. He combines these two together perfectly; and hardly anyone could have reached his heights. In addition, he has the strategic insight of 'visions beyond the vision range'. His international insight and vision has already exceeded the scope of ordinary scientists. He is just like a strategist. In the field of automation and robotics of China, nobody can compete with him."

In August 1986, in order to training talents in robotics, the Expert Committee of the Chinese Association of Automation held the First National Young Researchers Symposium on Robotics in Dalian City under the promotion and advocacy of Jiang. Qu, as a new prominent scholar, gave a presentation of his new paper 'Robot Control'. This paper, of high academic vale, pointed directly at the cutting-edge theory of robotics, as well as being one of the most representative papers in the robot application field, confirming that China's research into robotics has made an encouraging step.

Qu smiled after he recollected those energetic and vigorous years. "Actually, for me, it's nothing to step onto that stage. Making Chinese robots step onto the world stage has always been my dream."

Chapter II
We Have the "First Person"

Science without borders: when politicians open the door, scientists' spirits become the superpower that transcends time and space.

I. Transatlantic handshake

On 23rd November 2015, that year's World Robot Conference was ceremoniously held at the National Convention Centre, Beijing.

As the sun set on the Chinese capitals, lights shone spectacularly on the "Night of Innovation" event, during which 200 robot experts and scholars from all over the globe gathered for the signing ceremony for the Beijing Consensus on Robot Innovation and Cooperation.

Xu Xiaolan, member of the National Committee of the CPPCC and secretary general of both this conference and the Chinese Institute of Electronics, invited Professor Xi Ning from Michigan State University as to host the "Night of Innovation" together.

Qu Daokui told his friends, "Professor Xi has given unexpected help to the SIASUN company."

How did a college professor from the US give help to this Company?

Xi Ning was among the first Chinese college students when the college entrance examination was restored in 1977. His father was not only the chief designer of the Fourth Design Institute of the Ministry of the Aviation Industry, but also one of the founders of the ministry. Back then, Xi Ning had graduated from Beijing No. 11 Middle School, with extraordinary grades in the college entrance exams. His father expected Xi to take his career forward and advised him to apply to the Beijing Institute of Aeronautics (now known as Beihang University), majoring in automatic control. In 1987, Xi went to study abroad in the US where he is now a professor at Michigan State University.

Amid warm applause, Xi assisted an old man to the stage.

Academician Wang Tianran announced to the friends that, "He is a good friend of Jiang Xinsong and has also given unexpectedly major help to the SIA". One old friend had brought another old friend. What exactly is the story between them and China's robots? How did robots come to China?

History is not legend.

In the spring of 1979, a group of special guests from the US arrived in China, including renowned professors from several prestigious universities and authorities in their respective areas of expertise. One after another came to China to lecture, as well as complete an unusual mission, selecting college students to study in the US.

Since the mutual recognition and establishment of diplomatic relations between China and the US on 1st January 1979, the two countries' governments had signed, in person, the Agreement on Cooperation in Science and Technology and a Cultural Agreement (the Agreement for short). It was stated in the Agreement that China would select 50 college students for technological and academic exchanges in the science and technology field to study natural science, medicine and engineering in the US.

Such was the mission of these American guests' visit to China in the spring of 1979. Among the most highly anticipated of the first scientists who visited China was a Chinese American scientist, namely, Professor Tan Zizhong from Washington University in St. Louis (WUSTL).

Due to his unusual identity and academic status in the

automation area, Professor Tan seemed to trigger wider interest among the Chinese science community. He was invited to present a special report, entitled *Automation and Future Robots* to the Institute of Automation in the CAS.

Jiang Xinsong accompanied Professor Tan to this event as an expert in the automation field. Pursuing the same scientific goal allowed them to communicate effectively. At their first meeting, they were like old friends reunited after years of separation, with endless subjects of conversation and no distance between them. The ideals and feelings of the two scientists came together as one.

During Deng Xiaoping's visit to the US, Professor Tan was also invited to attend the signing ceremony of the Agreement. From the exchanges between experts in the technology area, Deng Xiaoping came to realize that Tan was Chinese American. He held Tan's hand and said, "You represent youth and strength in the American technology field. What about teaching some students for China?" Tan replied in a Sichuan dialect, "Of course I will contribute to my home country, that's without question". Deng Xiaoping smiled, with the rapport between them becoming more intimate, leading to the forging of a personal friendship.

In order to select Chinese students for studying abroad, Tan, after a long separation, returned to his motherland for the first time in 30 years. He first went to his hometown of Chongqing, as his father asked, to pay respects to his ancestors, then immediately arrived in Beijing to fulfil his commitment.

From the CAS, Tsinghua University and the University of Science and Technology Beijing, after careful consideration, he selected five distinguished students to study at WUSTL with full scholarships. This professor, who had lived overseas for many years while retaining an intense attachment to his motherland, was about to cultivate future robot experts for China.

II. Robot "friendly corridor"

Tan Zizhong is a famous tenured professor at WUSTL, dedicated to research on system science and control theory. He has made major accomplishments at a global level in intelligent control and international robot research and served as the president of the IEEE Robotics and Automation Society (IEEE RAS), from 1992-1993. He once received the Auto Soft Lifetime Achievement Award, the Pioneer in Robotics and Automation Award and the George Saridis Leadership Award from the IEEE RAS, together with other honours such as the John R. Ragazzini Award from the American Automatic Control Council. He has been repeatedly listed in any who's who of contemporary American science and technology and any who's who in the international engineering field. He was once the "star" from the scientific field according to the American mainstream media. As an influential scientist, he has been invited to teach at Tsinghua University and many other universities in China and received the Einstein Chair Professorship Award from the CAS.

Tan Zizhong was born in 1937 in what is now known as now Chongqing (Zhong County, Sichuan Province), where his father was an official in the salt industry at that time. He and his parents led an itinerant life through war and chaos, with his childhood filled with turmoil. According to his memory, in order to avoid bombardment from Japanese aircraft, his family was constantly on the move. Indeed, he had to transfer to six different elementary schools.

In 1946, his father was relocated to Taiwan and his entire family moved to Taipei. After graduating in 1959 from the National Cheng Kung University in Tainan, Tan was admitted to WUSTL, majoring in automation. He then remained in the US to teach at the school and engage in robot research. During his father's lifetime, Tan was told to never forget about his hometown in Sichuan and to support it when the time was right.

"Mr Jiang and I first met in China and became good friends at a conference in Japan. China was not as rich at that time and neither of them was familiar with the foreign environment, nor good at social communication. Therefore, I made connections to widen their opportunities. It was hard for them to entertain other people, while I enjoyed better conditions while living in the States. So, I organized meals, inviting some American experts over to get to know them and communicate. By having meals together, acquaintances, friendships and connections were made. At that time, I became familiar with everyone at international conferences. In order to improve the impact and international status of China's technological development achievements, I pushed Jiang's scientific achievements and papers towards the prize-awarding platform in the US, receiving the Leadership and Excellence in the Application and Development of Integrated Manufacturing Award from the Society of Manufacturing Engineers. After that, the world could never look down upon China's abilities in technological developments."

Professor Tan exhaled a long breath, saying, "Everyone was making an effort. China's abilities in technological developments were not strong enough. I also contributed by encouraging other people to vote. It was difficult to force other people to raise their hands. I was able to have a certain influence because of my familiarity with them and my adequate theoretical work in this field, the contribution I'd made and the authority I'd gained; otherwise, no one would have been convinced by my words, especially at academic conferences. I tried my best to establish connections, push forward China's achievements in this field and raise China's status and impact in the world. China was not to be looked down upon.

"Mr Jiang and I were both engaged in automation and robotics and we were good friends. It was natural to help him. Later, I invited him to be a visiting scholar at my university, engaging in technological and academic exchanges. I knew he really needed this."

Science without borders is an article of faith shared by all scientists around the world. In 1980s, Jiang and Tan grew increasingly intimate as a result of their frequent communications and academic exchanges. Thanks to their two-way communication and mutual assistance in technology, they manged to open up a robot "friendly corridor".

However, Jiang and Tan were not the only ones building this "friendly corridor". Rather, two politicians, Deng Xiaoping and Jimmy Carter, played the pivotal role. Seeing that the US was enjoying a potential profit stimulus from technological cooperation, President Carter finally decided to launch cultural and technological cooperation along with the establishment of China-US diplomatic relations.

In 1979, Carter and Deng signed the first agreement on cooperation in science, technology and culture between China and the US, opening a crack in the long-closed door between the two countries. Scientists' ideals and feelings were then transformed into the superpower that would transcend time and space. Technological cooperation brought enormous commercial profit to the US, while, at the same time, bringing in globally advanced science and technology, which increased the pace of China's opening-up progress and political developments between China and the US.

It took these two leaders' handshake in the US for the transatlantic handshake between the two aforementioned scientists to happen in China. Therefore, this invisible "friendly corridor" was built in the framework of legitimizing China-US cooperation in science, technology and culture. Chinese robots should salute them!

III. The birth

This is a story of how China's robot industry started from zero.

At an international seminar on AI in the late 1970s, some Japanese experts showed off their underwater vehicle, which could dive over 1,000 m below the sea surface and their unfinished remotely operated vehicle (ROV), "Kaiko", which would eventually dive deep into the Mariana Trench located over 10,000 m below the sea surface.

This worried Jiang Xinsong, because it meant that Japan had taken the lead in oceanic exploration while China had completely no say in this field.

Jiang was unsettled. China must do something in this field.

Thus, he started to study the underwater vehicle, hoping to make breakthroughs. Soon he brought up with the idea of developing "robots that are used in hazardous areas" to work in place of men under extreme environments, where there was high temperature or high pressure, in the deep sea or under toxic conditions.

Then news came that the South China Sea contained abundant oil and gas resources, which had immense development value and great prospect. That the South China Sea was safe meant a lot strategically to China's national defence.

Underwater vehicles are special robots, which are used for underwater detection, exploitation and missions. Despite their smaller application field and market demand, compared to industrial robots, they are important to China, a country with an oceanic territory of over 3 million km2, equal to one third of land coverage. Furthermore, there are some international disputes over some of the oceanic territory.

China was in the swirl of a fierce oceanic boundary dispute.

Jiang Xinsong had long-term strategic views and scientific acuity. Inspired by the discovery of rich resources in the South China Sea, he realized that he should perhaps start with underwater vehicles, which would support offshore oil exploitation and finally protect China's oceanic sovereignty.

In 1979, Jiang proposed that "the application of smart robots in oceanic development" should become a national key project, with developing underwater vehicles being the first objective. In 1980, Jiang was appointed as director of the SIA and chief designer of the aforementioned smart robots project.

After several visits to the South China Sea, Jiang found that it was difficult to see clearly when diving 20 m below the sea surface in order to rescue people or exploit offshore oil. Seawater over 50 m below the surface is in perpetual darkness. When workers work below the sea surface, they can only fumble about in the darkness and even face potential body damage caused by high water pressure. Besides, the cost of underwater missions is high in the sense that being able to breathe underwater for only a single minute is equivalent to the cost of 1 g of gold. As such, a large country like China must find ways to utilize underwater vehicles in developing oceanic resources and protecting national oceanic security.

Jiang analysed where other countries and China stood in terms of robotic development and came up with an overall plan. He led a team of 10 researchers to visit over 20 institutes nationwide, conducting feasibility investigations into underwater robots. This was his first step forward in creating underwater robots. When underwater vehicles were still in the pipeline, industrial robots had already been "born" in China.

In May 1981, Jiang received an invitation from Professor Tan Zizhong to visit WUSTL.

Soon after, Jiang arrived at Professor Tan's laboratory where he saw an industrial robot being trialled. While the robot did not seem intricate, it had the best controlling system he had seen, in which core technologies were applied, representing the world class in high technologies.

Professor Tan also accompanied him to see some of the advanced research institutes involved in electronic instruments and electronic technologies in St. Louis. These included the Emerson Co., one of the best global electronic enterprises offering advanced technologies in integrated manufacturing, as well as the McDonnell-Douglas Corporation, America's largest airplane production company, whose headquarters were in St. Louis, which had produced the world's first lunar spacecraft, "Apollo". From the mid-20th century onwards, St. Louis became the second largest American centre for automobile manufacturing after Detroit. It was a pioneer both in space robots and industrial robots.

Professor Tan introduced advanced robot technology to Jiang in detail. Jiang was truly inspired. After this visit, he realized how important and valuable it was to apply robots to future manufacturing, which would be the trend for any modern industry. He also clearly saw that China's manufacturing lagged far behind that of developed countries. Shenyang, though proudly recognized as China's flagship heavy-industrial centre, was in fact much more backward compared with many cities in other countries. Jiang felt he had to do something right away.

After returning home, Jiang talked about his experiences and reflections made during his visit to the US to his colleagues in the institute. He said "we must work hard and catch up. Otherwise, we will soon be disqualified as a game player in the arena." It didn't take long before Jiang drafted a plan to develop industrial robots and led his researcher team to work on it.

He always stayed up all night to build models and adjust the algorithms. After months of hard work, he and his team solved one technical problem after another and finally made key breakthroughs in core technologies applied in the controlling system.

In 1982, the SIA produced China's first industrial robot, a teaching-playback robot with a computerized system offering point-to-point control and speed and trajectory control. This robot was approved by the national authorities and won second prize in the Science and Technology Awards of the CAS.

By then, the robot was no longer a foreign innovation. China had one as well.

In fact, while the robot can perhaps nowadays be compared to a human, back then, it wasn't even at the "embryonic" stage, in the sense that it could only grasp things with instructions given by precoded programs in the teaching-playback box, thus possessing no "intelligence". It was still China's first industrial robot though.

That said, it was quite an achievement at that time for China to only spend slightly over a year to accomplish something that had taken other countries over a decade to create. It was impossible for international scientists to ignore China's scientific presence.

But Jiang was not satisfied with that. He had the ambition to nurture this "embryo" into a "baby" and then into a "man". His robots had to be applied beyond laboratories in the unmanned factory as commercial products in equipment manufacturing, so that they could support China's economic growth, locate China among the top economies and realize the true value of science.

Jiang declared with confidence, "20 years later, we will usher in the era of robots for China".

People looked forward to China's own robots. Meanwhile, underwater vehicles were being developed along with industrial robots. The success of teaching-playback robots represented a great breakthrough in the controlling system of robots, while also upgrading the status of the SIA in science circles and in turn increasing researchers' confidence. Jiang encouraged his team to carry on working without letting up. In 1983, the underwater vehicle was designated as a key research project of the CAS and named "HR 01". For Jiang, however, this was just the beginning of a long journey. An underwater robot involved certain interdisciplinary high technologies, meaning that researchers might face many technological difficulties that had been rarely seen before.

In December 1985, the first sample "HR 01" vehicle was successfully piloted in Dalian, Liaoning Province, diving as deep as 199 m below the sea surface to snare its target. It could therefore rival the same type of product anywhere in the world in terms of technical indexes.

Choosing to build robots that could work under extreme environments was an unprecedented milestone for China's robot research and application field. But the country still lagged behind developed countries such as the US, Japan and the Soviet Union, all of which already had underwater vehicles that could dive thousands of metres.

China had no other choice but to catch up.

Chapter III
The Combat Arena
for Smart Machines

Follow the trend of technology: technological competition worldwide is not only about technology, but also about wisdom and spirit.

In the "war" of technology, Chinese scientists have fought an arduous "battle".

I. The era of "863"

In early 1985, Jiang Xinsong visited WUSTL again and encountered the "flexible manufacturing system" or "agile manufacturing" concept, which was e popular abroad. With Professor Tan's introduction, Jiang went to see some of the manufacturing factories in St. Louis and observed something utterly surprising. There, the production and manufacturing process was automatically managed by computers, while the entire management and production process was integrated by a computing networking and robots were applied on some of the production lines. Those factories were nothing less than unmanned! Jiang felt that the progress made in one day in the States would take China years to catch up with.

Chinese people might have been satisfied with using motors to drive machines. But, compared to developed countries, China was still "primitive": while those developed countries were already in the Industry 3.0 phase, China was not even entering the 2.0 phase. Only by comparison would China realize the huge gap between itself and developed countries. Knowing this, Jiang felt quite depressed. How could China be a rival with other countries at this rate? China didn't even know what it should work on.

After he returned, Jiang reported immediately on what he had seen, heard and thought in the US to Song Jian, the new director of the State Scientific and Technological Commission. He also proposed the idea of a computer-integrated manufacturing system (CIMS) and suggested using it as the guideline for machine manufacturing.

Song Jian liked his idea and told him that Yang Jiachi, Chen Fangyun and several other senior scientists were also anxious about China's high-tech development and proposed that the country should invest heavily in capitals and talents and catch up with globally advanced technological progress. They thought about writing a proper report to the Communist Party of China (CPC) Central Committee about this, suggesting that China should catch up with technology development worldwide and become an integral part of the global technological network.

Science knows no boundaries. This notion has always received unanimous consensus among scientists. But, in the real world, a scientist's career often falls under political influence. The technological field will be an invisible battlefield once science becomes a weapon in international competition, with China, a developing world, being at a disadvantage. How would China break through all the discrimination and blockades and become not only part of the global technological network and but also a leader?

There was only one option, for Chinese scientists to fight against this predicament before finally seizing the vantage point in technology.

Therefore, four respectable scientists, Wang Daheng, Wang Ganchang, Yang Jiachi and Chen Fangyun, wrote a joint letter in March 1986 to the central authorities suggesting that China should track the world's most advanced technology and create the country's own high technology sector, so as to build a technical foundation for its economic development in the near future. This letter drew the attention of the CPC Central Committee and the State Council, which soon made the decision to draw up a plan for China's high technology development. The leading party group in the State

Scientific and Technological Commission immediately initiated this project and named it the 863 Programme after the date when the letter was written.

Jiang was very excited to learn about the plan. Under his leadership, his research team made ample preparation in terms of theories and technologies in order to include CIMS in the 863 plan.

Developing a CIMS was Jiang's solutions to upgrade the old north-eastern industrial bases. Applying information technology in traditional manufacturing was a new trend in the global automation circle.

Back then, computers were rarely applied, which meant that applying them in industrial circles was truly advanced. The CIMS concept was exactly what Industry 4.0 grew out of. It was the primary combination of informatization and industrialization. Now that the principles of the 863 Programme had been written up, even though the level of investment was not enough, projects needed to be strictly tested before being chosen to be on the final project list.

Jiang was recommended as the expert convener of the automation testing group when experts were discussing the details of the plan. His CIMS proposal won the approval of various experts and was chosen as the first shortlisted project in the automation field.

When the State Development Planning Commission was drafting the Seventh Five-year Plan, Jiang persuaded the CAS to allow the SIA to establish a robot demonstration project laboratory, which would provide the necessary equipment and environment for research.

In July 1986, the foundation stone ceremony for the laboratory was held at a new site chosen by the SIA, namely, 114 Nanta Street, Shenyang. Song Jian was there for the ceremony.

Robots were all that Jiang thought about. He had this creative idea to put a cartoon robot model in the middle of the gate of the new laboratory. That robot had a round prism in the middle as its body and two big circles above as its eyes. Its arms were stretched apart and its forearms were at its side, separating one doorway into two, which would allow people to enter and exit at the same time. The robot model was all in white, fashionably designed and eye-catching.

Song Jian enthused: "This is such a creative idea. Seeing this model, people will know that we are researching robots here."

"In early August, Wang Daheng, director of the Technological Sciences Department in the CAS, was here with officials from the People's Liberation Army General Staff Headquarters. They went to see the ocean robots that were successfully piloted in Dalian. When he saw the gate with a robot model designed by Jiang Xinsong, Wang Daheng showed his praise by saying, 'Well done! Scientists are really professionals, even at designing.' Today, that robot has become a household name. Shenyang people all know that that robot stands in front of the gate of the lab at 114 Nanta Street. It has become a historic landmark in the history of Chinese robots."

To make Chinese robots part of China's technology development strategies, they had to be included in the 863 Programme. If so, policymakers needed to face this prominent but practical problem: it might not have been the perfect time to develop robots when China was just beginning its reform and opening-up phase and had to satisfy the huge employment demand. China's national conditions were not good. The necessary market conditions weren't there yet. And it seemed too unrealistic.

But Jiang realized that science and technology development would never be made overnight but take time to grow. In other words, if China hadn't seized the opportunity at that time, it would have been too late and the country would have lagged behind. But not many people were able to realize and understand this.

In those days, many people didn't know much about strategic thinking and the macro management of a country's science and technology development, nor did they understand why their country would even have a strategic plan for investing heavily in capitals and human resources to develop high-tech robots.

What on earth is a robot? What is the role of a robot? At that time, some government agencies and enterprises did not know the answers. So, Jiang carried out a lot of publicity work to explain the project to people and win their support. His groundbreaking efforts made the establishment of the robot project much easier.

Jiang knew very clear that, although he was holding a robot "baby" in his arms, it would take a lot of effort to raise it into a "human". There was still a long way ahead.

To include robots in the 863 Programme, Jiang visited all departments of the CAS and relevant ministries and commissions of state. He explained with patience the position, function and value of robots in the equipment manufacturing industry and their significance to national industry and national economic development.

Where there's a will, there's a way. According to the motion of the State Council on making robots, and based on the actual situation in China, Jiang made great efforts to propose that intelligent robots should be the focus of the second shortlisted project, eventually including robot research in the 863 Programme.

The 863 Programme was officially launched in 1987. There were 15 themes, including CIMS and smart robots. The initial investment would reach 10 billion yuan. After this, robots became a huge force by which to strategically boost China's technological development. During the arduous journey, a group of scientists represented by Jiang finally paved the way for Chinese robots.

No other people but Jiang led two projects at the same time on the 863 Programme. Credit should go to Jiang's strong sense of responsibility, mission and spirit of commitment, as well as his dedication and obsession with his career.

The most important aspect of the 863 Programme was to choose the right direction and pathway for the scientific research. If the direction was wrong or the path deviated, the work would lead nowhere, while time-related cost is the costliest expense. This is the same as when Jiang reviewed students' papers: he always checked whether the conclusion was in line with the physical principles; if not, none of the designs or discussions would be meaningful.

With the 863 Programme, Jiang started to build a Chinese research and development system on robots with his influence, his authority, his superb organizational skills and his vision.

Thanks to Jiang's drive and others' cooperation, it took only five years for China to build 14 open laboratories, two engineering centres and nine application factories across the country, as well as establish a perfect three-level management system and carry out research and tests on five types of robots involving three models.

The 863 Programme was extremely important in the context of China's scientific and technological development. It shouldered the important task of promoting high technology and upgrading Chinese industries. Within the 20-plus years that this plan was implemented, China witnessed many high-tech talents who managed to narrow the gap with developed countries, as well as boost the Chinese high technology sector and industries in the interests of traditional industry transformation. This produced huge economic and social benefits.

China's robot industry wouldn't be where it is now if it hadn't been considered part of the 863 Programme back then. It was truly an extraordinary move to include robots in the plan! That plan also pursued two definite research directions, "core" and "brain", which actually initiated robot development in China. There is no doubt that Jiang should take the credit. As Qu Daokui put it, "Without someone like Jiang holding fast to the robotic industry, Chinese robots would be at least 10 or even 20 years behind the times."

II. Fantastic interaction with the world

At the Night of Innovation, an event held during the 2015 World Robot Conference in Beijing, Professor Tan Zizhong was invited onto the stage by Xi Ning, the guest host. He said to the audience, "It's my great honour to introduce Professor Tan Zizhong from WUSTL, who is my mentor. Over recent decades, Professor Tan has been highly concerned with and supported the development of China's robot endeavours. To attend this World Robot Conference, Mr Tan and his wife went out of their way to fly for over 20 hours before arriving in Beijing. Let's welcome Professor Tan on stage to make a speech."

Amid a burst of warm applause, Professor Tan took the

microphone, saying: "Thank you! Due to the heavy snow, it took seven or eight hours to transfer in Tokyo, Japan. I'm very sorry that we did not catch today's opening ceremony. When I was waiting for the plane, memories from 25 years ago flooded back to me. At that time, I also took a transfer in Tokyo to China, as had I invited nine world-class robot experts to give academic lectures in China. That academic exchange presented Chinese experts and scholars with the world's most cutting-edge theoretical technologies, exerting positive effects on the development of China's robots. We overseas Chinese scientists were then looking forward to the time when China's robots would soon be developed and step onto the world stage one day."

"Attending this World Robot Conference held here in Beijing, I feel that that day has come..."

The crowd broke into rapturous applause.

Why would nine world-class robot experts have come to China 25 years ago?

Organized by Jiang Xinsong and Professor Tan Zizhong, they were originally part of senior-level discussions between Chinese robot scholars and top world-class experts, which also represented a high-tech interaction between China and the world. The discussions exerted significant impacts on establishing the road map for robots on the 863 Programme. It was in fact Jiang Xinsong's wish that the invited world-class robot experts would revitalize robot development during China's Eighth Five-year Plan period with the input of advanced technological theories, so that further progress would be made in promoting the two themes of the programme.

That July, with his own academic status and influence in the area of robots worldwide, Tan helped Jiang Xinsong to invite these nine world-class robot experts to the SIA to give lectures and participate in discussions and exchanges concerning academic research. These experts were from the US, Japan, the UK, France and Italy, all of whom enjoyed great esteem in the robot research field. There was no doubt that such a group of people would provide China with insights into the most cutting-edge technological information on robots.

"Mr Jiang was a man with a serious attitude, who was wholeheartedly dedicated to his career. He has tried his utmost to advance the robot endeavours in China. It was strenuous for him to work his way up in that era and climate." Tan recalled that "at the time, our exchange was purely academic. Some thought that China was poor in terms of scientific and technological development. Far from what was assumed, I could see that China devoted much effort to scientific and technological areas. It had also made some progress in overcoming technological difficulties and cultivating talents. Take China's aerospace industry as an example. It is not solely about paying lip service to launch satellites. We all know that it requires talented engineers and scientists, who are key points in the whole process. China has done a great job in developing robots. It hopes to introduce its own robots to the world. China needs to learn from the world and the world also needs to learn more about China."

Tan recalled that "at the time in Shenyang, I invited the world's leading experts to China. As the saying goes, science knows no boundaries. We exchanged ideas and presented frontier theories in the academic field. It can be said that the experts who came greatly boosted and advanced the development of China's robot technology."

When Chinese scholars engaged with these world-class experts, one word confused them. An expert asked Jiang Xinsong, "Why do you call a robot a 'machine man' ('ji qi ren') in China?" Pondering carefully on a response, Jiang Xinsong was confused too. Who on earth translated robot into "machine man"? Literally, it's hard to relate "robot" to "machine man". So, why is "robot", rather than "machine man", used in English?

Let's go back to the very beginning. It all starts with *Rossum's Universal Robots*, the sci-fi stage play by Karel Čapek, a Czech writer. The main character in the play is called Robota. This Czech name soon crept into English as robot, to describe an automaton being, rather than "machine man". That's fine, but why was robot was translated into "machine man" in Chinese?

Back to his conversation with the expert, Jiang Xinsong explained that "the word 'robot' was introduced to China during the late 1960s and early 1970s, appearing in internal journals on science and technology. It's hard to find evidence to explain why robot was translated into 'machine man'. Maybe 'machine man' sounds more intuitive. The translation of this word has remained controversial ever since. However, it is so well known now that it can hardly be changed."

As a result, "machine man" ("ji qi ren") has become a distinctive Chinese expression.

As Jiang Xinsong later wrote in an article: "'robot' was translated into 'machine man' after reasonable considerations. The latter sounds more intuitive. However, it is also a bewildering decision to understand and has caused some negative effects. As 'machine man' is used in China, some have naturally come up with the question, with so large a population in China, does it need more machine men? The historical merits and demerits of this distinctive

Chinese expression may become an interesting research topic in the academic community for decades to come."

Jiang comments here ring true. As robot was translated into "machine man", misunderstandings have occurred from time to time and there have been problems in the promotion and application process of robotic technology. The issue as to why a robot wasn't called a "human machine" or an "intelligent machine" has been questioned by the academic community for a long time. Even at the 2015 World Robot Conference, there were still doubts about the translation: if translated into English, the Chinese expression "ji qi ren" means "machine man", rather than "robot". In international academic exchanges and technological cooperation, it is often a must for us to explain this to foreign friends who come to China for the first time.

In the mid-1980s when "robot" was a popular word, the Chinese expression "machine man" sparked controversy. As an authoritative expert who was well recognized in the robot community, Jiang Xinsong had the final word. The word "machine man" was gradually accepted by Chinese academic society.

In contrast to active academic discussions, that exchange also featured some thrilling moments. All foreign experts were unexpectedly caught up in "a heartbeat game", that is, an accident that was also an unforgettable memory.

According to Professor Tan's recollection: "The episode that happened during that exchange activity was really breathtaking. At that time, the SIA was only an old building without any magnificent offices like today. As some of the foreign experts took the lift to go down, it suddenly stopped, stuck between floors. Seeing them trapped in the lift, we were terrified. We asked others to call for rescue."

Jiang Xinsong was in the hallway. He heard the lift's emergency alarm and wondered what had happened. Someone shouted, "The lift stopped! Come quickly! The lift has broken down and it's stuck in the middle!" People ran up and down the stairs and found that the lift was stuck between the third and the fourth floors. Electricians in the institute were summoned. Jiang Xinsong stopped them: "That is not a solution! You should not attempt reckless measures. Go and find professionals."

They immediately realized that reckless measures wouldn't be an option. Things could get worse if other problems occurred. The people trapped inside were all world-class elites on robotic research. If something unfortunate happened to them, the consequence would be catastrophic!

If that's the case, even the CAS could not afford to shoulder the heavy responsibility, let alone the SIA! Jiang Xinsong felt a chill run down his spine. Standing on the third floor, Jiang comforted people inside the lift, reassuring them that he had already called for professional help, which would come very soon, so they should not worry. Wang Tianran, deputy director of the institute who accompanied the foreign experts, was also trapped. With a trembling voice, he said, "Don't move, don't move", again and again.

Not a moment later, professional technicians from the lift service company arrived. It turned out that the lift had a quality problem. The fault was soon cleared and the lift resumed normal operations. The foreign experts walked out of the lift, not yet recovered from the shock.

Wang Tianran looked extremely pale. The lift could have cost people's lives!

In order to calm nerves and extricate Jiang Xinsong from embarrassment, Professor Tan Zizhong, who always makes witty remarks, joked with Jiang that, "Since you are in the automation industry, why are you being so non-automatic now?" Wiping sweat from his forehead, Jiang repeated the word "sorry". Never has Jiang been so embarrassed. Afterwards, lingering concerns still haunted

Jiang. Therefore, leaders in the institute held a special conference to find out the causes and learn lessons.

Jiang Xinsong thumped on the desk, saying, "It is me who should carry out a review. At that time, it was my order to purchase lifts with domestic brands. And we chose the best domestic brand. That accident was the last thing we should have expected. If our country is able to apply robots in lift manufacturing, just like foreign countries, this kind of quality problem might not occur. I think the fundamental causes are that our country lags behind in manufacturing and the level of our technology is low, which results in poor product quality. It is our responsibility to speed up research on robots and develop an advanced equipment manufacturing industry. Only in this way can we fundamentally lift China out of such backwardness."

During that exchange activity, Jiang Xinsong and his colleagues were fully involved in discussions with foreign experts on subjects such as the application of robotic technology, cutting-edge theories and future directions. The foreign experts put forward valuable suggestions of critical importance for robot research and development in China.

Informed by the 863 Programme, Jiang Xinsong soon worked out an overall plan for a development strategy for China's robots, which fully covered the development directions of global robotic technology. A lesser-known fact was that, while researching and developing industrial and special robots, such as marine robots, the SIA has never given up on researching aerospace robots.

In 2014, the Exhibition of Scientific and Technological Achievements in Celebration of the 65th Anniversary of the National Day was held in the SIA. Besides industrial and marine robots and unmanned aerial vehicles, there was an aerospace robot, namely, a lunar rover. Small and exquisite, this space robot looked like a mantis. It was the twin sister of another moon rover Yutu (Jade Rabbit), which arrived on the surface of the moon carried by the Chang'e 3 lander on 15th December 2013. To meet the requirements of space project development, the SIA and the China Aerospace Science and Technology Corporation then simultaneously began research and development into a lunar rover. The performance of SIA's Yutu was no less than that of another rover that had reached on moon. This represents a landmark achievement for the SIA in the field of aerospace robots.

III. "Brain" and "hand"

A highly distinctive area of Heping District in Shenyang, Sanhao Street is known as the historic centre of China's robots, in other words, the place where the SIA was originally located.

Under the guidance of their supervisor Jiang Xinsong, Qu Daokui and Wang Yuechao graduated with excellent grades and then worked for the CAS Open Laboratory of Robotics, when newly built by the SIA, which went onto become the backbone of scientific research. Jiang Xinsong let them play a key role in undertaking the 863 Programme robot project.

Qu Daokui, the first man to obtain a master's degree in robotics in China, was directly appointed as the leader of the robot strand. Qu

Daokui said, "This was a really good chance to travel to the frontier of robotics after graduation and conduct research and development in this area on the 863 Programme. For me, it was a historic opportunity. So, I was really lucky."

Later on, Wang Yuechao became leader of another research strand. They were both working on robot control methods, which represent the core robotic technologies, such as the "brain" of robots. Although they were working in the same research area, their paths were quite different. There are many possible directions in research and development concerning control methods. Qu Daokui's research focused on adaptive control. With perception, robots can become more intelligent. Thus, adaptive control means robots can adapt themselves to the operating environment. Meanwhile, Wang Chaoyue concentrated on sensor-based control. The earliest industrial robot had no perception, which threw open the challenge about how to incorporate perception into the robotic system and control robots with the information from sensors. This is what is meant by sensor-based control. Both control methods were relatively cutting-edge; indeed, they laid a foundation for the following application and industrialization.

Qu Daokui and Wang Yuechao became Jiang Xinsong's right-hand man. The former recalled that: "Our group consisted of seven or eight people. The SIA was originally situated at 90 Sanhao Street in Heping District, Shenyang. In 1988, it was moved to the newly developed National Robotics Demonstration Engineering Centre at 114 Nanta Street in Shenyang, which is considered as the cradle of China's robotics."

"At that time, we had no idea about it and just applied to join the national research project when we were fresh out of graduate school. We didn't know that the project would require assessment, evaluation and acceptance tests. We just worked on it according to its content. There were no worries nor stresses."

The research subject that Jiang Xinsong assigned to Qu Daokui was the deep integration of CIMS and robot control, with the aim of studying the practical application of the robot hand in CIMS. That was to serve as the robot "chip". But Qu Daokui chose to work on the dual-arm collaborative control of robots, which was actually aimed at the development of their "brain".

The robot at that time was mostly the equivalent of one human hand. However, there were many restrictions in terms of the actions that could be performed with only one hand. Qu Daokui added, "I thought that a human with one hand could only do few things. If we can combine two robot hands together, they will be able to complete lots of operations, such as climbing up walls. With two hands, you can even climb over the wall. In other words, only with two hands working together can robots really behave like 'humans'. I started with dual-arm collaborative control when I was studying the neuron control methods of robots."

Qu went on: "But it was not easy because we had to start with algorithms and modelling. The technology was not growing as fast as it is now. There was no technological support in many relevant aspects, both at home and abroad. We needed all types of modelling and the corresponding communications technology to figure out how to coordinate two robot hands, including how to design the perception system. My mind was then full of strange ideas and all I wanted to do was surprise my supervisor."

When inspecting how the project was going, Jiang Xinsong found that Qu hadn't followed the research plan as scheduled and stormed off.

This reminded Jiang of his own youth when he was also capricious. Science needs this rebellious spirit, so later Jiang agreed with Qu's research.

In science, Qu tends to be along the lines of "love the new and hate the old". He has always been looking for and exploring new things. Once he finds them, he will feel dull and then advance into new areas.

Later, Qu Daokui realized that it was almost impossible to surpass Jiang Xinsong. When their group encountered an intractable problem, Jiang would appear in the laboratory and develop an algorithm to Qu Daokui recalled: "Mr Jiang was always helping us with some complex professional difficulties in scientific research and also been a real helper in life. Once, during a festival, he invited students, including Wang Chaoyue and me, to his house for dinner. We never thought that he would be able to cook a delicious meal. It is said that he always does the sewing at home and he can even knit a sweater. There are very few scientists as versatile as him. We all admire him very much."

Although Qu Daokui admired his teacher, he didn't hesitate to challenge him. Annually, there was a national acceptance test for projects of the 863 Programme. Would Qu Daokui make it with his "strange ideas" this time? In scientific research, Qu Daokui always broke away from the routine. But this time, he was very serious about the acceptance test. For once, by chance, he left a deep impression on the experts during the acceptance test.

For the acceptance test on the following evening, Qu Daokui

once again operated the "dual-arm collaborative control" system in line with the procedures. At that time, his studio had just moved to the newly built National Robot Demonstration Project Laboratory, where all the doors and windows were floor-to-ceiling glass. The whole design and construction were relatively advanced.

At about 10.00 p.m. one day, he had bumped into the glass door while walking out of the studio. There had previously been a desk near the door, but he hadn't realized it had been moved. With darkness outside, he thought the door was open. With a sudden crash, the door was shattered. His right hand, cut by the pieces of broken glasses, was streaming with blood.

He just ignored it. When he returned home, his wife, seeing the blood, was so scared that she took him to the emergency room of the Shenyang Military General Hospital, where he received 13 stitches.

The next day, Qu Daokui, with one hand bandaged, operated the keyboard with the other hand to show how the "dual-arm collaborative control" of robots worked. Not knowing what happened, the experts said that Qu performed "dual-arm collaborative control" for a robot while he turned himself into a "one-hand operator". Someone joked: "Qu, it is really something that one single hand can have two 'hands' under its disposal."

IV. Searching for "the elixir of life"

Although Qu Daokui could be quite wilful once he had some ideas, he still took the research topic assigned to him by his teacher seriously. Not only did Qu solve the issue of "dual-arm collaborative control", he also successfully completed the first stage of his 863 Programme research topic.

The research project on robotics of which Qu was in charge passed the acceptance inspection in 1988, representing an accomplishment of the Seventh Five-year Plan. As a result, the SIA was recognized by the CAS. Ordinarily, Qu would have pursued his PhD abroad. The institute's leadership could not decide whether or not to give Qu the opportunity to further his study abroad. Once Qu went abroad, the research process would be affected; however, if Qu were not given the chance to go abroad, it would be very difficult to keep pace with international cutting-edge technologies. At that time, the Chinese robot industry, which was in its early stages after all, lagged far behind the international advanced level. This kind of situation was a disadvantage to both the institute and Qu's personal development. In fact, what really concerned the leadership was whether or not Qu would come back after sending him abroad.

Qu had bought a set of industrial robot components on his business trip to America. After returning, he sighed that the technological gap between China and America was huge. Some heard Qu's comments and told Jiang Xinsong that he would never come back once he went abroad. "On my trip to America, when I got off the plane at San Francisco Airport, I was amazed by the size of the airport. And the highway was completely different from what we have here. I had this illusion before going abroad: I could not help thinking that our nation was in quite a good state. I used to think that China had developed at a very fast pace in those years. But, when I was in America, I realized that we were on totally different levels. During a month of training there, I have come to know how advanced this country is in developing new technologies and exploring new scientific fields." Qu recalled, "I feel kind of jealous of what America has achieved after I came back. I have told myself that I have to do something to catch up with America. But I also want to increase my own knowledge and gain some experiences abroad for sure."

Would Qu come back? At that time, studying abroad was becoming rather popular, with scientific and technological personnel eager to have this opportunity. Some of them had already decided to not come back once they left. Jiang was unable to let his student go. "Normally, I should have studied abroad after I finished my master's degree in 1986. As I had taken charge of a project under the 863 Programme, I was not able to go abroad, not until I finished the research project. At that time, there were several people in the institute who went abroad and never came back." Qu continued: "In that era, it was quite normal and convenient for those who worked in the scientific field to go abroad. I wouldn't have thought that studying abroad would have caused trouble in my case."

Jiang invited Qu to come to his office that day. He asked Qu, "Do you want to find 'the elixir of life'?"

Qu, who was famous for his quick thinking, could not decipher what Jiang meant. He was baffled and replied, "The elixir of life?" Jiang, who was always serious, became amused at seeing that his student was puzzled. He told Qu a story.

Deng Xiaoping, the paramount leader of the PRC at the time, visited Japan a decade ago. When he met with leaders from various parties and socialites in Japan, he could have recalled a story from history. Qin Shi Huang, the founder of the Qin Dynasty and the first emperor of a united China, commanded Xu Fu to cross over to Japan and find the elixir of life. Deng might also have wanted to use this story to let those Japanese leaders remember the ancient Sino-Japanese relationship. Deng switched the topic, which involved a play on words. He told everyone that he had heard that Japan had 'the elixir of life' and that the purpose of this visit was, firstly, to exchange approval letters for the Treaty of Peace and Friendship between China and Japan, secondly, to show gratitude to our Japanese friends who had made efforts to build such a friendship and, thirdly, to search for 'the elixir of life'."

As soon as he finished the sentence, laughter broke out. In fact, what Deng meant by saying "the elixir of life" was to reference Japan's rich experience in developing the nation rapidly and its modern technologies.

Hearing this, Qu's mind suddenly became clear. "The elixir of life" mentioned by his teacher actually referred to robot technology.

Grinning broadly, he said, "Who wouldn't want such a good thing? I think about it, even in my dreams."

"But it was such a pity that Xu Fu never came back after his eastward voyage to Japan, making Qin Shi Huang wait in vain." Leaning against the back of the seat and looking at the ceiling, Jiang reflected.

"We can't blame Xu alone. Qin Shi Huang was also responsible."

"Qin Shi Huang? Well, please continue." Jiang stood up immediately, with his eyes wide open and appearing to be slightly aggressive. Qu's unconventional thinking always surprised him.

"It was Qin Shi Huang who failed to pick the right person" said Qu brightly. He was proud of his answer.

"Qin Shi Huang would not have made a hasty decision on such an important matter." Jiang's smile faded. With a serious face, he said, "Isn't it more likely that the general wouldn't have taken orders from the emperor anymore, for he was far away from home and that Xu just indulged in pleasure and forgot about his country and duty?"

"In fact, it wasn't necessarily true that Xu didn't want to come back. It is possible that he couldn't find 'the elixir of life' anywhere, so there was nothing he could bring back home. Coming back with nothing to offer, he would only have been thrown into the prison and ended up in a desperate situation. So, he had no choice but to stay abroad."

"So, do you mean that Xu had his own reasons for not coming back?"

"Well, it's possible. If we think about it from a historical viewpoint, there are plenty of reasons to explain why he did not come back. However, if we take a look according to today's standards, there is only one reason that would have been enough for Xu to come back."

"What is it?" Jiang stared at his student.

"His loyalty." Qu answered unambiguously.

"Good point! I can let you go to search for 'the elixir of life' now."

"Aren't you afraid of me becoming the next Xu?" Qu had just resolved the difficulty in front of him before asking his teacher this question with a smile.

"Well, if you really become the next Xu, there is nothing I can do. But you're not going to Japan. You won't get the real 'elixir of life' in Japan. The Japanese won't give it to us anyway. This time you are going to study with Uncle Sam. Maybe you can bring some 'miracle cures' back."

It was quite unexpected that Uncle Sam had lost his temper for no reason and decided not to take Qu as one of his students.

V. The FBI's routine inspection

After Deng's visit to Japan, Sino-Japanese relations entered a new stage. The cooperation and exchange between the two countries had been very close, so why did Jiang want Qu to go to America instead of Japan? Besides the fact that America possessed the most advanced robot technologies, Jiang was quite clear about the Japanese attitude towards independent intellectual property rights. As an island country with inadequate resources, Japan had taken technologies very seriously. Its core technologies were particularly highly protected. Japan would never sell, transfer or reveal its technologies to the outside.

During Deng Xiaoping's visit to Japan, he visited the Panasonic company. Deng knew Matsushita Kōnosuke's reputation very well, calling him "the god of management". He wished that Panasonic would pass on its most advanced technologies to the Chinese people. Matsushita, however, was quite clear on this matter: "Private enterprises such as the Panasonic Cooperation get to survive by the ceaseless development of new technologies, which means that Japanese enterprises don't usually export their technologies and are even more unwilling to reveal their technologies to the world."

Obviously, Deng's advisors had not mentioned this information to him. He was not aware of such a characteristic of Japan, thus causing this moment of embarrassment to take place. For the sake of Deng, however, a compromise was made. Matsushita promised to help China develop advanced television manufacturing technology. Although Sino-Japanese relations became much closer following Deng's visit to Japan, the technological exchange between the two was quite limited. Japan had never shown flexibility towards China's technology blockade. It was absolutely fine if you just wanted to study or work in Japan; however, it was impossible to learn about Japan's advanced technologies. Those technologies were regarded as the key to survival in the market for Japanese enterprises. Jiang's request to buy Japan's robots used to be coldly rejected, so he knew that Japan would never easily sell its technologies. That's the reason why Qu eventually went to America to buy the industrial robot.

Jiang could not let go. "The Americans are more open than the Japanese people. Deng Xiaoping and Jimmy Carter signed an agreement on sci-tech communication, which provided us with an opportunity that we can take advantage of here" Jiang told Qu.

America was the birthplace of robots. Compared with Japan, which was known as "The Kingdom of Robots", America had developed robots much earlier. From the 1960s to 1970s, America had mainly focused on developing cutting-edge technologies in the field of robots. Only WUSTL and a few companies had pursued relevant application developments. At that time, the American government did not take the development of industrial robots seriously. Therefore, it was not regarded as one of the key development projects, causing America to miss out on the best time to develop industrial robots.

Such a strategic decision was definitely a mistake.

However, the craze for developing robots had overwhelmed the entire industry, inspired by the labour shortage in Japan.

In the 1980s, Japan truly deserved its reputation as "The Kingdom of Robots". Indeed, 1980 was known as "The First Year of Robots" in Japan.

It was at this time that the Americans realized how powerful robots were and began to feel the urgency to develop such technology. Both the government and enterprises' understanding of the manufacture and application of industrial robots had changed. They began to value robots and formulate policies and measures to develop this technology. As many factories had developed fairly mature robot technologies in the mid- to late 1980s, America began to develop and produce second-generation robots, which had vision and force sensing, as well as rapidly occupied 60% of the robot market in America. Although America initially took the wrong path, it never lost its leading status in the field of robot technologies on the international stage. Besides, intelligent technology had developed rapidly in America and been widely applied in the aerospace, automobile and military fields. Without doubt, America was one of the strongest countries that possessed the most advanced robot technology.

After all, Jiang was a strategic scientist who had a long-term vision. He had deliberated over Qu's overseas study with a long-term perspective. Jiang, who felt insulted and angry with Japan, was determined to win credit for his own country. Today, he would have asked Qu to make everything come true for him. But, back then, studying abroad in America was the best choice.

Jiang made contacts with those in America in person, making arrangements for Qu to further his study there.

In late 1988, Jiang arranged for Qu to study at Clemson University in New York City. Meanwhile, in order to prepare for studying in America, Qu was asked to take an intensive English language course for six months at the foreign language training centre in the CAS.

Why did Qu not go and study at WUSTL? Professor Tan Zizhong acknowledged the truth behind this decision. Among communications on scientific and technological issues between China and America, the frequent exchanges between Jiang and Tan had attracted the FBI's attention.

FBI officials were overly sensitive. They visited Tan's home frequently to conduct routine inspections, which had bothered his work and daily life.

Under such circumstances, it was inappropriate for Jiang to arrange for Qu to study at WUSTL. Instead, Qu chose Clemson University.

Nevertheless, when they dealt with all the procedures for going abroad, America suddenly began to refuse visas for Chinese students.

Uncle Sam had closed a door. Would God open another window?

Chapter IV
The Motherland is
Our Identity

Between family and country, what reality offers is always a zero-sum game. When serving one's nation with science becomes one's pursuit in life, the answer to this multivariate equation will become rather simple. However, one needs to use his or her spirit to do all of the modelling and spend his or her whole life to measure the results.

I. The sound of the wind on the Rhine

Later on, the scientific academy strengthened its communication with Europe, which led to a phenomenon whereby research institutes usually sent people to study in European countries. In this case, Jiang decided to send Qu to study in Germany.

Germany was still a young nation in terms of its robot manufacturing industry, but it was developing rapidly. The country was confronted by a labour shortage after World War II, so it paid full attention to improving its manufacturing process technique and constantly enhancing its production efficiency. The German government had made some effort to develop industrial robots. In the mid- to late 1970s, the German government implemented a working conditions improvement programme, which required certain jobs that could be dangerous, harmful or poisonous to the human body to be done by robots instead. Installing industrial robots throughout in traditional industries in Germany had actively driven the upgrade of these industries and led the development of industrial robots that were more intelligent, lightweight, flexible and efficient.

Germany began to develop intelligent robots in 1985. After years of efforts, KUKA, one of the representative industrial robot companies, had taken the leading position internationally. The arrangement that Jiang made for Qu to study in Germany had a clear purpose. The turning point in Qu's life was during the time he studied abroad in Germany.

In 1992, Qu attended a one-year intensive German training course in Hefei, the capital of Anhui Province in China, before travelling to Universitaet des Saarlandes in July. Universitaet des Saarlandes, one of the most well-known comprehensive universities in Germany, was founded in 1948. It was famous for its computer communication technology and mechatronics, among other majors offered by the university. Therefore, Qu chose to be a visiting scholar at its electronic technique laboratory in order to conduct research on the application of neural networks in robot control.

His mentor was H. Aschek, a celebrated robot expert in Germany and an authority on control system theory. When he read Qu's CV at first, he was not fully convinced by it, because he thought that China was still an "infant" in the field of robot development according to what he understood about the level of research and development in each country. The results and achievements that Qu provided in his CV was beyond the scope of his expectations.

When Qu met with Professor Aschek at Universitaet des Saarlandes for the first time, the communication between the two took the form of a strict "interview." Not only did this young scholar who came from the East calmly and fluently answer specialized and challenging questions posed by this German expert, but he also expressed his unique view on the current situation and the future trend concerning robotics on the international stage. Professor Aschek immediately realized that both this kind of wisdom from the East and Qu's extraordinary intelligence were exactly the qualities that robotics researchers needed to possess.

Not long after that discussion, Professor Aschek voluntarily applied for a change in status for Qu from a visiting scholar to an international student.

In this way, Qu could participate in Professor Aschek's research projects. Besides, he could work in the professor's laboratory at any time. It was quite an honour to enjoy such treatment at his research institute. Thus, Qu, who was especially appreciated by the professor, went onto become a very famous student during the time that he studied at Universitaet des Saarlandes.

II. A letter from home is worth 10,000 pieces of gold

Qu received a letter in July 1993, which explained the current situation in China and what had happened in the institute. The expectation that Qu would come home could be read between the lines. He was very moved reading this letter.

China had accelerated its reform and opened its door to the world after Deng's remarks during an inspection tour of the south of the country in the spring of 1992. More efforts were put into reforming scientific research field. The CAS announced promising news on a regular basis, in turn driving the marketization of scientific research achievements. Meanwhile, foreign enterprises, with the help of their advantages in advanced technologies, had forged a path into the Chinese market on a large-scale.

Jiang was keenly aware that it was time for the Chinese robots to leave the laboratory and enter the market as soon as possible. He decided to establish an engineering department for robot research and development. Many researchers on the frontline of scientific research were getting on in years, while most of the young technical talents had gone abroad to further their study. Meanwhile, youthful and energetic technicians were needed to support the robot division and solve the problem caused by the labour shortage in the robot field. Who was the right person? The answer was Jiang's student, Qu, for sure. Most of the people who went abroad chose to stay there, so everyone thought that Qu would not come back either. It was quite understandable that those who went abroad chose to stay abroad. The scientific and research environment was much better than that in China, meaning that staying aboard was better in personal development terms. In short, it was much easier for an individual to realize scientific achievements in the West.

It would indeed be surprising if, after studying abroad, students chose to come home. Those who did come back had to abandon whatever benefits and resist all the temptations they enjoyed in the West. Their career development would also be greatly affected.

Some people who came back had no choice but to become teachers, because a good scientific research environment was not available at home to help them carry on their research. Thus, returning to China from abroad was deemed to be abnormal.

In order to get a full picture of Qu's view on this matter, Jiang asked the institute to write a letter to him. Although Jiang's thoughts and intentions were not clearly expressed through those words, the implied message was quite straightforward. Qu felt the weight of this letter in his hands. He understood that the implication of this letter was to ask whether or not he would come back. Qu wrote his reply immediately, reporting on his studying and research in Germany and expressing an overseas student's inner thoughts and emotions.

According to the academician Wang Tianran, the letter was passed around the institute once the leadership had received it. Everyone was deeply moved. Frankly, it was fairly rare for those who went abroad to come back home. Jiang held the letter and said emotionally, "When Daokui comes back, we will have a successor in the field of robots. This letter should be published in our institute's journal."

An "editor's note" was published alongside this letter when it appeared in in the seventh issue of *Robot*, which was published in August 1993. An excerpt is given below:

"I have been working on robot simulation since I arrived in Germany. My main job is to build a robot simulation environment based on the C language and Microwindows in order to carry out research on applying neural networks to robots. This simulation environment consists of three parts: a robot database, neural network modelling and simulation, and output display. Obviously, everything is operated with Windows and most of the work has been completed. The next step is to expand and add some effective algorithms to the neural networks."

Qu said that he was quite moved when he received the letter and understood that the institute really needed him to come back. However, he could not leave Germany immediately because he had been there for less than a year and his research had not yet been completed. It was not easy for the government to sponsor students to study abroad, so he could not give up halfway. But he wanted to hurry up and finish his research. He wrote in reply:

"Despite the fact that my professor wishes me to stay to continue doing this research, and having already registered to study on campus for two semesters as my status was changed some time ago from a visiting scholar to a student, I plan to go back on schedule. But, if I cannot finish my work in time, I will stay for another couple of months. Besides, some other college professors have also agreed for me to work for them for a while or to obtain a degree. Nonetheless, I think that going back to China offers more advantages than staying in Germany based on my one-year personal experience here and the current rapid changes in China. I don't consider it patriotic to return home, nor do I think that someone who chooses to stay abroad has rejected his or her own country. We just choose to follow different paths because of the environment we are in and the status quo for us at the time. Living abroad is indeed wonderful, but it's never home after all. Going home earlier would be a better choice for me."

It was because of Qu's experience of studying abroad in Germany that the seeds were planted whereby he would serve his country through supporting industrial development and making the motherland stronger. "I have finally come to realize that a nation has to be strong. Only if a nation is powerful will it be qualified to be a member of the international community. In this way, a nation can retain its dignity" said Qu. It was also from that moment on that he was determined to develop China's own robots and make the nation celebrated for its robot development on the international stage. He wrote in reply:

"Robotics research has not been very popular internationally in recent years, including Germany. Many German universities nominally have departments for robotics research, but the scale of those are all very small and do not deserve the name they carry. The world is indeed interesting. You have to go and see the reality of it for yourself. Our institute is just as good as any institute abroad, based on facilities and research capability. But, we are not well informed in terms of robotics research elsewhere. There are only a few international articles available in China and the level of international academic communication is inadequate. So far, I have been to some robotics research institutes in Germany and I plan to get some information about relevant companies. I will share what I have learned later."

Qu recalled his research experience in Germany: "I have found that the Germans are very strict when it comes to orders and rules. They are all highly rigorous when doing scientific research. I was conducting research on neural networks at the time, applying this control technology to control robots. It was a new technology." As Qu furthered his study and research, he found that the technological difference between China and relevant foreign countries was narrow in respect of neural networks. As he had mastered this world-leading technique, there was nothing more for him to study.

Qu was quick to realize the industrialization potential by applying this technology in production. Indeed, he had made an inspection in Germany when he visited Volkswagen's manufacturing base in Wolfsburg. He was shocked with what was in front of him. In the automobile assembly workshop there, thousands of robots were working day and night.

It was here that he saw the potential of robots and a promising future, particularly the important function and huge industrial and economic value that these robots offered in developing a modern industrial country. He was desperate to return home so that he could apply robotics research to industrialization.

Qu's later research subject was not only limited to the neural networks of robots, but about how a Western country, such as Germany, achieved high-tech industrialization. He had conducted a great number of investigations and analysis, focusing on corporate giants including modern enterprises like Siemens. In this way, he had prepared himself for developing robots in China and found a way for the country to realize its own industrialization. In this case, Qu had proved himself to be Jiang's best student. They connected with each other and worked towards the same goal.

III. Spiritual purity

Qu received a telephone call from Jiang in October 1993. Jiang asked about his research process. Qu replied that it was almost complete. He had pretty much learned all the techniques but wanted to conduct some more research on the industrialization of robots. Germany had considerable experience in this field and there was much to learn from it.

"If that's the case, you should hurry up and finish your research, learn more about the industrialization of robots if you've got the chance and come back earlier" Jiang said in the telephone call. "We are going to establish a department for developing robotics research. Could you return home a bit sooner? The robotics research that the institute of automation is doing is not simply about theories. We want to produce products and enter the market."

"I was very excited when I heard what my teacher had said. I had the exact same idea as him" Qu recalled. "In fact, I was inspired to think about the real function of robots and where these robots could be applied because of what I had seen abroad. In the past, we had only considered robots to be a fun project. It was our interest alone that motivated us to carry out research on robots. Later, although I realized the applied value of robots, I did not quite think about their importance to industrialization, manufacturing industry, national economic development and even making the nation stronger. This kind of feeling became even stronger after studying abroad in Germany. As a result, I planned to return home earlier after making good use of my time to finish off my research."

Qu's mentor, Professor Aschek, on hearing the news that Qu was returning home, could not understand his decision and persuaded him to stay.

But Qu had his own dream. He politely declined the requests of his mentor and peers, stating that he was determined to go back home.

The institute of automation decided to let Qu establish a

department for robot development in the spring of 1994. Jiang gave Qu three months to draft a report on how to achieve the industrialization of robots based on his experience abroad, as well as asking him to propose a plan about how to develop a market for Chinese robots and how to achieve their industrialization.

Qu was completely devoted to planning the future. During that period of time, he was preoccupied with issues about developing robots, such as the status quo in China, analysing and making judgements on future trends, as well as identifying some countermeasures that the country needed to take when the time came. Qu finished this 20-page, 10,000-word report, entitled *Seize the Historic Opportunity and Drive the Application of Technology: Some Thoughts on the Industrialization Development of Industrial Robot*s, in less than two months. Jiang was very satisfied with the report and arranged for Qu to give a presentation at a kick-off and mobilization meeting.

Qu indeed lived up to his teacher's expectations. At this meeting, it was recognized that the report deeply and explicitly analysed the successful experience of and lessons from the industrialization of robots abroad and emphasized the measures and the path that China should take, with evidence and a rationale, in order to achieve this goal.

An older comrade then made a comment at the meeting: "It's a comprehensive, understandable, well-founded and eloquent presentation. Qu has proposed a very reasonable plan." Qu's great presentation had won everyone's admiration and appreciation.

His report was then published in *Robot* in January 1994 (12 issues in total). From today's point of view, this could be considered a "proclamation" announcing that Chinese robots had entered the market.

Chapter V
A Life's Devotion to Robots

Breaking the chain of blockade: with the help of others, Chinese robots took a giant leap onto the world stage; while facing the trap of an import project, the Chinese scientific community had no choice but to launch a counteroffensive.

The "father of Chinese robots" devoted his life to bringing glory to Chinese robots.

I. The CR-01 swims towards the Pacific Ocean

The shifting times provided Chinese robots with a historic opportunity.

In the 1980s, the US, former Soviet Union and Japan frequently dispatched their own underwater vehicles, which were able to dive to depths of up to 6,000 m, cruise across the oceans, explore the mysteries of the sea floor, and vie with each other to assert their hegemony over the underwater world.

Although China's underwater vehicle technologies were not well matched with those of the above-mentioned countries, it had already built a good foundation out of nothing in this field.

Through incessant hard work, Jiang Xinsong, along with

other technological personnel, successfully developed a series of underwater vehicles, among which was a 100 m and a 300 m deep-dive lightweight robot, which entered military service. Subsequently, he led the development of the Tansuo-1 underwater vehicle, which was used in offshore oil exploitation by China. In 1987, Tansuo-1 won second prize at the Scientific and Technological Progress Awards of the CAS. This robot not only satisfied urgent domestic needs but has also been exported to other countries.

At the same time, the SIA built the first domestic manufacturing base that was able to produce a series of underwater vehicles.

While formulating the Eighth Five-year Plan, Jiang confidently signed a written pledge to the State Scientific and Technological Commission, stating that, by 2010, during the 11th Five-year Plan period, Chinese underwater vehicles would reach the world's top-ranking level by diving to depths of over 6,000 m.

Jiang led domestic researchers to continue their research and development work. Soon, they created a type of medium-sized underwater detection vehicle. At that time, a total of six robots of this type was produced. Three of them were exported, while the others entered service on platforms in the South China Sea. The first of them had a service life of seven years. This project also won second prize in the National Scientific and Technological Progress Awards.

The development of underwater vehicles involved a combination of high technologies, including such complicated technologies as deep diving, sealing, automatic control, sonar, television, telephone, information transmission and liquid control. Based on China's technological capabilities at that time, each step forward required many breakthroughs in key technologies. What were the odds for realizing the goal of diving to a depth of 6,000 m within 20 years?

At this precise moment, the situation unexpectedly took a favourable turn. The change in the international situation had provided a historic opportunity for the development of Chinese underwater vehicles with Jiang choosing to take an unconventional approach.

In early 1991, faced with disintegration, the former Soviet Union plunged into chaos. At the annual World Robot Conference in Europe, G. Geralt, the director of the French National Centre for Scientific Research, told his old friend Jiang that the Far East Institute of Maritime Automation in the former Soviet Union was encountering a crisis of survival. In order to "fill their stomachs", experts at this institute considered transferring the deep-dive technology of their underwater vehicles. This piece of information instantly painted a beautiful picture in Jiang's mind: through cooperation with the former Soviet Union, China would be able to develop 6,000 m-class deep-dive underwater vehicles at one stroke. Therefore, this was a once-in-a-millennium opportunity. After returning to China, he immediately started to promote this cooperation.

Soon, experts from the Far East Institute of Maritime Automation came to negotiate with the SIA. During two days of arduous negotiation, these Soviet experts didn't accept the SIA's proposition. They thought that, as the amount of money offered by Jiang was too small, they would fail to recover the costs of so many years of hard work and suffer great losses.

However, the cooperation was very important for both sides: one wanted to "fill their stomachs" and resolve the crisis of survival, while the other wanted to seek help in realizing its ambition to reach the world's highest levels. As Jiang's limited budget could not satisfy the other side's requirements, the negotiation was extremely arduous. The two sides failed to reach a consensus after stalling for a long time, as both of them held their own trump cards without making any concessions. In the afternoon of the third day, the Soviet experts shook their heads and prepared to leave and the negotiations seemed to be ending with nothing to show for them. Suddenly, Jiang made an unexpected decision: inviting the guests to visit his underwater robot laboratory.

At that time, some people were confused. Would the visit turn out to be the SIA's last card? Yes. In fact, Jiang intended to use this last card as his trump in order to bring the negotiation to an end.

He had perceived that the other side wanted to manipulate the trump card in their hands to force the Chinese side to add more chips. However, what they didn't know was that the Chinese side also had a trump card, which was to prove decisive. Feng Xisheng, chief designer of the underwater robot project, instantly understood Jiang's intention and opened the laboratory's gate. When Jiang led these Soviet experts into the laboratory, they were amazed by its perfect facilities and experimental products and changed their minds at once. That very night, they called Jiang from their hotel and told him that they would like to stay and talk with him in the morning.

Upon visiting the SIA's laboratory, these Soviet experts felt that China had already created sufficient conditions for the development of 6,000 m-class deep-dive robots, which was merely a matter of time. If they lost this opportunity, they would hardly find another partner. Besides, these Soviet experts could never avoid the fact that their crisis of survival meant they had to solve the problem as soon as possible. As a result, they discussed and decided to show their trump card.

Hence, the SIA soon started its cooperation with the former Soviet Union in the development of a 6,000 m-class autonomous underwater vehicle (AUV). Jiang participated in and directed the preliminary overall design of the project, carried out a complete kinematic analysis and formulated a navigation and exploration plan under all kinds of circumstances.

Hearing about this information, two Japanese experts secretly arrived at the SIA and expressed their wish to cooperate with China in the field of underwater vehicles. The Japanese ROV "Kaiko" had successfully dived to a depth of 7,000 m near Guam and was sprinting towards the bottom of the Mariana Trench. It was, so to speak, second to none in the world.

Jiang immediately figured out the Japanese experts' intention. Obviously, the Japanese wanted to steal from the Russians. Indeed, the Japanese became more aggressive, daring to disrupt the cooperation project by pulling the rug out from under the Russians' feet. The logic was very simple: Russia was no longer as strong as the former Soviet Union.

Since a maritime dispute existed between China and Japan, was

Japan really sincere in working with China to develop underwater vehicles? Jiang politely declined the Japanese offer. Moreover, success was already in Jiang's grip. After that, the Japanese asked a US organization to seek cooperation with China. Soon, Jiang found out that Japan was involved in this manoeuvre.

However, instead of directly declining the "goodwill" gesture from the US, Jiang signed a memorandum of cooperation with the US in a tactical and friendly manner, so as to keep technical exchanges with the US in the field of robotics, rebuild the robot "friendly corridor" and seek out opportunities for further technological cooperation in his pursuit of world leadership in this field.

In 1995, the CR-01 AUV left Guangzhou for the Pacific Ocean to undertake a 6,000 m deep-dive experiment that would evaluate the performance and quality of the product. Sadly, due to overwork in the development of the CR-01, Jiang fell ill. When the CR-01 was loaded onto its test ship and prepared to depart for the Pacific Ocean, regardless of illness, he still came to the pier in Guangzhou to see it off.

On that day, he boarded the ship and softly patted the head of the CR-01, as if stroking his own child. "Sorry, little thing. I cannot swim to the Pacific Ocean along with you. I wish you a safe journey and a return in triumph" he said affectionately.

In August, the vast test area in the Pacific Ocean received a special guest

As stated, the CR-01, a 6,000 m deep-dive AUV, had been developed by China. Different from previous nomenclature, the first letter in its name was "C". When the CR-01 captured a clear picture of the sea floor and sent it back to the test ship, the deck crew burst into cheers. Chinese oceanic robots had finally broken the chain of technological blockade and leisurely roamed around the underwater world of the Pacific Ocean.

The CR-01 surprised the international community by undertaking a successful 6,000 m deepwater performance test in the Pacific Ocean. Immediately after that, the CR-01 successfully fulfilled a UN mission to detect 150,000 km^2 of deepwater seafloor, winning glory for its home country.

This important achievement not only allowed China to join the small group of world powers in the field of robotics, but also enabled it to carry out thorough detection of 97% of the world's ocean area. Jiang had gained technologies and, more importantly, time. Within just over four years, he had realized a 20-year goal and caught up with leading countries in the field, which had impressed the whole world. Furthermore, this underwater vehicle project, as part of the 863 Programme, had also been advanced by 15 years with immediate effect.

Hearing about the news, an old expert at the CAS burst into tears and said, "I never imagined that I would see a Chinese 6,000 m deep-dive underwater vehicle in my lifetime." Song Jian, then state councillor and director of the State Scientific and Technological Commission, highly rated this achievement, stating that: "The progress in robotics and its application are the most convincing achievements in the field of automatic control in the 20th century and the ultimate state of automation in modern times. China has gained hope and confidence in this field."

II. A bitter pill

In 1990s, with manufacturing industry prospering in every country around the world, the presence of industrial robots had mushroomed unexpectedly and the market space was expanding with speed. All of these factors made it a highly competitive technology field in all countries.

Therefore, industrial robots not only became the way in which developed countries could grab market share, but the essential tool for cracking down on manufacturing and exploiting resources in developing countries. It was the technological monopoly of foreign countries that suppressed China's automotive industry and left it with a memory filled with humiliation.

In accordance with the 863 Programme and the robot development proposals in the Seventh Five-year Plan set by Jiang Xinsong, the underwater vehicle and the industrial robot were to be pushed out altogether and promoted hand in hand. But the development of industrial robots was supposed to leave the lab during the Eighth Five-year Plan period, having achieved marketization.

In fact, under Jiang's decisive command, the order of this project was reversed. In the early 90s, research and development concerning an underwater vehicle was intensely promoted given the opportunity to cooperate with the former Soviet Union, with the expectation that the goal would be achieved ahead of time, while progress in the area of industrial robots lagged far behind. The cooperative unit, which was responsible for the research work on the industrial robot, fell behind schedule, with marketization within the Eighth Five-year Plan period almost collapsing.

China's industrial robots could not break through under the blockade of technical barriers imposed internationally. Wang Tianran was faced with such a problem after replacing Jiang as the director. He put it like this: "I am too worried to sleep or eat well." At that time, the failure to foster a Chinese and foreign technical cooperation project forced China's industrial robots out of the lab.

In 1991, the boss of Shenyang Jinbei Automobile Company paid a business visit to the US and was impressed by automated guided vehicle (AGV) robots, which were able to assemble good-quality engines automatically without workers' help. He was attracted to the concept right away.

Generally speaking, an AGV robot is like a porter on a dynamic assembly line, who carries engines, rear axles and oil tanks and moves the car bodies automatically once they are hanging above the assembly line.

An AGV is a type of industrial robot. It is controlled by a computer with moving automatic navigation and other functions. It can be widely applied to flexible handling and transmission in the machinery, electronics, paper and other industries. It can also be applied in automated warehouses, flexible processing systems and flexible assembly systems (AGVs as active assembly platforms) or utilized as a means of transportation at stations, airports and post offices for sorting goods.

In order to improve production efficiency and build a first-class automobile enterprise in China, Shenyang Jinbei Automobile Company decided to purchase foreign robots. The company got in contact with an assembly supplier in the US for developing a car assembly line. The US company was supposed to provide AGVs and introduce assembly line technology from Japan.

In reality, the US supplier simply wanted to test the water in the Chinese market with no intention of transferring its technology to China. The outcome was not hard to imagine.

The contract was signed and the car assembly line introduced from Japan was built halfway through the contract period. When it was the time for the US side to install the AGV control system, they unexpectedly announced, "We are sorry that the government restricts the export of technology. We cannot provide you with AGVs, we just cannot." Without AGVs, the production line bought from Japan was rendered useless and all the equipment became a pile of scrap iron.

Without AGVs from the US, the Japanese company broke off the contract unilaterally and stopped providing service support to Jinbei. All businesses know what an aborted project means to a company whose benefits are mainly derived through production. Aside from the initial investments in a project, delayed completion also represents heavy blow, let alone an abrupt termination.

As a pioneer in the automobile industry, Jinbei Auto appeared to be trapped by the US and Japanese companies. Indeed, it was obvious that some people with ulterior motives had already customized a "blockade chain" to prevent China from absorbing new technologies from overseas.

At the same time, Chinese scientists faced another humiliation. The subcompany of the China National Petroleum Corporation (CNPC), Bureau of Geophysical Prospecting Inc. (BGP), which was responsible for oil exploration during this period, needed to introduce IBM supercomputers from the US. Instead of selling the required number of computers, the US side only agreed to rent one of them to BGP, under the condition that US workers be sent along as supervisors.

CNPC had no choice but to set aside a room for US workers to operate the computer alone, with each calculation performed under the US workers' supervision. The Chinese side were never allowed to enter the operations room, even though they had to pay for these foreign supervisors.

This made Chinese people feel so wronged. Well, there was no way out of this situation. The home-made supercomputer was so unreliable that the lifeline was clenched in the hands of others. As the Chinese proverb says, "People have to head down under the eaves". Hearing this, Jiang Xinsong said with indignation: "You deserve to be bullied when you are lagged behind and you will be restricted if you rely on others. We should never let this happen in the robot sector."

This experience taught Chinese scientists a lesson and motivated them to catch up with world-class technologies, resulting in the development of China's own Yinhe series of supercomputers. In 2000, China's supercomputer Yinhe-IV was launched and its indicators reached the advanced international standards of that time. With it, China's high-end computer system stepped onto a new level and has been developing continuously ever since.

Later, speaking of this outcome, Song Jian, the former director of the State Science and Technology Commission, said with emotion, "It was originally a great shame for Chinese people. But we now own various kinds of supercomputers and they are mass produced. We no longer need to ask the Americans for help. Even if they want to sell them, the price should be decided by quality."

Jinbei's automated assembly line project ran aground due to the lack of AGVs. The company's boss had no choice but to seek help from another foreign company but he was also rejected. The automated assembly line at Jinbei was aborted, another victim of the business strategy pursued by the US and Japan. At that time, how to clean up the mess became a sore point for Jinbei executives. They could not litigate for compensation, only swallow the injustice.

Later, the boss of Jinbei heard about the domestic robot maker, namely, the SIA of the CAS. Given the urgency, general manager Zhao Xiyou came to the SIA and complained to Jiang Xinsong about the half-finished project, hoping they could lend a hand. On hearing this, Jiang was too angry to sit still. The US and Japan had pushed it too far!

He told Zhao Jinglun, Bai Xiaobo and several other technical backbones, "This production line is a 'feel-good line'. It produces ambition more than cars. It is one of the projects under the 863 Programme we have to tackle and you are in charge of it!"

Zhao Xiyou went to the Jinbei workshop together with the research staff, only to find various components scattering on the ground, some of which were still inside packages. Zhao Xiyou said to Zhao Jinglun: "Please just try your best. The budget is half spent and the rest is left to you." After careful examination, Zhao Jinglun replied: "Don't worry, we can handle it." With the support of Jiang Xinsong, Zhao Jinglun brought the staff together into a research group without delay, which studied new AGV technology in the automobile industry, tackling one problem after another like dissecting a sparrow.

At that time, the core "chip" and the controller "brain" for robots developed by the SIA were technically mature. However, the staff still needed to resolve a series of practical problems concerning robot assembly and assembly line construction.

III. The AGV's maiden show

The AGV is an exotic newborn in this world. How should we introduce it into China? It is a task demanding wisdom and determination.

A special team for AGV breakthroughs, consisting of Bai Xiaobo, Bian Guishi, Wang Hongyu, Zhou Guobin and Li Fengjun, was formed at the SIA. Bai Xiaobo was the team leader and Zhao Jinlun was the responsible person for the project.

At first, he had to start from scratch since no relevant information was available. News of the joint AGV production line between JiEr Machine-Tool Group Co., Ltd., and IAI America promoted Zhao Jinglun to send some team members to pay them a visit and learn about their technologies. However, the US side was in charge of the programme, which refused to share any information with outsiders. The Chinese side could do little about this. This angered Zhao Jinglun, who even swore. In turn, it was unanimously resolved that all members would strive to acquire the technology by themselves.

Thus, the team invited technicians from Jinbei to share what they had witnessed at the production site in US. But all they could prove was a description of the process rather than of the laws and principles. Starting from the stories that were shared, the special team tried to deduce the technological design.

Experiments were carried out by Zhao Jinglun and other members. But, in the early days, some prototypes in one lab simply could not function as planned. Somehow, the AGVs would stop at certain points. Neither the algorithms after multiple verifications and re-examinations nor the technological principles indicated that there was anything wrong. But, still, the AGVs would just not move.

The undiagnosed reasons worried the team to the extent that they skipped meals and sleep: "What on earth is wrong with you, AGV robots?"

Zhang Lei, a recent postgraduate who majored in software from

North-western Polytechnic University was assigned to the special team. Thanks to his complementary research subject, he joined as the youngest member. He still remembered those gloomy days: "We were almost desperate. The project could have been given up already if it were not led by Zhao Jinglun."

But Zhao Jinglun encouraged everyone: "Don't lose faith and don't give up. How can we simply throw it away after it was conceived by us? Like a child, it needs to be nurtured with patience." Could the immature mobile robot be affected by the environment like a human minor? This was the judgement of Zhao Jinglun, "The problem is not with the AGV itself. Let us switch to checking its working environment."

It turned out later that the AGV was oversensitive to the environment. The mysterious problem was caused by external signal interference. Problem solved. Thanks to the relentless efforts of the special team, the AGV went through operations testing in the production workshop following the successful lab tests in the presence of all members. The real operation was far more difficult than the lab test because, in real life, the vehicle had to withstand 24 hours of production while maintaining a high level of stability and reliability.

To everyone's surprise, the AGV became uncooperative on-site. Unused to the new environment, it twisted and turned all the time at work. The technical challenge lay on the assembly line.

It took more than one hour by bike and two hours by bus to arrive at the Jinbei factory from the institute. As a result, bike tyres needed frequent repairs. Imitating the factory workers, the team members learned the operation process by heart and improved their plans under the leadership of Zhao Jinglun. It was so chilly in the Jinbei workshop in winter that everyone's fingers were still frozen, even with gloves on, while typing on the keyboard.

Back then, many AGVs abroad could only walk straight along tracks on the ground. But the one developed by the institute could initiate navigation in assignment tracking. In addition to linear walking, it could also complete advanced tasks, such as turning on itself. It was the first to do so in China and among the best in the world. With model recognition, the robot could make judgements on the environment and walk independently. The technological breakthrough was based on the integration of machines and electronics, with expertise in mechanics, appliances, algorithms and sensing.

Two and a half years of arduous efforts finally led to a mature

AGV in 1993, which was ready to leave the lab. It was a Chinese robot, with our own technologies, born and raised in the country. On 30th November 1993, the first general assembly line for automobiles with the application of AGVs was established in the SIA and was applied in Jinbei's factory.

Shortly afterwards, the production line was put into full operation and approved by experts. With such advances, Jinbei buses were mass-produced and awarded first place in national competitions for light trucks and tourism buses.

The president of Jinbei came to the institute to express his gratitude in person, with he did wholeheartedly: "This batch of robots has pushed the technologies for the industrial production of automobiles in China to a higher level."

Hearing that Jinbei had adopted AGVs independently designed by China on its assembly line, the US company that had partnered with Jinbei sent a message that the US government now agreed to export the technology to China.

This is an old trick of offering an olive branch after a total blockade. "Thank you for your offer but we have our own AGVs" replied the president of Jinbei Auto.

Foreign AGV providers cut down the price from 1.5 million

yuan to less than one million per machine, having learned about the breakthroughs in China's AGVs. The magic of the market's "invisible hand" amazed Qu Daokui. When the technology was only exclusive to themselves, foreign companies were so arrogant that they did not care to share their price, let alone sell the machines. But they lowered their head once someone else had acquired the technology and entered the market. The market was so interesting.

This also taught Qu Daokui that technology-intensive products with innovations, which greatly impacted the market, would be chased after by market participants. Qu said, "This has proven that our technology is advanced. At the same time, it shows that we Chinese people are fully capable of reaching the frontline of the world's high technologies by ourselves. There is no reason why we would accept the superiority of foreign technologies."

Partnership at this most difficult time weighed heavier and consolidated mutual trust with which Jinbei introduced the second AGV auto general assembly line from the SIA in 1996. The testimony provided by the client can still be found in the archives of the institute:

"In the past, the operation required 28 people. The number is now down to six to eight. The output per shift was 800 units but has now increased to 1,600. Within one year, the new added turnover was 2.3 billion yuan and the new added profit (net income) was 230 million yuan. Conclusion: With the completed assembly line, the labour intensity is significantly lowered, reducing the stress of the undersupplied labour force and effectively ensuring the product quality. The price of the line was only one third of the foreign alternatives. The cost is coming down and profit is going up."

CAS academician Wang Tianran recalled: "The AGV assembly line in Shenyang Jinbei Auto was successfully developed in the 1990s and applied to the whole industry in the market against all odds. We can say we owe this success to the Americans. Their blockade and embargo in key technologies imposed on China pushed us to design our own."

In one science meeting in Beijing, the President of Shenyang Machine Tool Co., Ltd., said that the core parts of CNC machine tools were still monopolized by other countries as China had failed to obtain the technology after so many years. He went to Wang Tianran for a solution. Wang joked, "The best way out is to invite the US government to the negotiation table, where they will impose an embargo on China. Within three years, they will no longer want to return to the Chinese market even if they want to because, by then, we will have already designed our own." Everyone was amused.

Someone gave Wang Tianran a thumbs up amidst the laughter. "This is so true!" The conclusion triggered heated discussions and reflections among the scientists. Indeed, we should thank our opponents for what we are today.

IV. The debut of Chinese welding robots

In the mid-1990s, there were two major achievements that stood out in China's development of robots, namely, underwater vehicles and industrial robots. The latter had two landmark products: welding robots and AGVs.

In retrospect, Wang Tianran said, "The development of welding robots was our priority. Back then, there were too few auto industries that applied robots. Welding robots were mainly used in construction machinery industries where welding was in great demand. Technologies like spot welding and arc welding were very sophisticated and thus had higher requirements on robots. The plates in construction machinery are thick and big, the welding of which takes a long time. Besides, the high temperature and arc light are hazardous to the human body. At the same time, the quality of welding is crucial for a sizeable construction part. With the quality of human welding difficult to ensure, a single flaw may result in the abandonment of the whole piece. Foreign companies generally reject anything except products welded by robots for fear of substandard goods. So, we were convinced that welding robots had a considerable market."

In 1994, Qu Daokui, having completed his studies in Germany, brought home his research results, namely, the application of neural networks in simulation environments in order to control robots. In practice, he added some effective neural network algorithms, which achieved breakthroughs in the control technologies of Chinese robots, pushing China to the technological frontline in the world.

Wang Yuechao also returned to China after the completion of the research project with Professor Tan Zizhong in WUSTL. The "core and brain circuit" project was concluded. The world's most advanced technologies in the control system are now in the hands of SIA.

However, the body of the robots designed by the research partner of the institute failed to pass the quality examination. The brain and the core of the robots had no place to be detached from a body and limbs. Director Wang Tianran was very anxious that the robot control units, after so much human efforts and funds, could not be utilized. Without a body, the robot could never leave the lab and enter the market.

Wang Tianran said, "Auto manufacturing was thriving in the mid-1990s, which drove the demand for industrial robots. Foreign robots dominated the Chinese market at an overcharged price, but our hands were tied."

The cooperation with Russia in developing underwater robots gave Qu Daokui some inspiration. If the project succeeded, then China would instantly achieve something that took other countries 20 years. Could we find another partner to draw strength from in the same way?

He made a proposal to Jiang Xinsong and Wang Tianran that China could produce its own industrial robots with imported robotic bodies and our own control units. The idea was approved by Jiang and Wang, who believed that it was the only way out.

From whom should we purchase? After careful deliberation, the team agreed to buy Japanese robots, which were much cheaper than the European ones but with good quality. But would they sell them to us? As they spoke, the Japanese side came to the institute with an intention to cooperate. They hoped that they could sell their robots to China. It was exactly what Jiang Xinsong's team had wished for.

History just repeats itself. The same old story repeated but with roles reversed. The Japanese company that approached Mr Jiang was in fact the one that had rejected him 15 years ago on his first trip to Japan. No one expected that what Jiang said back then would became a reality 15 years later.

The representative of the company proposed to visit the institute but did not receive an immediate response. History evolves in a way that defies prediction. Like a magician, time seems to make random arrangements with destiny, which leads to constant changes. Sometimes, a person ends up falling into a trap that was dug by himself.

Wang Tianran and Qu Daokui assumed that Jiang the director had never forgot the humiliation 15 years ago. He was hurt and just could not pretend that it was all water under the bridge. But, to everyone's surprise, Jiang Xinsong invited the Japanese experts to the institute on the second day and made thoughtful arrangements, including a luncheon, for the visitors. During the discussion, the Japanese side, who finally remembered the ill treatment they gave to Mr Jiang 15 years ago, expressed their apologies. Jiang

Xinsong raised his glass and said, smilingly, "We hope that we, as neighbours, can become good friends. With friendly coexistence, we can cooperate with an open mind." But, for some reason, the professionals made their excuses and left the institute.

When everyone else was disappointed to see the loss of the opportunity, Jiang Xinsong comforted them with confidence: "Don't worry. The Japanese will come back to us." He was right. Yaskawa Electric and Nissei Electric made their way to the institute and expressed their cooperation intentions. Suddenly, the institute became a popular destination.

Someone exclaimed that Jiang Xinsong could foretell the future like a prophet! In fact, he made the right judgement, not because of some supernatural ability but because of his discernible observation.

The boom of the Japanese economy in the 1980s saw the accumulation of excess speculation, overcapacity and real-estate bubbles. But, as the illusions disappeared in the 1990s, the economy hit bottom where many companies could barely survive. To save themselves, they relied on exporting their technologies. With that, how could they say no to China, an emerging major market?

As Jiang Xinsong saw it, there would be an incessant flow of Japanese visitors. Before Jiang left for South Korea with a delegation,

Jiang told Wang Tianran to remain patient and talk through all the details with the other side because we had the upper hand. Thanks to the mutual visits of the two state leaders, China and South Korea reached a series of agreements on technological exchanges and had frequent communications. The successful trial of the new AGV designed by the institute aroused the interest of Samsung Techwin of South Korea. The delegation, which was led by Jiang Xinsong, was assigned to oversee the consultation related to the technological transfer.

An industrial welding robot takes the form of a robotic arm, which fulfils certain functions with its own power and control. Consisting of a control unit and a body, it is only a shell without a core and a brain.

Qu Daokui believed that we should synergize our own advanced robot controlling system with the cost-effective robotic body from Japan in order to develop our robot industry in our own way.

Back then, the worry was concerned with compatibility between the body, which cost hundreds of thousands of yuan, and our own control unit. But Qu Daokui was confident that our controlling system could adapt to any bodies. There were also propositions that we should buy one body to experiment with first of all.

Wang Tianran and Qu Daokui both reckoned that such a practice would raise the cost and delay a full-scale rollout. In support, Jiang Xinsong said, "If we decide to buy, then we should buy a batch". In 1994, the institute made a big and bold move. It spent 15 million yuan in purchasing 19 robotic bodies from Yaskawa Electric in one breath. Applied with self-designed control units, the industrial welding robots were produced and entered the market.

"It was risky decision. We did not have any fixed clients so we would have not broken even, thus endangering the institute if we had failed to sell the 19 robots. I would have become the culprit and that amount of money was almost astronomical in those days." Wang Tianran was still excited when recalling the old times. "Despite the possible risks, Jiang Xinsong and the whole institute were determined. Our courage derived from the confidence in the performance of our control units. Qu Daokui, a fresh graduate back from Germany, was assigned to the production of the spot and arc welding robots and supporting equipment, as well as their introduction on the market."

As the head of the programme, Qu Daokui took over responsibility. The hard nuts in technologies were cracked by a team of over 10. Finally, the first batch of high-functioning welding robots was produced, which combined the Japanese bodies and Chinese control units. Without the controlling system or its Chinese spirit, the bodies were no more than a bunch of scattered parts. There was no reason why they couldn't be called Chinese robots with a Chinese identity.

The first three welding robots were operating smoothly on production lines that made perfect products. "We made it!" cried the science professionals and workers on-site.

By the end of 1995, all the robots were sold and the investment of 15 million yuan was recouped. Eventually, the worries of Wang Tianran were dispelled. The first battle was a success, which boosted the confidence and courage of the professionals in the institute and marked a watershed moment in the automation history of China. In fact, China needed to produce its own robotic body in addition to its own control units before it could make genuine Chinese robots. That is to say, developing robotic bodies became a must.

Shortly afterwards, more good news came in. The robotic lab at the Harbin Institute of Technology produced a robotic body with key parts produced in China. Here they were, welding robots that were authentic Chinese.

V. Gold-digging abroad

In September 1994, Jiang Xinsong introduced to Samsung Techwin the superiority of Chinese-developed AGVs during his visit to South Korea.

At that time, China and South Korea maintained a good relationship and close ties. Leaders of both countries took the initiative to advance bilateral economic, trade, cultural and technological cooperation during mutual visits. As experts of Samsung Techwin arrived at the SIA, they were so surprised by the AGVs because they never imagined that China had such advanced mobile robots.

Foreign AGVs used for assembly in automobile factories ran on tracks, while Chinese AGVs were automatic and free from tracks, making them superior to similar products found in the international equipment manufacturing industry in terms of technology level and leading the way in this field. The senior management of Samsung Techwin was very interested and decided on the spot to cooperate with China. On 30th October 1994, it entered into a technology transfer agreement with the SIA.

After learning that the Chinese welding robot developed by the SIA had taken the spotlight in the Changchun First Automobile Workshop and that the AGV was officially put into operation at Jinbei and ready to be exported to South Korea, Song Jian, state councillor and director of the State Scientific and Technological Commission, could not wait to see it. On 30th September 1996, Song Jian made a special trip to the SIA to inspect the progress of the national 863 Programme key projects.

"This is Qu Daokui, leader of the 863 Programme research team and director of the Robot Engineering Development Department. He is also my first postgraduate student in robotics. He will give the report today" Jiang Xinsong said to Song Jian. "Good. You are the first postgraduate of director Jiang and probably the first postgraduate in robotics in China" said Song Jian, holding the hands of Qu Daokui.

Qu Daokui talked about the principle structure, performance characteristics and manufacturers' application of welding robots and AGVs with great familiarity. Song Jian nodded from time to time. As Qu Daokui stated that they were preparing for batch production and moving towards industrialization through market exploitation, Song Jian said cheerily, "It's our fundamental aim and direction to realize the industrialization of scientific and technological achievements and turn them into productive forces to serve national economic development. The State Council was working out policies and measures to reform the science and technology systems. You can take a bold step, beat a path and explore experience!"

On 30th October 1996, Chinese mobile robot technology was exported to South Korea. On that day, the staff of the SIA ornately decorated the AGVs as daughters to be married off and held a brief seeing-off ceremony for them before being exported abroad for the first time.

With only a small disk installed on a vehicle with an area of 2 m², the export of AGV technology was a big deal worth 350 thousand US dollars to the scientific academy back then. For the first time, Chinese researchers were amazed by the endless charm of technology. Once you create a new technology, you will have a say and hold a dominant position in the market, followed by great economic benefits. Chinese robots rose to fame. The scientific and technological personnel of the SIA were highly inspired.

Chinese AGV technology had reached a certain level and outshone others in the industry. It had a great impact on the foreign monopoly in the robot market and attracted a crowd of foreign enterprises.

Qu Daokui explained to foreign travelling businessmen that the AGV technology had been sold to South Korea. The funny thing was that these businessmen thought they heard it wrong and that Qu Daokui had actually bought the technology from Samsung. Americans and Europeans especially did not buy it. They sought confirmation from Qu Daokui over and over again. "We are the seller, not the buyer of the technology" replied Qu Daokui. They still did not believe it entirely, for they thought Samsung's technology must be more advanced than that of China. They then continued to seek answers from South Korea, which greatly upset them. Not long after, the price of foreign robots on the Chinese market went down by one third.

At that moment, Chinese robots began to enter the market. They were qualified and competitive enough to withstand the test of the market tide.

Chapter VI
"Birth Certificate"
Granted by the State

Launching a market model: the opportunities to enter the market

had come. It was time for Chinese robots to take action.

How could scientific and technological personnel act after

declaring war on the market?

I. Science researchers and businessmen

In the late 1990s, the Chinese automobile manufacture industry was booming. Chinese manufacture industries overall started a new round of transformation and upgrades, while foreign robots strove to make their way into the Chinese market. Having kept a close eye on market trends, Qu Daokui realized that the moment to put Chinese robots on the market had arrived. It was the time.

Since October 1997, under the guidance of Qu Daokui, Chinese robots began to move out of the lab and into the market. The institute decided that director Qu Daokui and deputy director Hu Bingde should implement a "one institute, two systems" principle within the Robot Engineering Development Department, which meant independent management and separate accounts identical to the running model of a company. They should develop technologies and exploit the market and seek out users at the same time.

As a group of young science researchers, their passion and dreams were critical in creating their robots for a sea trial. But, how could these science researcher-business operators manage business activities? Since Qu Daokui's team had carried out the sea trial, all of them should have considered themselves an operator. Being "landlubbers" though, they had been put out to sea with their robots.

Once, an engineer called Li Qingjie was working on an S78080 project led by an elderly veteran aimed at designing and installing a welding robot for an enterprise. The price of the design was 400,000 yuan. During negotiations with the enterprise, the veteran was quite honest. He just quoted as per the price of the design and ignored profits and tax, leaving no room for accounting for the cost of the project. When they bargained with each other, the enterprise cut down the price by a half and said that it could only offer 200,000 at most. To everyone's surprise, the veteran could not help but strike the bargain. The enterprise concluded the transaction at half price with such words.

On second thoughts, Li Qingjie realized that the project would not make any profits. Instead, it would lose money. The veteran said that he felt shy bargaining with the enterprise.

Li Qingjie could not hold it any more. This would only result in a double loss. How could this help to develop robots? He suggested that any quotation should make allowances for profits and tax apart from cost. Upon hearing this, the veteran said to Li, "Good point. You do it then". At this point, then, Li Qingjie was assigned to negotiating contracts for projects.

Li Qingjie not only had professional technology expertise, he also had a strong sense of business acumen during the running of the whole project. The marketing genius of Li Qingjie was discovered by Qu Daokui.

Li Qingjie was an engineer born in Anshan in 1962. He graduated from Dalian University of Technology in 1984 and assigned to the SIA in 1993 for researching robotic welding technologies. In terms of some key projects, Qu Daokui would let Li Qingjie negotiate quality and price with buyers and sign contracts.

There was an occasion when a project was taking a long time to set up. So, Qu Daokui asked Li Qingjie to manage the design, calculation and negotiation of the whole plan as well as the installation and operations of the project. The project was a great success, which not only satisfied the client very much but also delivered huge profits. Later on, frequent contacts made Li Qingjie and the client very familiar with each other. "We did not know you technical people and your technologies so well during early negotiations, so we felt insecure and ruled you out. Then we found you were too deskbound and honest. That's why we just gave up bargaining with you anymore" said the client.

That is what technical personnel are like. Honesty is one of their merits, while too much honesty is among their demerits. Once recognized, such honesty leads to trust, a resource and an advantage.

Scientists are not businessmen. Cultural ideas and rules in the scientific field and the market are different. Complete solutions could become fragmented information and plans when presented to the client due to a lack of communication skills. In business negotiations, scientific researchers are not good at bargaining, so they often lose money when dealing with clients.

Qu Daokui decided to set up a marketing department to eliminate such differences. At the beginning of 1999, Qu Daokui and Hu Bingde, deputy director of the Technical Research and Development Department went to talk with Li Qingjie, telling him that they were going to set up a company and a marketing department and inviting him to serve as general manager. Li Qingjie kept shaking his head after hearing this and said, "I am a technical person. How could I know about marketing?" Meanwhile, Qu Daojie was trying to play to Li Qingjie's strengths in developing marketing.

A marketing department was a must after establishing the company. Qu Daokui and Hu Bingde thought over and over again that hardly any of these immersed scientific researchers had a gift for marketing; but Li Qingjie did, even though he did not enjoy engaging in marketing. He came to the SIA in the first place because of professional robotic technologies. Psychologically, he could not accept this change in role from a researcher to a salesman. Qu Daokui and Hu Bingde did not succeed in persuading Li Qingjie after talking to him twice. On the third occasion, Qu Daokui told Li Qingjie, "We work together to develop the market and we are going to set up a robots company. No matter how good your product is, you will also lose money if you cannot sell it. How do we enter the market? Marketing is the vanguard, which has vital importance. If you are not up to it, then who is? I believe you can do it. This is a great cause." The words of Qu Daokui were full of trust.

Li Qingjie understood Qu Daokui's concerns. He knew that everyone was in the same boat and playing an indispensable role and that everyone should submit to the overall situation. Unwillingly, though, Li Qingjie nodded at last and set up the marketing team.

Could these "scientific researchers" become excellent salesmen in the market?

II. Surviving in the cracks

In the late 1990s, robotic technologies in the auto manufacturing industry were monopolized by some large foreign companies, leaving no entry for Chinese robots that had just rolled out of the lab. After the financial storm, robotic technologies that had been left out for a long while rapidly came back to life in the auto manufacturing industry.

How could Chinese robots find a place in the market?

Qu Daokui found that the AGV technology that they had developed in the very beginning was relatively synchronous with that found in foreign countries, whose mobile robots were just about to be put on the market. Their AGVs had no new clients for several years after being put into production in the assembly shop at Jinbei. At that time, most robots used for assembly in auto factories still needed tracks, but their AGVs did not. In comparison, their technology was more advanced than that of foreign countries.

After a market survey and analysis, Qu Daokui found that their AGVs possessed technological strengths and superiority in service convenience. It's just that the distance was too far to let others know and advertising was insufficient to let clients know about these products. Actually, they had the strength already to rival foreign enterprises in this field. Qu Daokui made up his mind to let Chinese robots stand up and go global.

At the end of 1997, Qu Daokui heard that Liuzhou Minicar Company was going to cooperate with America on a new car, so he led the engineering technicians to recommend their AGVs. After listening to the presentation, the company found that the offer was everything they needed and came to the SIA for a site survey there and then.

Seeing that the AGVs were automatically running around in the shop without any tracks, the foreign experts were so interested that they signed a purchase contract with Qu Daokui for nine sets of AGVs. Their AGVs quickly became minor celebrities in the domestic auto industry. Soon afterwards, the bid was won for a tender issued by the Chang'an Automobile Group. Chinese robots began to be seen in the domestic market.

Inspired by this, Qu Daokui decided to try and live in the cracks of the market and gain a foothold in heedless areas of his rivals. If one could not gain access to big orders in the mainstream market, he or she should seek to secure small orders in the cracks of the market. They used "outflanking tactics", starting with foreign enterprises and gradually opening the breakthrough point. Chinese robots began to leap onto the market stage.

In 1998, American Tenneco (Walker) Auto Parts Company in Shanghai was in urgent need of arc welding robots to manufacture the Passat vehicle exhaust system. After learning that the SIA was specialized in robot development, experts from Tenneco (Walker) made a trip here.

They were very interested in the welding robot created by Qu Daokui's team. Through mutual communication, they proposed to try out the robot in their shop for four months.

Back then, all robots manufactured by the SIA had been put to use. New products could not be released in only four months. But it was a shame to let go of this "fish".

Relying on quick-wittedness, Qu Daokui thought of a welding robot they had provided to the lab of Shanghai Jiao Tong University for a teaching experiment not long ago. Shanghai Jiao Tong University was the alma mater of Jiang Xinsong. They had been maintaining close cooperation and offering mutual support over many years. He contacted Shanghai Jiao Tong University immediately to borrow the welding robot to test it at Tenneco (Walker).

The trial was a big success. Tenneco (Walker) signed a 10-set purchase contract with the SIA. As such, following the AGVs, Chinese welding robots emerged and entered the market and gradually gained fame.

Qu Daokui and his team gave play to strong points, avoided shortcomings and mainly advertised self-developed AGVs in the market. These AGVs were cheaper than foreign counterparts and had lower maintenance costs. A set of such AGVs could be used for more than a decade. A large amount of money could be saved in maintenance. In the Chinese market, it is economic to use AGVs developed by a Chinese company. If there is a problem, the maintenance service is responsive. Qu Daokui's commitment to clients is to arrive on-site in two hours.

As Qu Daokui organized the market team and actively carried

out the marketing of AGVs, in turn receiving other orders from several auto manufacturers before long for a batch of customized AGVs. It was in this way that Chinese robots stepped into the market of the automobile manufacturing industry.

Adopting such methods, they started by obtaining small projects and small orders, accumulating technological strengths and a reputation step by step. They gradually won big projects and big orders, thus breaking the curse that Chinese people could not make robots with greater success than foreign rivals.

Although Chinese robots stood out, they could have been stifled in the cradle when they sought to live in the cracks of the market. Faced with competition from international giants, Qu Daokui sighed: "Just like a race between a newborn baby and a robust adult, it's a very tough battle. It will become more and more fierce and leave you with slow growth from time to time. Only through sustainable technical innovation and market exploitation can Chinese robots become stronger and invincible."

III. Outwitting an "old master"

At that time, Shanghai's auto industry started to surge like the rising tide of the sea. If Chinese robots wanted a place on the international stage, it had to gain a foothold in Shanghai, an international metropolis. As a consequence, Qu Daokui and Li Zhenggang, an engineer, decided to travel all the way to Shanghai. They hoped that Chinese robots would take a foothold here.

This visit came after Qu learned that the Shanghai Volkswagen (SVW) was considering upgrading and equipping its assembly line with welding robots. Introducing his welding robot to his new clients, he showed them a photo taken of the one demonstrated at Tenneco (Walker), which was a novelty to his clients.

At that time, compared with robots produced by the SIA, the foreign equipment used at SVW was rather backward. Welding robots had not yet been applied on their production lines. After much product presentation, Qu and Li finally persuaded experts from SVW, a Sino-foreign joint venture. However, these experts were not confident and asked them to provide a welding robot for testing before negotiating a mass production contract.

Unexpectedly, during this process, Li was at loggerheads with an "old master". Both sides were locked in a fierce struggle, role-playing a tale in which the "old master" was outwitted.

This corporation had a senior technician who was called the "old master" by people in Shanghai. The "old master" was more than 10 years older than Li. Seeing himself as a senior technician and a "big potato" with rich experience, he was somewhat arrogant and looked down on Li.

In the beginning, the "old master" told Li the way in which he used to assemble machines and demanded Li follow his old ways. But Li wanted to make some improvements. However, the master said he could only accept his own ways, not allowing Li to make any adjustment. After Li produced a workpiece according to his own design plan, the "old master" was defiant and made every effort to find faults in it. Li was also defiant, saying in his mind, "What makes you so arrogant? Aren't you Chinese as well? Why are you so proud of working for foreigners?"

The "old master" said that Li's workpiece was irrational and demanded it be constructed the other way around. But Li was rather stubborn and made no adjustment. When Li was absent, the "old master" asked two of his apprentices to disassemble the workpiece and turn it around. As a result, Li's design plan was completely disrupted.

Li was very annoyed with it. Although the master's technical approach was able to meet the prevailing requirements in certain respects, it had led to the sacrifice of other functions. Being unable to operate in a coordinated way, the product would be prone to running into trouble.

Nevertheless, it would be unwise for Li to deface the "old master", as he was an elusive client. So, he chose not to take it too seriously. But, what if the product ran into trouble in the future? In the end, Li would be to blame. People would say that Li's technology was defective, which would discredit the SIA. So, Li must be responsible for his clients as well as himself and put it right: this represented the professional ethics to which he had always adhered.

Engineers and technicians in the scientific research field shared a common faith: you can disrespect me, but I must gain your respect for my profession; you can look down on me, but I won't let you look down on my team and technology.

"Please give me half an hour and I will work out a solution that meets your requirements" Li said patiently to the "old master". Actually, what Li wanted was to change the master's methodology again. Both of them tensed themselves in the mind to struggle with each other. While one said this, the other would insist on another way. So long as they were struggling with each other, Li had to work out a perfect solution to gain the upper hand.

Half an hour later, Li worked out a plan. The original materials were not wasted at all. Requirements were met by adding a lath and changing the position of the robot. The performance of the robot was perfect. "It's good for us to compete in the technical field. The 'old master' is very proud and I should show him respect" said Li.

Soon, Li took charge of a follow-up project for them, which was a new project launched by the SVW. The "old master" said to Li, "This project is completely new to me. I'm afraid that I will not be able to help you. Now it's all up to you."

Li was very glad that he could carry on with the whole project in his own way. In the end, he produced a set of welding robots, whose performance was excellent. The "old master" could not help but hold up his thumb in approval. "Youth is to be regarded with respect" he proclaimed.

Li said, "No fists, no friends. We became good friends out of admiration for each other. Both of us respected science and technology. After the establishment of SIASUN, I was appointed as the general manager of its Shanghai branch. We became friends and our relationship was always very good. After retirement, he was employed as an adviser by other companies. When running into technical problems or difficulties, he often asked me for help. Besides, he has introduced many clients to me, helping my company expand its market in Shanghai. Gradually, we got a firm foothold in Shanghai."

At the end of 1998, Qu Daokui complied with the trend and led the SIA to cooperate with the local government in Jinqiao, Shanghai, and jointly registered a robot company. They rented a model house covering an area of about 100 m2 in a green belt located at 51 Hongfeng Road, Shanghai. Although the house was not eye-catching, Qu, along with his team, had succeeded in bringing Chinese robots into the market.

Chapter VII
Flexing Muscles on
a Grand Stage

A competitive market: the "lucky dog" grew strong

through trials and hardships in the market.

How did Chinese robots get onto the world stage?

I. Let the spirit stand up first

Although Jiang Xinsong has passed away, his spirit was still living in his dreams and in an era that he had foreseen...

In April 2000, at the first plenary meeting of SIASUN, Wang Tianran, president of the company and director of the SIA, said emotively to over 30 scientific researchers in the SIA: "Twenty years ago, our former director Jiang Xinsong had dreamed of developing Chinese robots and bringing China into an era of robots within two decades. Today, we have realized his dream. But this is just the very beginning of the dream. To fulfil this dream, we have to realize two more dreams: one is to promote China's robot research and development capabilities to a world-leading level, the other is to develop China's own robot industry as soon as possible."

Wang explained that, in the era of the knowledge economy, the most important thing is obtaining leading science and technology with independent intellectual property rights. If other people have already obtained a certain technology and we catch up with them, this is indeed remarkable. However, it can only be rated as an "advanced world level". In fact, the "world-leading level" must be based on our "own pioneering work". Real "self-empowerment" must be based on "independence". As Wang said, "I hope that all of us will pursue this dream as our eternal cause".

After its establishment, SIASUN rented a workshop in the SIA as its office. Upon entering the door, staff could see Jiang's familiar figure in a photo taken when he was giving a lecture. Beneath it were the core values of the company's corporate culture as formulated by Qu Daokui: striving for excellence, creating perfection, honesty and dedication, and serving the homeland. This was the "SIASUN gene".

At that time, dozens of people worked in a big room. All of them focused on their own work. The room was so quiet that people could almost hear the sound of a fallen needle. When people needed to discuss problems or difficulties, they always tried their best to lower the voice. They were very enthusiastic and highly efficient.

Everybody worked wholeheartedly, trying hard to be the fastest, the best and perfect. Overtime work had become the norm. Lights in the design hall never went out before 10 p.m., while the graphic plotter never stopped, with people lining up for plotting. Many people couldn't fall asleep even when they returned to their dorms from work, because they were in high spirits and unable to relax. Hence, they had to watch TV before falling asleep. They had never experienced such a working tempo and state.

At 6 a.m., they would start a busy day all over again. Day in and day out, people worked like this all the time, without feeling bored. All of them were immersed in a proactive and hardworking atmosphere, without interference from negative factors. The whole team showed unprecedented passion and vigour for the cause. Each of them had a strong feeling of urgency to focus on building a strong SIASUN. In the face of increasingly fierce market competition, these ambitious SIASUN employees could not relax at all. They wanted to join hands with Chinese robots and run together.

Each year, SIASUN would recruit a number of new employees, most of whom had recently completed their postgraduate or undergraduate studies.

At each opening ceremony of the new employee training

session, Qu would always say to the novice recruits: "As the saying aptly goes, men are afraid of choosing the wrong profession, while women are afraid of choosing the wrong husband. Since you have chosen SIASUN, you will enjoy success. Since you have chosen SIASUN, you have chosen a life of serving the homeland and the responsibility to carry on the spirit of science. The 'SIASUN gene' will be unconsciously integrated into your body. If Chinese robots are to stand up, our scientific and technological personnel shall stand up straight first. If a person is to stand up, his/her spirit shall stand up straight first. The SIASUN spirit is the key to its employees' invincibility."

At that moment, Chinese robots had already walked out of the laboratory and into the vast territory of China. However, it must take an industrialized approach to form real science and technology productivity. Although SIASUN had the "noble blood" of the CAS and made a series of national-level scientific research achievements, it must develop independently, instead of always living on the nutrition of its matrix.

SIASUN's employees were well aware that they would independently face the test of the market and create a new enterprise. But the market showed little appreciation in return. Under the aura of its past glory, SIASUN's zealous employees were rebuffed again and again before getting into the market.

It seemed that, when an inexperienced young fellow set foot into the market, his capabilities could not be enhanced without tough trials and tribulations.

Just as Qu expected, as the world economy recovered from the financial crisis, foreign companies rushed back to the Chinese market. The market was like a battlefield. In a fiercely contested market, how could the newborn SIASUN fight those international giants?

In the new century, China's manufacturing industry has embarked on a fast track. Manufacturers' demand for industrial robots has been growing with each passing day. However, this opportunity was not grasped easily. For a long time, China's industrial robot market has been monopolized by foreign companies. Under the circumstances of that time, competing with foreign companies in such a high-tech field as robotics was only a beautiful and idealistic dream.

The dream was ideal, yet reality was cruel. Soon, these passionate people found out the cruelty of this reality. The opponents they faced were such world-class companies as Sweden's ABB, German's KUKA, Japan's Fanuc and Yaskawa, and Italy's Comau. Compared with these companies, SIASUN's robots had much leeway to make up in terms of technology accumulation, scale of production, brand strength and engineering experience on large-scale projects. Users always valued the fame and brand when they bought robots. So, it was impossible to keep down opponents through price competition. The domestic market was firmly controlled by foreign robot companies, while domestic clients, out of prejudice towards domestic equipment, lacked confidence in domestic robots.

The truth could never be found out without painful experiences. Every mythology has a legend behind it.

When SIASUN's people promoted their technological products to clients, they often encountered the embarrassment of being turned down. Upon hearing that SIASUN was a domestic company, the clients unexceptionally showed a sceptical look. What the clients doubted most were along the lines of "Is SIASUN a robot company?" or "Are there any robot companies in our country?". Some clients even didn't have the patience to listen to the product briefing. They would wave their hands and say goodbye to SIASUN staff before they had finished the briefing.

As a "green hand" in this field, SIASUN was not yet well-known and nobody would show any respect to it. While a company could not prove itself with solid achievements for the time being, who dared to use its products? Moreover, robots were high-end and complicated equipment. Users could get extra benefits from cooperation with foreign companies, such as going abroad for training, which represented glory to them. What kind of benefit could they get from cooperation with SIASUN? Naturally, the company was often left out in the cold, which deeply undermined the self-esteem of the employees. Furthermore, the company's business ran into many difficulties.

Once upon a time, Qu Daokui, along with several technicians, participated in the bidding for an auto manufacturer's project. The manufacturer was very happy that there was a bid from SIASUN, thinking it was a Japanese company. After meeting Qu and finding out that he was not a Japanese, the manufacturer was a bit disappointed. But the manufacturer still asked him, "Which Japanese company do you joint-venture with?" Qu was dumbfounded and depressed. This was an identical situation to that experienced by Qu during his study in Germany. At that time, foreigners didn't believe that China could develop robots. This time, however even a Chinese company wasn't prepared to believe it. To Qu's surprise, upon realizing that SIASUN was a Chinese company, the manufacturer declined his offer.

II. Ways cannot be changed

The SIASUN company was still struggling to get orders in the competitive business pool, unable to make a breakthrough. It was only at this point that they discovered that this was an unequal war with huge discrepancy in power.

On one side were China's small and weak enterprises, which had not yet understood what the market was all about, while, on the other side, there were the multinational companies that had fought for many years for beneficial positioning in a market economy. There are no compromises or agreements in market competition, the only thing that counts is whether you succeed or fail as a result. Examinations before learning anything, being put on the battlefield without knowing how to shoot: this was exact the grim situation that SIASUN's people, who lacked marketization operation experience, were facing.

From being mainly engaged in the field of robotics research to leading an enterprise amid the wind and waves of the market, what could Qu Daokui do to ensure that the SIASUN company he led would achieve the dual objectives of national mission and enterprise development?

Qu Daokui was visibly emaciated during this period. Some people advised him to learn from the Lenovo Group, that if projects fail, just turn to commerce and trade, doing technology research and development after making a fortune. Liu Chuanzhi (former president of Lenovo) enjoyed great financial success using this business model. Qu had also thought about it. Before SIASUN started, he had done a thorough analysis and designed the SIASUN development path. He had also conducted an in-depth study on Lenovo's success as a typical case.

Lenovo is an example of the successful undertaking of an enterprise of the CAS in the 1980s and the pride of the scientific academic community. Qu Daokui believes that SIASUN and Lenovo represent two different types of company.

Lenovo, which started in the 1980s, is a model enterprise with the pooled resources of the CAS in terms of talents, finance and property, among others. Before the 1990s, Lenovo had completed primitive accumulation based on its trading business, which enabled it to follow the "trade-manufacture-research" development path. Until 2001, Lenovo, starting with trade, could proudly claim to have begun to rely on technology to make money after the development of a high-performance computer, meaning that its product line could be fully improved. Lenovo had started a new page in the case of China's IT progress.

SIASUN's beginnings are different to those of Lenovo. SIASUN, starting with technology, has had to find new ways and take a new path that is guided by technology. What SIASUN has in its favour is technology. With market demand dictating direction and technology innovation as the driving force, SIASUN's headquarters is responsible for research and development and project design, with the aim of providing solutions for customers, which forms a customization business model.

Soon after the foundation of the SIASUN company, Lenovo's then president Liu Chuanzhi met Wang Tianran in Beijing. He knew that the SIA had set up a robot company, the business model of which was quite different. "Do you think it's going to work?" Liu asked Wang.

"Why is it not going to work? Technology is always the point in this field. Who is going to activate the marketization of China's self-developed robots if we are not?" Wang confidently answered.

"You are enlightening the market" Liu Chuanzhi said.

"We should not only enlighten but also develop and lead the market." Wang Tianran was full of longing for the future of SIASUN.

However, while SIASUN was struggling, should it go back to the path that Lenovo took in the past? In the 1980s, it was faster to make money from trade and easier to succeed than relying on research and development. Given that, in the initial stage of reform and opening-up, there was shortage of goods and material circulation was not smooth, it was not necessary to carry out more technical research and innovation for making a profit at that time. Thus, if you were to organize some people and start up a trading company, breaking the gap between different industries and dredge the field of circulation to meet market demand, you could succeed. At that time, agents mainly made money on the basis of information asymmetry. Making money was as simple as selling a commodity for 20 yuan that only cost 10.

Now, in the 21st century, we are in a totally different age with a glutted market, while the shortage economy is outdated and everything is transparent. With an improvement in people's living standard and the change in social demand, many products appear with high-tech features. There are more requirements for technicians and technology companies in the market.

Many people tried to advise Qu Daokui to change ways, but in vain. Every success and setback he endured had already sown the seeds of tenacity in his soul. He certainly said as much: "The path cannot be changed! An eye should be kept on technical research and development based on the market demand. Our products should provide solutions for customers."

Qu Daokui had already made sure about the path to take. He wanted to work out a unique route in the business world with his technology as a trump card! Success shows up when the right person does the right thing at the right time. As for failure, excuses are not needed and meaningless. The value of failure is the lesson you learn from it.

SIASUN's staff firmly believe that it is always necessary to stand at the forefront of market trends, of technological development and of the development pattern! Let the robots grip the "invisible hand" of the market and they will create magical charm and unlimited vitality!

Now, Qu Daokui has some regrets: "SIASUN is a very lucky enterprise, it is the survivor in the tide of the market. The luckiest thing about it is that it is going in the right direction, on the right path, and doing just about everything at just the right moment."

What determines success or failure? In the chain of logic concerning success, some people say that the details determine success or failure, other say that the strategy determines success or failure, or that attitude does. In fact, every single factor is key to success or failure. Just think about it, even if the strategy is right, but there is something wrong with the details, the path to success will be blocked; and, if the strategy is wrong, and there is deviation in the direction towards the success of the goal, the efforts made in terms of the details will be meaningless. Therefore, only if every single step in the logic chain is correct will success show up as a big probability event.

SIASUN's employees today are entitled to proudly say that we have been on the right path for our own good.

But, 15 years ago, the path was still unclear and uncertain. "The Chinese can never create a good robot!" This is the kind of prejudice or deep-rooted traditional assumption about foreigners and the Chinese that saddens Qu Daokui the most. "We are faced with a number of well-known domestic enterprises. When they hear that the Chinese have made their own robots, they all ask with a sneer on their face, 'Can you really build robots?'" Qu Daokui recalls that there was even a customer who malicious said, "Stop talking, please, even if you give me the products without any costs, I won't dare to use them."

III. Commando

During the difficult period when SIASUN entered the market, a special opportunity presented itself linked to national defence projects.

In the spring of 2001, an automatic storage system was needed to be built in the logistics warehouse of the Chengdu Military Region for combat readiness training under the new situation. Although foreign companies with a keen sense of smell had long been eyeing up projects such as this, the Chinese military, for national defence security considerations, red-lighted them.

Among domestic enterprises, who would be willing to immediately take on the challenge? This kind of high-tech project was not what average enterprises could undertake; rather, this was a modernized unmanned warehouse or intelligent warehousing as it should be known. After the Military Intelligence Department came across SIASUN, a consensus was quickly reached after contact and inspections were made. The Chengdu Military Region handed over the project of creating the Automated Storage and Retrieval System (ASRS) to SIASUN.

The hands of Qu Daokui and of a Chinese military senior colonel were tightly held together. This was not only a harmonious connection between a scientist's feelings to serve the country through industry and the military's patriotic feelings, but also a blood oath to facilitate cooperation between state-owned enterprise and the armed forces.

The core technology of the intelligent warehousing system is the AGVs that can carry the goods automatically, representing the exclusive technique that evolved out of the first development work by SIASUN. In the mid-1990s, although SIASUN's AGVs were applied on the Jinbei assembly line as soon as they were created and then favoured by Samsung, this technology had somehow remained hidden in the country thereafter.

When an AGV receives a command, it travels at a magical

speed in a warehouse, putting munitions one by one in the designated positions or taking it out to a transport vehicle. This kind of project has become an important symbol of the automation of national defence security.

Soon they were hit by a shock. That day, when Wang Jiabao, the general manager of the Intelligent Logistics Division, was planning and designing an intelligent warehouse in Chengdu with his team, he suddenly received a report from an engineer that the confidential computer had disappeared! Wang Jiabao immediately broke out in a cold sweat. The entire intelligent warehouse design model and a large number of operating data and software were in the confidential computer. Once lost, years of data accumulation and painstaking efforts would be wasted; furthermore, as it contained a lot of highly sensitive information, there would have been disastrous consequences once it was uncovered.

Wang Jiabao really was in big trouble! Fortunately, he did not lose his mind and his brain still worked in orderly fashion in accordance with the procedures. His first reaction was to immediately report the matter to the military, who quickly blocked the site. At the same time, the local police deployed more than 100 people to urgently track the missing computer until it was found. Fortunately, it was quickly discovered by the police that the computer was taken into the shed as a toy by a migrant worker at the site in a safe and undamaged condition.

Wang Jiabao still has a lingering fear when he recalls it: "Alas, we were all inexperienced at that time and we will never forget about this lesson." Since then, security has become the top priority, no matter whether it is a military, local or foreign project.

Now, visitors who want to visit military-related projects being undertaken by SIASUN have to subject themselves to an "all-round" security check and training on safety, as well as visit the site accompanied by special safety supervision staff the entire time.

Since then, the high-tech products of SIASUN have been able to serve China's national defence modernization, which makes SIASUN's employees feel honoured and proud.

The successful operation of the ASRS at the Chengdu Military Logistics Warehouse helped SIASUN gain much more popularity. In autumn 2001, when it became known that SIASUN could handle intelligent warehousing, the general director of Shenyang Liming Automobile Engine came to visit the company with suspicion. As soon as he met with Qu Daokui, he asked to see SIASUN's intelligent warehousing.

When Qu Daokui brought him to the Intelligent Logistics Division, the general director of Liming burst into a big smile and said: "I have seen this in other countries before and longed for it with my life." This was even before Wang Jiabao had finished playing the computer demo. "Then I thought, when can our country also have intelligent warehouse? I never imagined that our self-developed products would be neck and neck with the foreign ones. We must have something wrong with our mind if we Chinese do not use our own products." He grabbed Qu Daokui's arm and pulled him into the car, "Let's go, go and see my place first. 'First come, first served', you have to get me a set first."

At that time, Shandong Sun Paper Corporation also came to SIASUN. As the company wanted to purchase some AGVs for their production lines, SIASUN's robots was also invited into the Sun Paper's handling workshop. Since then, the robots have been tirelessly working for Sun Paper, with the original employees no longer sweating but sitting in front of computers in the control room, admiring the landscape.

Thus, both the Shenyang Liming Automobile Engine and Shandong Sun Paper Corporation became the first customers of SIASUN. "Every project we complete will be a step forward on the basis of the original technology. Although the projects of Shenyang Liming Automobile Engine and Sun Paper do not compare with current intelligence, at that time, they were indeed very advanced. The more valuable thing is that we offer more reliable quality, more convenient home servicing and higher efficiency than they have abroad" said Wang Jiabao with confidence.

That said, SIASUN was still a novice in this field back then. In the domestic market, it was very difficult for its products and technology to enjoy more trust from domestic enterprises. Furthermore, SIASUN also suffered from being excluded by foreign giants in this industry. Some rivals were anxious to put this "little company" down.

IV. Foreign robots are acclimatized

Although foreign robot enterprises were scrambling to join the competition in the Chinese market with the growth of China's automobile industry, not all the foreign robots that flooded in could be adapted to the production environment of Chinese enterprises, with many of them appearing "acclimatized".

Foreign robots were too "standard", while the requirements for the production environment and the original spare parts for processing were relatively high. Everything around had to be standardized and normalized; otherwise the robots would not operate as normal. The production equipment and environment in Chinese factories were still not sufficiently standardized: when a little bit of end-to-end welding was needed between pieces, foreign robots could not handle it or even missed, resulting in the weldments being scrapped.

SIASUN's welding robots were different; as China's own robots, their requirements concerning the production environment were not so high.

Domestic welding robots were tailored to reflect China's national conditions, very easy to operate, more adaptable and come with a wider range than foreign products. Chinese welding robots can handle a lot of work that foreign robots cannot. Customers gradually found that Chinese robots are more effective.

At that time, numerous enterprises could not operate well due to the problems caused by foreign robots, while the costs were very high when foreign technicians came to China for overhauling, troubleshooting or after-sales servicing. Many Chinese and foreign enterprises wanted to find a suitable partner in China to ensure the normal operation of robots.

Although Chinese robots did not look especially advanced, they worked well. Some foreign companies sniffed the strength of SIASUN. Indeed, they hoped that the company could help to fit foreign robots in, getting rid of the status of "acclimatization". Taking advantage of congenital defects in the acclimatization of foreign robots, Chinese robots confidently walked into the foreign auto companies that came to China to snatch their share of the market.

At the end of 2001, Shanghai Yanfeng Jiangsen Auto Parts Co., Ltd., knocked on the door of the Shanghai branch of SIASUN for welding robots. Shanghai Yanfeng Jiangsen Auto Parts Co., Ltd., is one of the world's top 500 companies and one of the largest auto parts suppliers, meaning that they are very picky about production matters. Their previous production lines were all imported. Despite producing cars in China, they had never used Chinese equipment until then. As the foreign robots turned out to be acclimatized, they had to consider the locally available resources.

The president of Yanfeng Jiangsen came to visit SIASUN in person, which made the company overjoyed. Welding robots are SIASUN's forte.

Qu Daokui allowed the American experts to experience SIASUN's robots in the production workshop. When they saw these products, the experts showed their appreciation as well as expressed worries; after all, they were still laboratory robots. The customer was very harsh, insisting on "no down payment" as a term of cooperation. In other words, the terminal charge would only be made after the completion and approval of the project, meaning that SIASUN had to bear the full risk of the completed products not reaching the required standard.

SIASUN's manager was shocked after calculating that at least 500,000 US dollars were needed to finish a whole production set. This was an enormous figure for SIASUN, as a new start-up, and the risks were extremely high.

"Let's do it!" Qu Daokui said decisively. His boldness came from his confidence in SIASUN technology. The reason why Qu Daokui made concessions to them was not to fight for just a project, but that SIASUN needed a chance to make a breakthrough for Chinese robots to enter foreign enterprises.

The engineers Liu Changyong and Qiu Jihong teamed up with the technical staff, who, stationed in Yanfeng Jiangsen, starting to plan and design.

Liu Changyong is now the president's assistant and senior engineer. "In September 2001, I had just come back from America" he recalls. "Dr Qiu Jihong is now the general manager of the Rail Transport Division. At that time, we were both engineers and too stressed to fall asleep at night after receiving this assignment. We undertook this project with about eight technicians who had just graduated from university. We completed the final design and on-site installation within five months. We probably invested 60 to 70% of our budget, which was nearly 400,000 US dollars, into the project, which would be for nothing if we failed. It was our first time to work on this kind of automobile production line. Although the overall automation level of the system was not particularly high, it contained a lot of applications. The design concept was also very advanced for the time. The American experts were highly convinced when they saw the efforts that we had made towards error prevention, loopholes prevention etc."

When these Chinese welding robots completed the delicate parts one by one, the discerning American customer was heartily convinced. In turn, Chinese robots had finally entered the "battlefield" of foreign companies.

In August 2002, SIASUN's "120 kg Welding Robot Project" received second prize at the National Scientific and Technological Progress Awards.

That same summer, Beijing King Tiger Radiator Co., Ltd., was unable to recruit enough welders, which meant that the breach of a group of contracts was in sight. Entering the new century, a peculiar phenomenon has appeared in the Chinese equipment manufacturing industry. In the 1990s, welders born the 1960s were working in equipment manufacturing workshops; after 2000, it was those who were born in the 1970s. After that, no one was willing to be a welder any more. It was getting more difficult to recruit employees to do this tough and hard physical work. As such, general director Zhang of Beijing King Tiger Radiator was very anxious. The company had heard that robots could do welding, so it had tried to ask some companies for help. But, as none of them could take on the business, it attempted to purchase foreign robots.

Zhang was shocked when he saw how the welding robots worked in Yanfeng Jiangsen, and he was even more shocked when he was told that these were all Chinese robots developed by SIASUN.

Then Zhang went up to Qu Daokui and expressed the hope that SIASUN would quickly equip his company with a robot welding production line. Otherwise, if this batch of radiators could not be produced, not only would orders be wasted, but also the scheduled delivery in a residential area of Beijing would be affected.

Shortly afterwards, SIASUN's technicians came to Beijing with the company's own welding robot. In a test presentation, the welding robot completed the welding of a group of radiators perfectly within a very short period of time. The testing site was surrounded by staff from Beijing King Tiger Radiator. It was the first time they had seen welding robots; indeed, everybody was too shocked to move and applauded: "This guy works well!" SIASUN then got a purchase order worth 13 million yuan from King Tiger Radiator.

The most unforgettable thing for Zhang Lei, the general manager of the AGV Department, is that, during a bidding fair organized by the Hualing company in 2002, Guo Jinjun, a senior expert of the FAW, said to the Hualing's president: "SIASUN's people are scholarly businessmen, you can relax when you cooperate with them."

Guo Jinjun said that for a reason. In 1998, when the SIA was designing AGVs for FAW, Zhang Lei, along with his colleagues, and Guo Jinjun became good friends. The engineers and technicians in the SIA left FAW with a good impression of adhering to the scientific spirit. Their rigorous, honest, solid and meticulous work attitude and style won a lot of praise from the staff at FAW. The SIA was hailed as a trustworthy partner.

That was why Guo Jinjun said such kind words about SIASUN in the bidding fair of Hualing. A reputable expert's words may not play a decisive role, but an enterprise's good reputation can help it be viewed as a positive brand in the industry. SIASUN's enterprise image went onto win wide acclaim from customers and the market share, as well as bids for projects with Hualing, Cyma and other companies, constantly consolidating and expanding the market.

It is safe to say that the SIASUN has come to the point where it fits the market. It has also become an advanced model of marketization in the CAS, while factory directors and managers keep flooding through SIASUN's doors to learn from its experience.

V. Venturing in Shanghai

As SIASUN continued to grow, Qu Daokui began to look far beyond the current business scope.

When venturing into the market, SIASUN targeted two directions: Shanghai, where the automotive industry had rapidly grown, and Guangdong, where the electronics industry had boomed. It aimed to establish an international "base area" on the market frontier.

SIASUN decided to further develop the Shanghai market by leveraging a robot company that it had registered in Jinqiao, Shanghai. Thanks to sound cooperation with SVW, Qu Daokui and Li Zhenggang once again took on the project of an SVW subsidiary involving the design and installation of eight welding robots. Once again, welding robots that were "made in China" entered SVW.

At that time, Santana products were made by SVW with second-hand foreign special equipment, rather than robots. Only a few Chinese welding robots that had been designed by Li Zhenggang a few years before were still working tirelessly and efficiently. With the advent of the age of automobiles in China, SVW's ageing equipment was in urgent need of a higher production capacity. An SVW engineer once told Li Zhenggang that the company's production equipment was too old to continue in service. An awful defect linked to the age of the equipment concerned a part that had dropped off the steering wheel of a Santana car on its first day of service in Hainan. As its failing and outdated production equipment could no longer guarantee quality, it had to update its equipment.

The welding robot for the SVW project was firstly designed according to the features of the new model production and tested by SIASUN before being installed for use in SVW.

Qu Daokui told Li Zhenggang: "Only by doing a good job on this project can we gain a firm foothold in Shanghai." To save time, Li Zhenggang did not go back home for meals after taking over the project. Sometimes, when he missed a meal, he just bought a pancake and two salted duck eggs at a street vendor's stall in front of the company and ate while keeping busy with work in the workshop. Watching him eating dry food, the gatekeeper at the SIA sympathetically poured him water every day. Although working in harsh conditions, he was very happy, from deep within his heart, to witness the market application of the technology. He worked without any rest from morning until 10 p.m. when he went home to sleep. But he never felt bitter. Instead, fighting alongside his colleagues, he felt fulfilled.

When designing and manufacturing the first welding robot, the client demanded to verify the product first and approve it later, which involved a verification process. When verifying, the client strictly took a batch of German samples as a standard. The Chinese welding robot was ordered to weld hundreds of parts without stopping for 24 consecutive hours. Li Zhenggang worked continuously for two days and nights to ensure that the product successfully passed the verification and acceptance stage.

This welding robot was remarkably capable, compared with the original model, such that the client spoke highly of it and ordered 10 sets on the spot. Using this batch of welding robots, the SVW production capacity has greatly improved. The Santana 2000 was upgraded to Santana 3000, with the production capacity continuously expanded and the quality improved. With extremely handsome benefits, SVW recovered the equipment costs almost within a year.

This project once again demonstrated the capability of Chinese robots and further enhance SIASUN's excellent reputation, leading to a large number of follow-up orders as a result. Later, with the rapid development of Shanghai's automobile manufacturing industry, SIASUN made even more progress in the Shanghai market, as week as carried out process integration for the Shanghai Huizhong Automotive Manufacturing Co., Ltd., including robots for producing automotive components.

With SIASUN's market expansion in the Shanghai market, Qu Daokui detected the increasingly prominent location advantage of this city and the huge and emerging robot market. SIASUN was devoted to pushing itself to the market forefront and implementing its internationalization strategy by transforming the Shanghai branch into a gateway to the world as part of a "going global" process.

SIASUN's goal was to develop the company into an enterprise group to engage in international competition. In response, Qu Daokui decisively set up a subsidiary of Shenyang SIASUN Robot & Automation Co., Ltd., in Shanghai, which was the company known as the Shanghai SIASUN Co., Ltd. This subsidiary, targeting the huge market in the "Yangtze River Delta" region, has been serving as a base for SIASUN's strategy of internationalization ever since.

SIASUN felt financially constrained by investing a vast amount of money in establishing the SIASUN Industrial Park in the high-tech zone of Shenyang. Was it realistic to set up a branch in Shanghai?

"The decision-making process for setting up a company in Shanghai went through some ups and downs and it was understandable that there was disagreement among the group leadership" recalled Yang Luo, who is now deputy general manager of Shanghai SIASUN Co., Ltd. "We faced harsh challenges and unsatisfying operations in the early days of Shanghai market development in 2002. As a result, some colleagues were not optimistic about prioritizing Shanghai as a key area. But Qu fought back the opposition and insisted we enter the Shanghai market, believing that the company should take a long-term approach to Shanghai instead of being limited to immediate interests, as the city was crucial to the future development of SIASUN with its great influence and strong 'radiation effect'."

In August 2002, Li Zhenggang, general manager of Shanghai SIASUN, and Yang Luo took up their new positions in Shanghai.

Shanghai SIASUN had only three employees back then: one financier, one cashier and one salesperson. The only assets they had included a Santana 2000, several computers, and hundreds of thousands of yuan in cash. The office rented by the company was a model house temporarily built by a sales office with such a small yard that was impossible for it to serve as a production site. This "house on stilts" on the Shanghai Bund seemed nothing like a base for internationalization strategy. However, Qu Daokui encouraged his team, saying, "Don't underestimate this 'house on stilts' on the Bund. It stands at the forefront and faces the world."

This "house on stilts" has become a clear landmark in the history of Shanghai. Located at 51, Hongfeng Road, Shanghai, this model house in the green belt has since been turned into an international dental clinic. Li Zhenggang said: "The house is of great significance to me and I often go to visit this place. I always want to buy it but the owner doesn't want to sell."

Many conditions restricted business development in Shanghai. If Li Zhenggang and Yang Luo failed to get orders and kick-start business, they would use up all the several hundred thousand yuan by the end of the year. Developing Shanghai SIASUN was equivalent to starting a new business. Therefore, they attended to everything by themselves at the beginning, including cleaning the weeds and painting the rusted railings in the yard at the weekend. Fearing that the equipment transported from Shenyang to Shanghai would be damaged by being left outdoors for a long time and unwilling to pay for porters, they carried the equipment indoors with their hands and on their shoulders. Due to the hard labour involved, the feeble intellectuals suffered from aches in their stomachs and backs for several days.

At the beginning, Li Zhenggang and Yang Luo won several small projects worth several hundred thousand yuan. Gradually, they got their hands on multimillion-yuan projects. The large-scale projects were transferred to the Shenyang SIASUN headquarters. As Shanghai SIASUN continued to grow and develop, its engineering technology system was gradually established and the company built up the capacity to carry out general projects. It later developed many foreign-funded enterprise clients in Shanghai. Now, with the majority of clients being foreign enterprises, Shanghai SIASUN leverages geographical advantage to connect to the international market.

When SAISUN employees promoted the company at the client's office, the client was not sure about its capacity due to a lack of understanding. The company's scale was indeed too small at that time and lacked all the necessary resources, just like a dummy company. The office was so small and simple that they dared not to invite clients there to negotiate business in case it raised any doubts about the capacity of the company. It took a lot of efforts for Li Zhenggang to finally approach the UAES, a Germany-dominated Sino-German joint venture, and win a small order. As he personally engaged in every business niche, from marketing to design and production, the client suspiciously asked, "For such a small order, why do you, as the general manager, personally carry out the project?"

Li Zhenggang blushed. Fearing that the client might think the company was too small, he braced himself before making a reply: "The big boss is behind the scene and I am just a technician." The client only came to know everything about Li Zhenggang on completing the project. The client said with emotion, "I never imagined that only a few of you would have accomplished such a high-tech project. Awesome!" Li Zhenggang smiled and said, "If you need a long spoon to sup with the devil, we need the capacity to take on the job!"

This is how Shanghai SIASUN started its market development. On receiving an order, the first step its employees took was to make plans. Based on different needs, they needed to initiative new ideas and make completely individualized designs; but they had so few references at their disposal and only a few staff. However, guided by the spirit of the company, concrete progress was incrementally made.

Yang Luo recalled: "As orders increase, we often work overtime to meet the deadlines. At the beginning, clients were doubtful about our ability and tested us with only small projects. But, with excellent products and technology, we have won the trust of the clients. And bigger and bigger projects and bigger orders followed. Thanks to this process, we have accumulated more technologies and experience and built a solid foundation for the integration and optimization of technologies, as well as developed the capacity to implement large-scale engineering projects. This model allowed the company to start from scratch and develop from a small to a large scale, just like it takes a great many grains of sand to be grouped together and form a pagoda. Step by step, we gradually expanded the market. In turn, market demand has also boosted the scientific and technological innovation and enabled continuous technological improvement. As a result, the overall strength of the company has become stronger."

Shanghai SIASUN started to make profits in 2003. In 2004, a year that witnessed the rapid development of the automotive industry, Shanghai SIASUN opened up a new business space and soon became the largest robot supplier in East China.

Seeing foreign enterprises adopt SIASUN technology, Chinese enterprises have also shown their respect, many of which have made gestures about cooperation and expressed the intention to support joint efforts to build up a brand for China's advanced manufacturing industry.

This little company grew up without being noticed, with the "house on stilts" on the Bund being transformed into an international "base area". Furthermore, Chinese robots have entered the international arena and been able to "flex their muscles" with major players in the world's robotics industry.

Chapter VIII
"Magical Change"

The SIASUN family: just like the Monkey King, who could pluck off a hair and turn it into a small monkey, this company has established many small "SIASUNs" and turned them into a "kingdom" of robots.

Chinese robots can also transform, in the same way that Hercules was transformed into the "Vajradhara".

I. The eyas leaves the nest

Suffering and glory are almost must-have experiences for all successful people. Today's "kingdom of robots" has gone through a difficult take-off just like the eyas leaving the nest.

After two years of strenuous efforts to open up the market, SIASUN finally ushered in the harvest season. By the end of 2002, it had achieved contract orders worth 200 million yuan throughout the year. While gaining market share, it also reaped real profits. If merely considering the amount, the earnings were not really impressive. But, for SIASUN, a rookie in the vast sea of business, achieving a per capita output value of more than one million yuan is worthy of pride.

Qu Daokui believed that the benefits created by SIASUN staff should be shared by all those who had put in the work. He decided to allocate a car to each middle-level executive, aiming to make the technicians live a more dignified and rewarding life.

This was also delivering on a promise that Qu had made to everyone when SIASUN was established. However, this arrangement immediately caused a disturbance in the SIA.

"Did you see? The car driven by SIASUN staff is better than that of the head of the institute!" There were various discussions in the institute, with some people experiencing an unbalanced mentality.

A deputy director of the SIA of the CAS, who had a good personal relationship with Qu Daokui, said to him in private: "It is fair that you allocate cars to the executives. But the cars are so fabulous that the staff in the science institutes feel jealous." Qu replied: "They are different cases in the company and the institute. Cars are necessary for us to carry out work."

When the company was established, more than 30 people collectively "went into the vast sea of business" to fight their way out of difficulties. Qu once said to them: "We will be the pioneers starting from scratch. Once the company is well developed, we will reward each and every one of you. We must work hard so that you can afford cars and houses within four years. And within seven to eight years, you won't be distracted by extraneous worries at home."

By buying cars, the company fulfilled its first promise, but it also caused troubles. The company allocated Qu Daokui a Chrysler worth more than 600,000 yuan. One day, he parked his car in front of the No. 5 Building and, when he was about to drive away after a day's work, noticed that "kiss-ass" followed by three exclamation marks had been carved on the bonnet. Qu Daoqiu smiled reluctantly and then shook his head.

Wang Tianran called Qu Daokui to his office and said: "Daokui! You must deal with the impact."

"What impact?" Qu Daokui asked with disapproval.

"The company has so more cars that are more attractive that those of the institute. The institute only has two or three cars. Some people are so envious that they are making sarcastic comments to me."

"Don't listen to them. We need cars at work. The cars can also win credit for the institute, proving that those engaging in science and technology studies can live a dignified life."

"You always have reason working on your side" Wang said with smile.

At that time, there was a saying in society that "those selling tea-flavoured boiled eggs lived a better life than those conducting missile research, and those working with a barber's razor lived a better life than those with a surgical knife". Such beliefs hurt the pride of scientists and technicians and made them feel worthless. If the cars could make the scientists and technicians working in the institute feel proud, isn't it a good thing?

Wang Tianran added, in a proactive and encouraging way, "Don't show off for the moment. If you are capable, help all the scientists and technicians in our institute live a prosperous life."

"My old leader, you can rest assured. This is not difficult. The company cannot achieve so much without the support of the institute. We do not aim to make big money from developing robots. But, as long as we accomplish something meaningful, money will naturally follow as reward" Qu said, brimming with confidence.

At this time, Shenyang was planning to set up the Hunnan Hi-tech Development Zone, while Li Zhenggang and Yang Luo, together with technicians, had completed several projects for foreign enterprises in Shanghai. Qu Daokui keenly sensed that Shenyang had advantages in the timing of opportunities, geographical location and human resources, while Shanghai had wide-ranging prospects for market development. The company would embrace major opportunities for development in both Shenyang and Shanghai.

Qu Daogui and his team began to plan a new take-off. It didn't take long for Qu Daokui to approach Wang Tianran again when he proposed to move SIASUN's office from the SIA to Shenyang's Hunnan Hi-tech Development Zone.

Upon hearing that, Wang Tianran said: "You do have many ideas! You now have good days operating here. Aren't you making things complicated by removing the company from the Institute?" He persuaded Qu in the way that adults did babies: "You enjoy cheaper rent, free water and electricity as well as reliable logistics support. You are still unsatisfied? It is better to stay here safe and sound."

"SIASUN needs to a bigger platform to achieve further developments. Otherwise, how can we help all the scientists and technicians in our institute live a prosperous life? At the time of its establishment, you personally positioned SIASUN as a company that is able to 'lead modern industry, stand tall amidst the world's advanced equipment manufacturing industry with outstanding technologies and products, and glorify China.' This is no trick. If we stay here all along, what can we expect to achieve? My old leader, it is time to let us go and venture out into the wild world! Otherwise, SIASUN will never mature."

Wang pondered for a moment and said, "Well! You're right. I won't stop you. How much land do you want?"

"236 mu with two pieces combined."

"What are you going to do with such a large amount of land? Raise horses?"

"If we are to build an industrial park, it has to be a large and decent one" Qu Daokui said with audacity. "SIASUN needs a prominent arena, just like Mount Huaguo for the Monkey King to realize 'magical change'. We have been working in the institute since SIASUN's establishment in 2000. Despite working as two separate entities, we will never enjoy real independence as long as we stick together with the institute. It's just like a person who still lives with and depends on his parents after marriage. To truly establish itself, SIASUN has to move out to start its own business. When SIASUN had just been established, we shared the same model as the institute and were bonded together by an umbilical cord of culture. As a result, it is difficult for SIASUN to stretch its legs and develop into a big company."

China was designing and planning a strategy of revitalizing the old industrial bases in the north-east of the country. Shenyang decided to develop an area to the south of the Hun River by establishing the Hunnan Hi-tech Industrial Development Zone. The leader of Shenyang municipal government approached Wang Tianran and Qu Daokui and encouraged them with generous offers by saying: "You represent a high-tech company with huge influence; we hope you can be a pioneer that resides in the Hunnan Development Zone. We can offer 1,000 mu of land for free wherever you would like in the development zone. And Shenyang has set up a big stage for you to show off whatever you are capable of."

Wang Tianran thought it was a good idea to break away from its original office at 114 Nanta Street, which was so small that it restrained the company from growing bigger. This was a rare historic opportunity that should not be ignored. With strong support from local government, both the SIA and SIASUN were relocated to Hunnan to create a new platform for the development of robotics.

As such, Shenyang Advanced Manufacturing Technology Industrial Park and Shenyang SIASUN Robot & Automation Co., Ltd., held a grand foundation ceremony in the Shenyang Hunnan High-tech Development Zone.

When SIASUN employees broke the soil for the first time with a shovel on vast wasteland, they firmly believed that, on this land, with the "SIASUN gene", a "giant" could be grown. This would be fertile ground for the growth of Chinese robots.

Soon, the north-east launched the new-century "battle" to revitalize its old industrial bases, which was vividly described as the "third move" for China's coordinated regional economic development. As the assembling trumpet for the battle sounded, SIASUN, as a symbol of the high-tech enterprises in North-east China, took the lead and rushed ahead.

With such a big platform to soar above, SIASUN has fully displayed what it is capable of.

Qu Daokui said: "SIASUN's rapid expansion strategy began at a time when it 'broke away from the parent institute'. In China's new round of development strategy, whose aim was to revitalize old industrial bases in North-east China, SIASUN seized the moment and made full use of the advantageous situation to achieve its own development."

Marching to the music of time, SIASUN has made great strides forward.

II. A great rival

Qu went to the meeting room that day and said, "Here's good news for everyone. We are a hit on the charts." The Chinese version of *Forbes* had published an article entitled 'Top 100 China's Potential Enterprises' in 2004, of which SIASUN was ranked in 48th place. A quiver of excitement ran through the entire meeting room immediately when the news was delivered.

The remarkable achievements that SIASUN had made had captured the attention of many mainstream media outlets at home and abroad. Forbes Inc., a media mogul, was not an ordinary media company in America; rather, it was somewhat of an authority in commercial circles. The company's flagship publication, *Forbes*, was one of the oldest business magazines in America. It had a circulation of one million copies worldwide and a high-level business readership of almost five million internationally.

The Chinese version of *Forbes* was first released by Forbes Inc. in 2003, whose charts soon become an indication of economic trend. Those that made the *Forbes* charts were definitely not ordinary companies.

It was only the fifth year since SIASUN was founded and the fact that this company had become famous in *Forbes* was not groundless. After the hardship in its early stages, the company's annual compound growth rate exceeded 40%, a stepped increase at a steady pace. In 2004, the company had over 300 million yuan in sales revenue. Nowadays, with its complete coverage of products in the international robotics industry, SIASUN is truly active in the robot field.

Those international giants had always expected the failure of this small company, but SIASUN was like the fast-growing bamboos after the rain. Such a rapid development of this company had truly surprised its opponents. At this point, SIASUN had begun to work on its second-phase project to establish an industrialized base for robots. Once this base was established and later put into use, SIASUN's future operation target would change diametrically in comparison with the previous record. The annual output value would be expected to reach billions of yuan in five years.

Thus, *Forbes* would never ignore SIASUN. With its own unique view and powerful influence, *Forbes* publishes the most authoritative business information and in-depth observations. It is a great honour, according to all enterprises in the world, to be mentioned in *Forbes*. The fact that SIASUN appeared in *Forbes* was encouraging, something that was at least worth being proud of, as it indicated that, as a strong company, it had rapidly gained its own place in China's potential robot field.

"Is it something that we all should be proud of?" asked Qu, who looked at everyone. People glanced questioningly at one another. They did not understand what he meant, so nobody responded. Qu kept saying, "There is an old saying in my hometown. 'Those who were overweight in their early age would not necessarily be the same when they grew up.' What does number 48 prove? We still fall far behind number one." Those who were present laughed. Qu adopted a serious face. "And now is the bad news for everyone. We might have been watched." Looking at Qu, everybody seemed confused. "You don't believe it? Well, we'll see." It was not as though Qu intended to keep people guessing. Instead, he looked like a prophet who could clearly see the future. Soon afterwards, information from the other side of the world confirmed Qu's "bad news".

SIASUN had got into "trouble".

It was April 2005, SIASUN's fifth anniversary, that Qu unexpectedly received a "gift" from "Uncle Sam": a 158-page report on the development of science and technology in China from the United States-China Economic and Security Review Commission.

This report had collected a great amount of information on scientific and technological improvements from 2003 to 2005 in China, putting forward 17 scientific achievements and plans that were considered worth paying attention to. SIASUN Robot & Automation Co., Ltd., was ranked in first place. This report far outweighed the importance of *Forbes*. The company had just shown what it could do when someone had already noticed. Qu had loads of questions in his mind in this moment. "Is this sincere compliment from America? Do we actually need such a compliment from them? It is necessary to encourage an enterprise from time to time, but this report means something else."

In fact, SIASUN did not have any secrets. Jiang Xinsong, known as the "father of China's robotics", intended to show the development of Chinese robots to the world since he had established a robotics laboratory in the 1980s. In this way, the world would know China better and China would also be able to connect to the world.

In the 1990s, Jiang led the research on the CR-01 AUV, which would automatically go underwater to a depth of 6,000 m, thereby pushing China's underwater vehicle research to the highest level in the world. Obviously, everything was on the table. Nothing was hidden behind the scenes. Western countries did not take China seriously at that time. However, China had already shown its strength in scientific and technological development, with Jiang never wanting to keep a low profile from the very beginning.

Things had changed with a very fast pace. The Western world had become quite sensitive to the fact that China was becoming stronger every day. The rise of China definitely meant that scientific and technological development was taking place. As Western countries would never ignore Chinese achievements in the robot field, this explained why they thought highly of SIASUN. It was impossible then for SIASUN to keep a low profile even if it wanted to now. Having his own ideas in mind, Qu was very calm when facing all sorts of compliments. The old parable of the fox and the crow came into his mind.

This report, different from *Forbes*, was scientific and technological intelligence provided by America in an official way. Some people believed that China had improved its scientific and technological competitiveness so that it was necessary to re-evaluate such progress and discuss the possibility for China to become a powerful country in the scientific and technological field. The report mentioned an alarming fact: the day when China would become a strong country in terms of science and technology would occur once it had overcome certain scientific and technological difficulties. This country could become the most powerful rival America would face.

At an internal meeting with executives, Qu reminded everyone to stay clear-minded. He quoted an idiom he had heard in his hometown: "A weasel giving new year's greetings to a hen has ulterior motives. Don't take it as an honour." Nevertheless, SIASUN in its current form was indeed a rival that could not be underestimated. According to the company's age, SIASUN was only five years old, so it was like a child in a kindergarten. This company, considered as a "small child" by those corporations that had achieved a lot in robotics research, had already become a strong "young man" now. Its fast growth had become China's growing strength.

If Qu had already expected that SIASUN would be watched, it

was indeed beyond his expectation that the day for the company's rivals to knock on the door would come this soon.

Qu returned from a business trip that day. As usual, he went to the company directly from the airport. Along Jinhui Avenue, Qu noticed two mansions near SIASUN by chance. Over there, two huge billboards were built to advertise another two foreign robot companies' logos, which were quite eye-catching. These two enterprises were among the "Four Big Families" in the field of robots worldwide. Qu pointed to the billboards and told a few executives beside him: "Look! Our rivals are knocking on the door now. What shall we do?"

The exponential growth in China's robot market came after the financial storm and when all of those powerful international actors tried to occupy the market first. Dozens of foreign enterprises began to enter the Chinese market one after another, including the "Four Big Families", the well-known robot companies around the world. Almost all of these companies had built their own factories in China. The fact that these foreign robot companies had entered the Chinese market would definitely make the competition even more intensive. There was a rapid growth in Shenzhen's robot market. KUKA, Fanuc, Yaskawa and ABB were the four top foreign robot enterprises that had owned more than 80% of Shenzhen's robot market in comparison to a market share of only 10% to 15% for domestic robots. Developed countries and regions such as America and EU member states had also considered the development of robots to be a national strategy, which again had increased competition.

Those international powers had moved in alongside SIASUN, watching its robot development work on a daily basis. Sooner or later, there would be an unavoidably cruel competition between those foreign companies and SIASUN. China's robot companies were facing a huge challenge and an increasingly competitive market.

SIASUN was just in its early stage of development when it was already surrounded by quite a few rivals. How would it handle this situation? This would definitely become a "life or death" technological struggle and a commercial war. Qu Daokui remained calm despite this situation. He clearly knew that the company's survival was not in rivals' hands. It was only the company itself that could determine its future. China's robots would demonstrate the country's determination and strength to the world.

The Volvo Group, a Swedish multinational manufacturing company, conducted a tender for the procurement of industrial robots in Sweden. A crowd of globally advanced robot companies had participated in this tender. Would SIASUN take part in this intensive competition? Some were afraid that it was not even qualified to compete with those powerful international actors. Qu said: "There is nothing to be afraid of. If we win, great. If we lose, there is nothing to be ashamed of. We can increase our knowledge and broaden our views instead."

The rivals were right in front of SIASUN, so it had to make the best out of such a competitive situation.

Qu said, "We have been emphasizing that SIASUN should act just like a wolf that dares to attack and fight. We can't hide ourselves at home. As a real fighter, we shall die on the battlefield. We can't be scared to death at home. Besides, we shall never take part in low-level competitions and repeatedly compete among ourselves. SIASUN should never do this kind of thing."

Qu added that SIASUN had to take responsibility for developing the entire nation. It had to think, make policies and act for the sake of the whole country. On the one hand, the company had to think about how to advance technology and industry in China's interests; on the other hand, it was necessary for SIASUN to offer enough space for domestic companies to survive. There was nothing much to be proud of when competing with domestic companies, even if those domestic rivals were to be pushed out of the market.

SIASUN's new products were supposed to aim at reaching the international advanced level. Its core technology, team and capital were also supposed to be improved in order to get closer to the international advanced standard. It intended to become a high-end enterprise, which would never produce low-quality products. High-end companies should not be afraid of competing with powerful rivals.

SIASUN set its foot down overseas bravely through that competitive tender, appearing on the international stage and entering the European market. Shortly afterwards, SIASUN made its first appearance in Northern Europe and at its first successful show on the international stage. After intensive competition, the Volvo Group surprisingly chose the solutions offered by SIASUN. Even ABB, a Swedish-Swiss multinational corporation that had achieved a great deal in the robotics field, did not see such a result coming. SIASUN's AGVs had lived up to everyone's expectations and won this bid. This intensive competition confirmed that China has finally accomplished something in the robotics field.

The SIASUN employees felt proud of such a great achievement. Qu said that this was how SIASUN responded to the challenges posed by those international robot powers. In turn, these global enterprises found that SIASUN was already able to compete with them.

The SIASUN employees did not get carried away. Qu knew very well that the market was quite unpredictable. It was impossible to become a real power with only one or two achievements. SIASUN had to improve itself more in order to be even much stronger.

What was the next step that SIASUN would take?

III. Successful business model innovation

In order to confront those 100-year-old strong companies on the international stage, China's robot enterprises had to keep expanding their own mass.

SIASUN's "magic" was its business model innovation. During its own transformation in the technological field, it seized the opportunity to change its business model and thus gained the capability to develop rapidly.

In 2006, SIASUN was in the "fast lane". While it proposed to respect the market, it had transformed itself in order to gather talents to work on the front line of the market. A new sales model was thus created: all of SIASUN's employees would undertake marketing and cooperate with each other. The SIASUN company had adjusted the organizational structure to a great deal, which was called "a reconstructed process".

vice general director Hu Bingde went to talk with Li Qingjie, the manager of the Sales Department, and told him that his department would be disbanded. Li wanted to get angry but he could only feel disappointed and hopeless. He just could not figure out why this would happen at that moment.

When the Sales Department was established, Li was unwilling to be the manager. Qu had persuaded him to take on this position for quite a long time before he left his specialized field and started working as a marketer. Facing the difficulties in expanding the market, Li had led the team in securing quite a few orders, which met expectations. At the same time, based on the characteristics of different technicians' positions, he had created a complete performance management system and implemented many innovative evaluation methods. In general, Li's contribution to SIASUN's market development was considerable. He could not accept the fact that this well-functioning department would be closed down.

Although the transformation of structure could be effective and useful, the process would never be easy.

Li was genuinely sad that night. He did not even go home after work. A few colleagues noticed that Li was not in a good mood and asked him what had happened. Li answered that the Sales Department would be dismissed soon. Li's answer created a heated discussion. Many of his colleagues asked, "Why does the company dismiss our department? Is it because we've failed our company? Are we going to be fired?" Some young men got very angry, yelling to reason with the executive.

Li and his colleagues in the Sales Department had got along very well in the past six or seven years. Those young men went through quite a lot for the sake of SIASUN's market development. They had spent a great amount of time and efforts in such a cause and never felt regretful, not even for a minute. In order to market the products, these young men had been coldly refused many times, with waiting in vain already a routine. In order to market the product, they asked people to do them a favour and put in a good word for others, experiencing every kind of situation that a salesperson could face. However, they had never whined about their work and no complaints had ever been made. These young men had the same dream and a firm faith and hope in the promising future of SIASUN. This prevailed even during the struggling and difficult time when Li and his colleagues built this kind of brotherhood and created the team's unique strength. How could they accept the fact that their department would soon be no more?

Qu told Li, "Man, when SIASUN was founded, you once said at a meeting, 'Isn't it like chickens leaving the roost that our division left the research institute to manage this company?' You were right then. SIASUN is going to 'hatch more chickens' this time and it will keep 'hatching chickens'. SIASUN will always have something new to produce in this way."

This was the first step that SIASUN had taken to transform its business model. In turn, the company was able to divide the market in a more specific way so that the potential customers could be better targeted. Based on business development and market demand, the company decided to disband the Sales Department and establish the Rail Transport Department and the Automatic Storage Department instead, with marketers would be dispatched to other departments.

Li asked all his colleagues in the Sales Department to have dinner together. Everyone, believing that this was a farewell dinner, was in a gloomy mood with their head down. The atmosphere was very depressing.

"What happened? Our men should never look like this! Come

on, fill your glass with wine." Li was exceptionally agitated. The kind of low spirit that he was in the day before was no longer there. Instead, he appeared to be forthright and bright, just like a guy from the north-east of China. He held the glass and said in a loud voice, "Look, this is not a farewell dinner. We are here to actually wish for more victories ahead of us! Our department should respect and accept the company's decision for its better development. Even if the Sales Department no longer exists, we are still here and SIASUN's spirit is still here. We will never give up. We are all technicians. Even if we lose our job in the Sales Department, we will find one in another department. From now on, we will gain more market share with our technologies and products on new paths. What was that old saying? Those who keep struggling will finally win? Those who are willing to keep working here, come and work with me tomorrow! Those who were dissatisfied with the company's decision can leave for other opportunities. I'd like to propose a toast to everyone." Li emptied the glass and those who were present applauded. They were all energetic young men after all. They were all smiling.

This adjustment was both a "process reconstruction" in SIASUN and an institutional innovation. The company could better serve its customers and enter the market by realizing direct communication between technicians, the company's products and the customers. In this way, SIASUN's scientific and technological achievements could be efficiently transformed into products, which could create more opportunities in the market. In the end, SIASUN had expanded the company through successful business model innovation.

IV. "The iron god"

Some people in the Sales Department were dispatched to other divisions in accordance with their specialties. Li established a new division with five people, but they felt confused because they did not exactly know what they were supposed to do. Would they be able to achieve something? Some said that this was a great age, but others said that it might be the worst. The key was concerned with what kind of attitude you took on to deal with this age: whether you would see that everything was changing constantly and whether you might feel overwhelmed sometimes. The rise and decline in this age were just like a person's life, which is full of ups and downs. Once you step foot into such a field, you have to do whatever is necessary regardless of the consequences.

It was with the new business model that SIASUN had gradually grown up. This was a reflection of its wisdom and flexibility. Li led his team to analyse the current market to better demonstrate their technological advantage. In this way, they could avoid the existent business scope and find a completely new area that nobody had ever set foot in. Although they could not determine a specific target market, Li had been very familiar with the market and learned a lot of information after a few years' research. They began to attempt selling some small products in the market.

Later, Li found that the hydraulic robot techniques that the company had mastered had not been applied in the oil industry. Therefore, they developed a special robot, which was called a heavy-duty hydraulic grab. It was quite an effort for dozens of oil workers to move around steel pipes that were over 10 t. If oil workers were working in the freezing winter, they had to make even more efforts to overcome unimaginably huge difficulties. However, it was just a piece of cake for the robots to pick up those steel pipes, which not only saved quite a lot manpower but also enhanced construction efficiency. Those oil workers were very glad to get help from the robots, all of which they named "Hercules".

"Hercules" was very popular among SIASUN's customers. The Liaohe Oilfield of CNPC and SIASUN had signed a contract that was worth over three million yuan. The appearance and application of "Hercules" had opened a new market.

In this way, Li led his team to find an energy supply division. They had developed a dozen robot products including ones for removing pipes, transporting and arranging goods, as well as a two-tier robot system. Thanks to heavy-duty hydraulic robotics, the robots in the energy industry were then developed into a series of products.

Take the heavy duty hydraulic robot as an example. It had six degrees of freedom and its load capacity was 3 t, while its repeatability was between 0.08 and 0.5 mm, which represented cutting-edge technology both at home and abroad.

During the process of developing petroleum resources in the South China Sea, SIASUN was responsible for developing a heavy-duty robot, which could remove pipes for the Hai Yang Shi You 981 oil platform. The company had to develop a hydraulic robot that could bear a weight of over 20 t.

When the technicians conducted relevant applied experiments, "Hercules" suddenly made a terrible noise, suggesting that one of the mechanical arms had snapped while transporting heavy objects.

Everyone was surprised and turned off the robot immediately. The technicians began to feel very anxious because they could not find the cause for such a weird sound after repeated examinations. "Hercules" seemed to be perfectly fine, but Li discovered blisters all over his mouth.

At that time, the snapping sound would wake him up in the middle of the night. Sometimes, he would even wake up feeling pain in his arm. Some people who felt discouraged believed that such a weight had exceeded the load limit of "Hercules", so it was impossible for the robot to carry such a heavy object.

SIASUN's spirit was to never give up. Dong Cunxian, the vice president of Central Research Institute of SIASUN, and a few other experienced experts had also joined the team to resolve the problem. Later, they discovered that it was the inadequacy of the technological control that caused some problems in joint lubrication.

On the eve of the 2012 Spring Festival, Li and his team created a low-speed, heavy-duty hydraulic robot whose load capacity was 40 t.

In 2013, "Hercules" was proudly "recruited" as a soldier for national defence and became an effective tool to protect the nation. Although "Hercules" had great strength, it had to survive the extreme weather in the frigid zone. The chief engineer, Xie Bing, and Li Qingjie led a group of nine technicians to the Tibetan Plateau where they conducted experiments on "Hercules" under extreme environmental conditions. This "new recruit" enjoyed special treatment before taking over the post officially. Escorted by police and military cars, "Hercules" was on the way to the Tibetan Plateau.

The weather was changing constantly. After experiencing dust storms from the nearby Gobi Desert and the environmental changes of the four seasons during the trip, they finally climbed to the top of the soaring Tanggula Mountain. Everyone, including "Hercules", went through quite an adventure including a series of physical challenges. When this group of people returned to Shenyang, their faces bore "rosy cheeks". "Hercules", with its great performance, passed the assessment straightaway, which lived up to everyone's expectation, thereby becoming an "iron god" in the military field and a great soldier for national defence.

This heavy-duty hydraulic robot, which was considered a globally advanced technology, went into mass production in 2014. Li's team was expanding at the same time.

Today, the "iron god" has become a strong soldier for national defence and is on duty day and night to protect the nation.

At SIASUN's annual summary commendation congress, Li received the Outstanding Achievement Award. The award citation that the congress gave to Li was as follows: "With faith and persistence, Li Qingjie and his team have solved the technological problem of heavy-duty hydraulic robots and developed a series of robot products that could be applied in the oil and marine fields and under extreme conditions. It was their deep technical knowledge, good professional ethics, great determination and strong faith in SIASUN's spirit that helped them gain such accomplishments. They have indeed achieved a great deal on the road towards realizing their own dreams."

V. Competition on the same platform

One day in 2006, SIASUN's AGV Business Department received an email from a technical staff member at Weisente, part of General Motors (GM). It said that experts from Weisente had carried out a survey in China not long ago and spoke highly of SIASUN's robots applied in the Liuzhou Auto factory. They also hoped that there would be opportunities for cooperation.

Why did Liuzhou Auto replace the robots from the US and Germany with domestic robots? Actually, it was because of the typical inadaptability of the foreign robots. The first batch of robots used by Liuzhou Auto were from the US, but they went wrong after only a few days for some reason. Then the company tried German robots. However, these robots required a demanding working environment, so they went wrong as well soon after installation. Liuzhou Auto had no choice but to turn to SIASUN.

The experts from the GM Global Equipment Purchasing Department unexpectedly found that the average operational time of the SIASUN AGVs was much greater than that of foreign counterparts. The production and delivery cycle was, on average, about four months, which is about half that of foreign counterparts. Besides, the price was much the same. Thus, one of the experts from GM emailed Zhang Lei asking for more information about SIASUN.

They started to communicate with each other electronically mails. At that time, Zhang was engaged in another project, so his schedule was much too tight. But, every day after work, he would communicate with the expert in the evening, answering every question in a careful and polite way. At the beginning, the expert just expressed his interest in SIASUN products, but later on he raised a series of questions, hoping that Zhang could provide some solutions and evaluate the flexibility of the plans. Without too much hope, Zhang still made plans in details to meet the expert's demands out of respect for science and technology and the knowledge of his correspondent.

Zhang's parents were both university lecturers. The family

environment nurtured his elegance, steadiness and passion for work. The tenacity demonstrated in his work was reflected in his intelligence and smart eyes. Through sincere communications, Zhang had narrowed the gap between him and the American colleague. They talked in more and more specific detail, with cooperation more and more likely to take place.

They communicated with each other for about half a year using email. Later on, the American expert asked Zhang for a quote. It was going to work out! Zhang excitedly told his boss, Wang Hongyu, who was surprised to hear that, for this was the first time, a foreign expert would receive technical support from SIASUN and, what's more, it was an expert from GM.

The cooperation began to take shape after further email communication.

On May 2007, a group of technical experts from GM paid a special visit to SIASUN for a survey. After negotiations, SIASUN's products entered the GM manufacturing factory in Shanghai. In due course, SIASUN as astonished when their former rival showed their respect. It was definitely of importance to take a large order from Weisente; what's more, Chinese robots confidently entered foreign enterprises, thus making SIASUN employees feel proud and elated.

Soon, they found that, although the quoted price was higher than that of domestic enterprises, it was still far lower than that of foreign companies. After that, when they were engaged in overseas projects, their price got higher, as did the profit rate.

In October 2007, GM, an American company with over 100 years of history, released the international bid document for the public procurement of AGVs. This was another project to compete with foreign "giants" in the robot industry. SIASUN's employees designed the bid document elaborately. Chinese robots stepped onto the international stage with the strength of their unique techniques and super quality to accept challenges.

Victory belongs to the stronger. After a few rounds, SIASUN defeated its rivals one after another, eventually winning over the global tycoons. It won a purchase order for around 70 AGVs, which was worth over 70,000,000 yuan. Later on, SIASUN was approved as the global cooperation supplier of GM.

After several years of accumulation, the technology and market share of SIASUN's AGVs dominated the field, making rivals green with envy. The precision, weight and speed of these AGV robots all reached the international advanced level. SIASUN also took on projects in Mexico, India, Russia, Canada, Uzbekistan etc. in succession. Soon afterwards, its robots were not only introduced into GM factories in India, South Korea and Europe, but into the core factory in Detroit, USA. This confirmed that Chinese robots were not only taking their rightful place in the international market but playing an important role. It set off a great wave in the industrial robot field. Could Chinese robots survive in foreign countries and get a firm foothold on the international stage? Soon, a crucible presented itself.

On Christmas Eve 2008, Zhang could not enjoy the celebrations as he had received an urgent email from Detroit sent by the engineering technicians Cui Canglong and Shao Ming, saying that the AGVs were not working properly and an expert was demanded on-site.

After receiving it, Zhang became very anxious. Unfortunately, the senior engineer in charge of this project was in hospital, meaning that no one was available to travel to the Detroit factory. Even if there was someone in China who could go to the US, the passport and visa process would take a very long time. However, the customer was urgently asking for an expert. How could it not be urgent? The Detroit automobile factory produced one automobile every 46 s. Once a tiny mistake occurred in the system, there would be a great loss. Zhang knew very clearly that if the AGVs broke down, a huge cost would have to be paid.

Detroit that Christmas Eve was lit up by beautiful lights and filled with a joyous and romantic aroma. However, in the GM assembly workshop, the foreign staff did not care about what presents they would be giving their children later on. They gathered around the Chinese AGVs, scratching their heads and looking at the abnormal movements they were making. Then they gazed at each other with a desperate look and shrugged their shoulders.

When some of Zhang's friends, who were just back from abroad, invited him to enjoy Christmas together, he refused with a wry smile: "My 'kids' are sick, so how can I enjoy Christmas now?" He saw each AGV as his own child and his friends fell for it.

After Qu Daokui heard about this situation, he immediately called the experts at the Central Research Institute of SIASUN and Zhang Lei to discuss a solution based on the information in the email from the Detroit factory.

How could this solution be sent to the other side of the Pacific Ocean? Qu Daokui told Zhang to send the solution through the relevant networks, as well as asked Cui and Shao to carry out the necessary adjustments and send feedback based on the solution and the AGVs' status. Internet technology connected Motor City in Detroit with the robot kingdom in China, via remote real-time docking across the Pacific Ocean. In the assembly workshop of GM in Detroit, Cui and Shao were nervously debugging the AGVs following the instructions sent by Zhang. A group of foreign staff was waiting on-site for the result.

The problems of SIASUN's products must be addressed by the company itself. This was a basic promise that SIASUN had made to the customers. This was also the first time that SIASUN had encountered this kind of situation, with special timing and location. All of the foreign experts were watching on the spot, putting SIASUN's technicians under great pressure. With the help of Qu Daokui and other experts, Zhang was constantly sending software instructions to Detroit via the Internet. After adjusting the software for over 10 hours, the problem was finally solved.

AGVs ran cheerfully again. When the "OK" that had been typed by Cui from Detroit showed up on the screen in front of Zhang, everybody was relieved. After experiencing high tension for over two days, Zhang sighed with relief and sank into the chair, as if he had just struggled out of the water.

OK! It's time for Christmas! At the workshop in Detroit, the American experts gave their applause. This Christmas, Westerners were saluting Eastern wisdom.

VI. The cute "Song Song"

On 15th May 2016, Song Song, a SIASUN robot, became the "host" of *Voice* on China Central Television (CCTV). On that day, the show's topic was "The era of the robot is coming". Before the hosts, Qu Daokui and Sa Beining appeared, Song Song stepped onto the stage first, bringing down the house. His "cosmos blue" cartoon clothing represented a model of the 'future man', provoking infinite imagination.

After Sa showed up, Song Song started to joke with him. This "Mr Manners" said that he would kick Sa out and replace him, which made Sa pretty confused. The IQ of Song Song amazed every audience member at the show.

When we consider the smart Xin Xin and Song Song, we also have to talk about their predecessors.

On 28th April 2006, two newcomers, Yue Yue and Liang Liang, were born to the SIASUN robot family. They were pursued by the media from the moment they were created, frequently appearing on TV programmes. They were also very cute. However, their names were often mistaken by many journalists, for example, they referred to 月月 (Yue Yue, meaning the moon) instead of 悦悦 (Yue Yue, the correct one, meaning happy).

Why should it be the latter? There was a story in there.

Jia Kai and Du Zhenjun were both engineers in the SIASUN Central Research Institute who developed a pair of household service robots based on the development pattern of the company. The robots were 0.8 m tall and grey and looked as chubby as penguins. They could swing their arms, spin around to music, sing, forecast the weather, and even text messages to their owners. They had four functions: education, entertainment, security and personal assistance.

These two little chaps should have a name, their creators thought. Compared to industrial robots, these two robots were not only delightful (shang xin yue mu in Chinese), but also cute, and they were going to be a big hit in the world (xiang liang shi jie in

Chinese). At that time, everyone agreed to give names to them, so they picked two Chinese characters from the meanings above, Yue Yue and Liang Liang. They were not only newcomers, but symbolized a new group. Yue Yue and Liang Liang were a sensation when performing in companies and grand shows. On hearing the news, journalists immediately wanted to know more, putting the robots in the celebrity spotlight.

Due to the huge potential market of service robots, SIASUN Central Research Institute opened the Service Robot Business Department, where a group of young qualified scientists and technicians wielded their talents and upgraded the software and intelligent technology again and again, inserting their wisdom into the brains of service robots. They let the robots step into thousands of households, enabling the general public to enjoy this beautiful life built by high-tech.

The demands for robots would naturally go up as more and more people experienced the superior possibilities offered by robots. Qu Daokui said, "The robot industry has a promising future and will become the next development stage in intelligent manufacturing in China."

What actually made the SIASUN interested in service robots

was that they could be excellent assistants for the old and the disabled, which made their market potentiality huge. Qu said, "Many people don't know anything about Chinese robots. This is because the robots we are currently developing and applying are basically industrial robots, engaged in the manufacturing and production in factories. Our next step is to develop a large number of consumer robots such as robots for smart services, making this high-tech step into thousands of households, and making these kinds of robots the most popular technological products, which will enable the public to experience the achievements of high-tech development."

In those years, when Jiang Xinsong did his utmost to hold his own opinion against that of the majority, scheduling robot technology into the 863 Programme, he said, "When we grow old, maybe we will have to invite robots to take care of us". Now it seems that his prediction has come true. The number of those aged over 60 years in China has exceeded 200 million. The trend of an ageing society is inevitable. Besides, there are still over 80 million who are disabled. Smart service robots can provide a solution to the problem of supporting the old and the disabled.

In 2009, the second phase of the intelligent industrial park was built by SIASUN, facilitating production of five series of robots in three categories (industrial, life service and special purpose), which covered all kinds of foreign robots. Thus, SIASUN has become true to its name as the "Kingdom of Robots". Nowadays, when people step into its intelligent industrial park, the ceremonial usher and ceremonial usherette they see are already the third-generation versions of Yue Yue and Liang Liang.

Their costumes are ultra-cool. Yue Yue is wearing a skirt in Chinese red, which is the typical colour of SIASUN's robots. Yue Yue is a guide in the form of an appealing angel. Liang Liang is taller than Yue Yue by half a head and wears a spacesuit comprising a vest of Cosmos blue, which is another symbolic colour of SIASUN. Liang Liang is very masculine, hence the name of the ceremonial usher. When they speak, their voices are cute and beautiful; when they walk, their stride is elegant and fancy.

When Yue Yue meets a guest, she will blink her big eyes, as if she is thinking of something for a moment, and then she will kindly greet the guest, "Hello! Welcome to SIASUN!" She can also graciously shake hands with guests, only without human temperature on her hands. However, her warmth makes some compensation.

Look! When the song "Little Apple" starts, eight robots start to dance and sing along. Their dancing postures are graceful and their tempos are perfect, just like professional dancers.

Have you ever imagined this kind of smart steward: he can do some cleaning, serve drinks, chat with you when you are in bad mood, play with the children and take care of the old... It is the greatest achievement for SIASUN to have enabled these kinds of robots to step into thousands of households.

Now, the fourth-generation housekeeping smart robots, Xin Xin and Song Song, are available to public, becoming the apple of their owners' eyes all over the world.

Based on the branch approach, SIASUN has created several robot families in just a few years including the AGVs, welding robots, military heavy-duty robots, service robots, cleaning robot and 3D printing robots. The scale of SIASUN has grown from three business departments in the beginning to 11 departments currently, and it is still growing.

Chapter IX
Three Breathtaking Attempts

Against all odds: connected to the capital market, SIASUN leapfrogged and aspired to achieve primacy.

Foreign robots made their way into the Chinese market. How should Chinese robots take advantage amid the fierce competition?

I. Several crushes

Parked in front of the office building of SIASUN, the cars of the presidents, with interesting licence plates, attract curious observers. Uniformly numbered with 1545, the plates only differ alphabetically: the first letter of the pinyin of the owner's surname is inserted among the numbers.

Why did they do that? "1545 shows how tall Mount Tai is, the most famous mountain in China. We look up to this mountain for its primacy, not for its height, which is dwarfed by other mountains in China. Our company aspires to gain a profile as high as Mount Tai" explained Qu Daokui.

The pursuit of primacy is more than an objective. It is, in fact, a state of existence that is based on self-confidence and self-respect. It was also what drove SIASUN to make new plans towards the goal.

The first quarter of 2005 was a good start for SIASUN, which not only gained a foothold in the Chinese market, but also expanded the market share of robots. It was time to go public.

The company had to set up a positive profile in society. At first, the logo of the company was not SIASUN. Instead, it was composed of a rising sun, which is also an eye, along with the company. This graphic logo was settled after collecting and selecting ideas from inside the company shortly after its establishment.

This is how SIASUN employees view the logo: SIA is the abbreviation of Shenyang Institute of Automation and indicates its role in initiating the company; SUN was adopted with an expectation that the company would move upwards like a rising sun; in addition, the pronunciation of SIASUN is very similar to Xinsong in Chinese. Therefore, this design was well received.

Later, Qu Daokui suggested that the company remove the image and solely use SIASUN. This involved a redefinition of S, I and A, referring to strength, information and automation, respectively, while SUN would indicate a combination of the elements. He expected that the company, with the new logo, could emerge as a powerful entity of information and automation. This is how the logo of SIASUN came into being. Qu added that, perhaps, colours and artistic forms could be added but the numbers would not be changed in the future.

A company's logo also demonstrates its corporate culture. What role and responsibility should SIASUN take as it positioned itself as a combination of information and automation? Back then, the company identified its mission as "leading advanced manufacturing technologies and driving modern industrial culture".

In this way, before its listing, SIASUN had a clear picture of its profile, responsibility and philosophy.

Since its inception, it has formulated a three-step strategy including technology-based foundations, industrial expansion and capital and international operations. An entry into the capital market is thus well grounded with the inclusion of the market into the development plan and strict compliance with the requirements imposed on public companies involved in corporate operations and management.

With such preparations in place, Qu Daokui decided to make the company public. His proposal was immediately welcomed by the board of directors. This was a leapfrog moment for this rapidly growing company in the capital market.

The listing made SIASUN's employees the richest team in the Chinese high-tech world overnight. But there was hardly any excitement on Qu Daokui's part. He shook his head and said, "The listing was exhausting. What people could see was my smiling face but not my unsettled mind."

What was on his mind? At first, Qu Daokui was convinced that going public was just about low-hanging fruit. However, constant failures defied his expectations. Accidents caught him unguarded. Since 2000, when the company was founded, the way was already paved towards the capital market. Three years of technological accumulation and discreet management earned the company the necessary qualifications to make an IPO application.

In July 2003, SIASUN filed its first application to be listed on the Small and Medium Enterprise Board of Shenzhen Stocks Exchange with the China Securities Regulatory Commission (CSRC). Qu Daokui and Zhao Liguo, the board secretary responsible for the listing, were in charge of document compilation, file submission and problem handling. Though intense and demanding, the work made smooth progress.

To everyone's surprise, during the review of SIASUN's IPO application, CSRC received an anonymous report prepared by business rivals or other parties that cut the ground from under the company's feet. The trick suspended the company's advances towards the capital market.

Disappointed and angry, some directors called for an all-in investigation. But, President Wang Yue set the tone: "We should cool things down. As long as we improve the management, rules and regulations of our company, there will be plenty of opportunities to come."

Back then, the IPO in China still had to go through certain designated channels. To find out the truth of the mysterious letter, the company had to wait for a long process of investigation. Going public was therefore put on hold. Still finding it hard to accept, Qu Daokui had to let this matter go.

The nomadic institution that was responsible for SIASUN's IPO was very concerned due to the cost and commercial interests. Then, following a comprehensive study and evaluation, SIASUN decided to withdraw its IPO application. This marked the abandonment of SIASUN's first IPO endeavour.

In 2007, it decided to make its second attempt.

To avoid a similar problem, SIASUN set up a special working group to ensure that every step towards listing was solid and concrete. Zhao Liguo, the secretary of the board of directors, took over the leadership and worked around the clock with all the team members. Going public was the only thing on their mind. For two months, thousands of pages of documents went through discussions and revisions more than once for further improvement. Sharing the same dream, everyone was fully convinced that they could make it!

One day in December, Qu Daokui and Zhao Liguo waited outside a conference room at the Beijing Stock Exchange for the final decision on the listing of SIASUN by experts at the institution.

The agenda was simple. CITIC Securities, as the sponsor of SIASUN's listing, made a presentation on the issue and responded to enquiries from experts. Then, after a joint review by the experts, voting would decide the fate of this attempt.

Everything seemed to go as well as Qu Daokui had expected. They thought it was just a matter of time before they could celebrate the good news. Three hours passed but the result had still not been announced. Qu Daokui and Zhao Liguo sensed that something was not right. Could there be something unexpected again? At last, the result of the review was read out by a staff member of the CSRC. Shenyang SIASUN Robot & Automation Co., Ltd., did not pass the review.

The second try was also without luck. Devastation welled up in Qu Daokui and Zhao Liguo's hearts. Later, the reason for the denial became clear. One subsidiary, Beijing SIASUN Electronic System Co., Ltd., had already been listed on Zhongguancun National Equities Exchange and Quotations. Although this had been presented in the submitted materials, SIASUN was accused of the "omission of significant information". Qu Daokui, when recalling that incident, said pitifully that, "We were rejected the second time over this small matter".

At that time, the financial crisis was already showing its impact. SIASUN tried to be involved in the capital platform through financing and looked for a leapfrog development and expansion via a merger. The financial crisis was critical to narrowing the gap between China and the giants in robotics around the world because the cost of a merger was at its lowest. However, this chance slipped away due to the failed attempt of going public.

Qu Daokui got the hump. How should he report to the board of directors when he went back? On the way to the Stock Exchange, he has told Wang Yuechao: "Don't worry, we can do it this time."

Qu Daokui has valued his reputation all his life. But his face was totally lost after the two unfortunate listings. Apart from his own name, what about that of the company? "The reputation of SIASUN will never be ruined by me or anyone" thought Qu Daokui "because the company has been built on the contributions of so many people for such a long time."

II. Going public against all odds

"I'll be back!" This is a catchphrase associated with Arnold Schwarzenegger and a classic line he utters in *The Terminator*. It is a promise made by the robot T-850 to end the life of his rival John when he "recalls" the future.

This line is not especially relevant to the financial crisis, as it comes from the decade before (i.e., 1997). This time, however, the crisis was triggered by the subprime crisis. But whose life would it terminate? Whose "terminator" was it?

Half of a year after thoughtful preparations, SIASUN was ready to go public once again. This time, it coincided with the overwhelming 2008 financial crisis. Could SIASUN march forward steadily against the tide and step onto the capital platform?

In the second half of 2008, the business volume slumped all of a sudden. This was the first volatility in the company's performance after so many years.

Triggered by the subprime situation in the US, the financial crisis swept across the whole world and threatened the entire manufacturing sector, resulting in a drastic fall in the number of clients in the robotic business world. SIASUN was no exception. All the overseas projects of major clients were suspended. This included the project of a foreign company in Suzhou, which was about to be constructed after land acquisition. The intention of the company and SIASUN to cooperate was underway when the financial storm struck. As a result, the company preferred to withdraw and pay the default charge than continue with construction. Due to the huge loss, the general manager and vice general manager of that company were both sacked. The majority of companies in robotics chose to downsize and cut their business in response to the crisis.

This time, Qu Daokui held a face-to-face meeting with employees of SIASUN in Shanghai. He also visited some client companies to keep up with new trends in the business and the market in Shanghai. A full picture was crucial to the mapping process for a new future for SIASUN.

Shanghai SIASUN has expanded rapidly prior to the 2008 financial crisis. The stocktaking of over 80 million yuan at the end of 2007 boosted the confidence of the whole company, leading to the expectation that 2008 would see an even better achievement. At the annual conference, Li Zhenggang told everyone, "If we can exceed 100 million in turnover in the coming year, then we will all go to the Maldives for our annual conference. My treat."

Shanghai SIASUN started out to be quite small but went through a rapid expansion. The passion for and dedication towards making the company bigger and stronger almost reached the point of impatience. The number of business divisions was on the rise. Human resources, in particular, led on programmes it was responsible for and naturally recruited more people.

The rapid growth of the company also kept everyone on full alert. "Despite the surge in the quantities of the projects, our capability was more than saturated. In fact, almost all the sectors were sprawling in an unhealthy manner. Now, if I think about it, it was a sign of the upcoming financial crisis" said Li Zhenggang, recalling the old days.

You never know what life will bring. At the end of 2008,

Li Zhenggang told everyone at the conference, which included all employees, that the turnover had not reached 100 million yuan. In fact, it even dropped. Instead of flying to the Maldives, they sat in the company offices to discuss how to overcome the crisis and withstand the downward economic pressure. Li Zhenggang had a firm belief that they should keep focusing on their expertise, which is the core for any extension. The 2008 financial crisis could cool things down by offering a gap in which to streamline the technologies. Vertically, they could lengthen the industry chain of robotics to solidify the foundation.

There was a cloud hanging over the conference room where the meeting among middle- and high-level managers in SIASUN was taking place. There were diverging views on the response: suggestions on reducing cost, improving efficiency, compressing industrial parks and cutting spending to make their way through the crisis. Making cuts in the number of employees to improve performance was especially popular.

But Qu Daokui believed that robotics was an emerging industry where industrial transformation and upgrading would usher in more opportunities. The market would continue to witness growing demand. In other words, the temporary recession presented both a challenge and an opportunity.

"We cannot go for lay-offs or reducing the size of the industrial parks. Shouldn't we walk together through thick and thin? We should be responsible to society in addition to our own people. We are morally bound and socially obligated to deal with this burden and not to transfer it to other entities in society in such difficult times." Everyone gained a peace of mind as Qu Daokui spoke these words. "Instead of making the industrial parks smaller, we should have a grander plan for the future. The economic crisis should not blind us to the immediate challenges. Rather, we should keep the pursuit of success in mind. The crisis is itself an opportunity. When our profit is at the lowest point, so is the cost of expanding and developing the industrial parks."

SIASUN decided not to reduce staff numbers or suspend the building of a new industrial park. Both the number of employees and the salary remained at the same level despite the sliding profits. So how did Qu Daokui manage to keep the company running? Where did money come from? These were problems to consider.

Zhao Liguo, the secretary of the board of directors said: "We did not stop straining the resources including human capital and finance, as everyone became frivolous and impatient, until the financial crisis was over. During the crisis, we adopted a strategy centred on resilience by reducing spending. It was a critical period for wrapping up previous projects, such as concluding the unfinished ones and organizing the others. Although there was a drop in the number of new orders, our projects became more quality-guaranteed. The supposed challenge became an opportunity for restructuring and therefore had very little impact on the company's operation."

On the afternoon of 13th December 2008, then president and chairman of the CPC Central Committee Hu Jintao paid a visit to SIASUN in the company of the academician Bai Chunli, the vice secretary general and vice standing president of the CAS. In the spacious workshop, Chairman Hu learned in detail about every product and observed and experienced the latest launching system for laser welding beams before he gave his significant approval for the innovative products. Back then, the world was trapped in the financial crisis. Having heard the report from Qu Daokui, Chairman Hu said, "When it is dark in the West, it is bright in the East. China's future development relies on technological support. I hope that you keep forging ahead towards the best in the world."

Mr Hu's remarks sent out a strong signal from the CPC Central Committee. Facing the difficulties posed by the financial crisis to the country's economy, the Chinese leaders paid more attention and bolstered high-tech industries, with the hope that the robotics industry could shake off the negative impacts and revitalize the Chinese economy. The chairman's remarks encouraged SIASUN.

As the economy recovered in 2009, demand surged in the robot markets, outpacing supply. As a result, another investment craze for robots re-emerged in the industrial manufacturing sector. But SIASUN advanced steadily while meeting clients' demand. At the beginning of that year, China set up the Growth Enterprise Board to inject impetus into the recovery of businesses in response to the financial crisis.

The former two failures did not exhaust the expectations and aspirations for robotics development among SIASUN employees. Therefore, they went ahead with a third plan for listing.

With lessons learned from the previous two unfortunate IPO applications, Qu Daokui and Zhao Liguo, together with the working group, made sure that every item and piece of material was examined more carefully by themselves. The thoughtful preparations paved the way for the third Small and Medium Enterprise Board listing application submitted to the CSRC.

The president of CITIC Securities called Qu Daokui to say that SIASUN should file an application for the Growth Enterprise Board than the Small and Medium Enterprise Board. The president felt sorry about the last attempt and tried to do his best to upgrade SIASUN and, at the same time, make himself look better. However, no one could say for sure if the new board worked. It contained so much risk that companies listed on that board could see their demise if they lacked vitality. SIASUN was therefore in a dilemma.

Qu Daokui also found himself in a difficult position. He was still haunted by the memories of 2003 and 2007, although the two setbacks did not deter the company from thriving afterwards. However, the situation was worse due to the financial storm. To start with, the performance of the company was in a downward trend. He literally would lose face if he failed another time.

Before he made any decisions, Mr Qu invited the general manager of CITIC Securities from Beijing to Shenyang to report directly to the board of directors. Chaired by Wang Yuechao, the meeting was held in order to acquire information and suggestions from the CITIC president. Given the huge risks and uncertainties, going public would led to an unknown territory. Everyone on the board had different opinions so an agreement could not be reached easily.

Wang Yuechao and Qu Daokui supported each other all the way. But it was a tough call on that occasion. So, Wang Yuechao let Qu

Daokui to make the final decision. "Considering the disagreements, the listing issue is therefore in the hands of the senior management level of the company" Wang Yuechao told the directors.

Consenting, the directors looked at Qu Daokui. The hard nut to crack was then passed to Qu Daokui, who had to comply with what President Wang Yuechao said, even if he was the elder.

But that was also what Wang Yuechao could only do when opinions were so sharply divergent. At that point, no one knew the conditions better than Qu Daokui. In addition, the final decision had to be duly made by the CEO, who had to rise up to the challenge with responsibility, broad-mindedness and resilience. Wang Yuechao was fully confident that Qu Daokui could do his part.

Qu Daokui examined the past two setbacks thoroughly. Even so, he could only resign if another mistake happened. Only NASDAQ saw successful listings of growth enterprises, while those in Singapore, Germany and the UK were not in a good shape. Could the newly established Growth Enterprise Board in China be as active as the main board? No one was sure of the answer.

If it were not for the past two failures, quick-tempered Qu Daokui would have immediately decided. But, this time, the issue took him two days to ponder on. What went through his mind?

III. Every step involved risks

Qu Daokui was very anxious.

The Jinchangpu Company of the Institute of Metal Research of Shenyang used to enjoy transient fame thanks to its plant building and expansion. However, the financing failure concerning the IPO in 2008 led to a broken capital chain that choked the company's survival. This evoked mixed feelings among the public.

The Chemphy Chemical Company of the Dalian Institute of Chemical Physics, part of the CAS, was set up at roughly the same time as SIASUN and once enjoyed a good momentum for growth. However, its products failed to adapt to the changes in the market, thus resulting in a downturn in its business performance. In 2005, it attempted to resurrect itself by going public, but with no luck. The passion for revival was thus curbed. The science professionals had no choice but to return to where they were.

As for management, Qu Daokui believes that there are thousands of paths to success, which means that your way should not be copied by another. The recipe of success involves different ingredients. For example, a helping hand can push you ahead, a precious opportunity offers a favourable momentum and a good idea provides a shortcut to the destination. These are all factors leading to success but are not the things that can be easily duplicated. However, failures share similar patterns and features. Understanding the underlying reasons is like setting up warning signs on the road ahead. With that, you can avoid the misfortunes and achieve smooth progress.

Lenovo rose to the top among the companies under the CAS by going public, while Huawei managed to secure its prominence without going public. In other words, you can only be in awe at their success but not the specific way they did it. The waters they have crossed are not the same as those crossed on foot. You are not stepping into the same river.

Which way should SIASUN take? Success cannot be copied but failures will re-emerge. There is a saying on the Stock Market that goes, "Be cautious about investments as the market involves risks". In fact, it also works for going public. Different paths lead to the same destination. Qu Daokui must make his own decision for the company.

After two days of evaluation and reflection, he made up his mind.

Qu Daokui trusted his judgement. "As a high-tech company, SIASUN should engage in the first round of IPO in the Growth Enterprise Board as other high-tech businesses do. The new models and types of business determine their great chance of success. That's why I bet on the Growth Enterprise Board."

The decision was secured in July 2009 and the listing was finalized in September. Qu said: "Three months of paperwork modifications, roadshows and prospectuses ensured that the company joined the first listing group. Our bottom line was to be part of the first round or optimal timing would be missed. In China, the first ones always reap more benefits than the latecomers. So, we became one of the 28 pioneers."

This major decision to go public shocked many. Some shared their worries privately that luck might not be in their favour at the third attempt after two failures.

Beneath Qu's composure lies a thorough understanding of the international market of industrial robots through research, reflection and anticipation.

According to the 2008 statistics of the International Federation of Robotics (IFR), an upward momentum of Chinese industrial robots was to remain in the coming years. Such a trend and prospects offered a precious growth prospect for SIASUN. Against such a backdrop, the company had to clear the way for financing in order to make a leap forward. They would never let this golden opportunity slip away.

Going public was the only thing on Qu Daokui's mind. He believed that the financial crisis offered more opportunities to high-tech companies with core technologies. Equipped with cutting edge technologies, the company was embarking upon a smooth path in the forward direction. What came with the international financial crisis was the chance to realize new business for SIASUN in a faster and desirable manner, thanks to the reshuffling of market orders.

Would reality follow the planned road map? Before being listed, SIASUN had to undergo the "roadshow" test, that is, presenting itself to the public. This determined whether the company would gain the trust of stock investors and receive the listing.

Qu Daokui was prepared to take the test.

On 29th September 2009, a representative of the CSRC announced that the company's listing was successful. The conference was brimming with applause and cheers. It was a delayed comfort because people responsible for the listing had been waiting for far too long.

But there was still much to do. Due to the narrow window, the company chose to do roadshows in Beijing and Shanghai to impress more investors with materials verified on multiple occasions. Led by President Qu Daokui, the features of the business, operational models, the company's prospects as well as the future trend of the industry were all on display and part of the demonstration.

To increase publicity for the listing and encourage more investors to further learn and participate, the organizer maximized media coverage via its affiliated resources including webpages, print and broadcast media, networks, audio messages and SMS. Both traditional and new media conducted an all-round and in-depth report from the beginning of the road show.

In terms of online communication, investors could ask people from the company questions that they were interested in and receive detailed answers. This "face-to-face" communication in virtual reality provided a comprehensive picture of robotics. A little more communication and understanding could increase the probability of a successful listing.

In addition to the questions about basic information, investors and netizens also proposed tough ones that may have caught the company representatives by surprise. This was not personal, but a natural query that tested the mindset and sophistication of the entrepreneur. If the representative was not careful enough, then what they would be left with would be nothing but regret. Experienced stock investors value the character and intelligence of business leaders and teams over booms in the market because a smart leader will always build up a successful team in any business.

On the surface, roadshows seem to represent fierce arguments between business leaders, stock investors and other people online. In reality, however, the potential investors will not be fooled by sugar-coated words. Persuasion derives from sincerity and capability. Otherwise, there is always a point when some badly answered questions give you away.

This is not something new. Staggered by the firing of questions, some presidents of companies show very painful facial expressions. It goes without saying that it cannot end well.

Sincerity is the building block for success and also the strength of humanity. When it is absent, the confidence of investors will crumble. In SIASUN's case, the investor who asked the first question of the roadshow wanted to know about the position of the product units in the competitive robotics industry, including the technological level of SIASUN compared to the whole sector. This question seemed simple, but was actually very technical, indicating that the audience was a professional one.

What are product units? The term refers to the collection of the key parts of robots, including reducers and actuating motors. They were the weakest links in Chinese robotics.

Qu Daokui answered that the US, Japan and European companies dominated the market. For all the progress made among the suppliers of product units, China was still lagging far behind. In recent years, most Chinese product units shattered the blockade and SIASUN's independently developed products entered the key production round. Thanks to the development of robotic technologies and the industry, the competition landscape would witness a rapid shift with a larger share of products by domestic companies. "We should be confident about that" Qu said.

Qu had hardly finished his sentence before another question

popped up from another audience member. "What did you learn after years of corporate management as a successful entrepreneur?"

Qu Daokui answered: "A strong sense of responsibility, well-trained decision-making abilities, a good grasp of opportunities and the lowering of risks. The leader should also build a united team of talented people. Besides, this group of people should do the right thing at the proper time."

"How do you see your employees?"

"Employees are the most valuable assets of the company. We cannot achieve what we have today without their efforts, passion about work and love for the company. I feel extremely proud to have these people in my company."

"President Qu, whose interests come first, stakeholders, clients or employees? What is it like in your company?"

"As a general manager, I am responsible to the board of directors. It is my job to maximize the benefits of stakeholders through good production, management and output. But, to me, these three aspects are equally important and highly complementary. We will try our best to achieve synchronized growth in the interests of stakeholders, clients and employees in addition to the company. Thank you."

Then came another question. "The introduction of the Growth Enterprise Board in China will generate about another 3,000 billionaires. What will you do about it as you are one of the group? How do you feel about it?"

It seemed that the bombardment of questions tried to corner Qu Daokui. But he remained calm, which came from sincerity and openness. He answered: "After the listing, some companies indeed become rich overnight. But, to me, the profit belongs to everyone. I always believe the saying that 'When the benefits are distributed, then people come together'. Everything has two sides and wealth is no exception. For me, money is no more than a figure. There will be hardly any difference if I become super rich. I will still live and work the same way as I do now. Money should be taken less seriously. It does not matter that much to me so I never pursue profit in business. We want the company to be listed to acquire more capital for its growth and then take on more social responsibilities. To us, going public is never about gaining more money or enriching ourselves."

"Why do you call your shares in the listed company 'robots'? Are you taking advantage of this fashionable concept?"

Qu Daokui answered: "My mentor the academician Jiang Xinsong, along with science professionals of the SIA of the CAS, has dedicated his life to research on robotics since the 1970s and kept his eyes on the world's leading technologies. Since the foundation of SIASUN, we have had nothing else on our minds but developing robots and automated equipment. Robots, as our primary products, are now manufactured in five series across three categories. So far, there is not another company of the same type. It is sensible to name our shares as robots."

Qu Daokui had a candid discussion with netizens and investors over the 2 h roadshow. Without stopping, Qu Daokui answered nearly 100 questions with a steady hand.

It takes 10 years to grind a sword. On 30th October 2009, SIASUN (stock code: 300024) was among the first 28 companies that went public on the Growth Enterprise Board in the Shenzhen Stock Exchange. SIASUN issued the first share of "robots", thus kicking off the international operation of the company that is leveraged on capital.

Unlike the majority of entrepreneurs who expressed their joy and pride following the success of the listing, Qu Daokui was very peaceful. His response to the reporters asking about his feelings was as simple as this: "It all came naturally without any surprise."

IV. Embrace "paradise on earth"

In 2009, the SIASUN company was successfully listed, entering into an economic recovery after the financial crisis. Within six months, SIASUN's shares (under the name of "robots") doubled again. Qu Daokui believed that the world was in constant development and that the cycle of new ideas, new concepts and new knowledge converted into technology was increasingly shorter. Opportunity determines success or failure; only by seizing the market opportunities and reacting immediately can we win over the market's initiative.

As a result, a strategic layout of "2+N+M", which broke the market competitors grip, started its formation in Qu Daokui's mind:

"2" means setting up two headquarters for SIASUN, one domestic location in Shenyang and one international one in Shanghai; "N" means building multiple regional headquarters or robot industrial parks in cities below the headquarters level, such as in Hangzhou, Qingdao, Chongqing and Guangzhou, forming "N" numbers of layouts; "M" means, below the level of every "N" industrial park layout, setting up different subsidiaries for engineering applications and services, establishing "M" numbers of the company's business supporting points. The implementation of the "2+N+M" strategic development layout created the general plan for SIASUN, allowing the "SIASUN System" to become the big network pattern that covered the entire country. This was the upgraded version of SIASUN's new strategies.

SIASUN then started its enclosure and construction in cities such as Beijing, Shanghai, Guangzhou, Hangzhou and Qingdao. Those who didn't know the true story thought Qu was actually doing real-estate work. In fact, Qu was making efforts and breakthroughs in carrying out the "2+N+M" strategic layout. Focusing on the four major business segments of industry, national defence, consumption and education, he drew a new blueprint for SIASUN.

China has already become the world's fastest-growing industrial robot market. The IFR statistics showed that, in 2013, China was the biggest robot market in the world. Since then, China has continued to grow at a speed exceeding 30% over the years. The high-speed growth that has attracted broad attention has made China's market the most desirable among the world's major robot manufacturers.

Statistics show that all the international manufacturers of robot bodies that occupy more than 85% of the global robot market share have set up branches in China, have their own factories in the country or are planning on building factories there. China's market is at an aggressive stage.

Hangzhou, hailed as "paradise on earth", is also the "resort" that attracts Chinese robots.

"Embracing" the "paradise on earth" is a crucial campaign in SIASUN's "2+N+M" strategic layout. In the first stage of the campaign, Li Zhenggang suffered a setback and was nearly defeated. Indeed, as he said, he almost became a deserter.

For the SIASUN company, 3rd December 2010 is a date destined to go down in history! On this day, the signing ceremony for SIASUN's Hangzhou Research and Innovation Centre and Industrialized Base Construction was held. In order to reflect the great importance on both sides, SIASUN's chairman Wang Yuechao and the leaders of the Hangzhou Municipal Party Committee signed the contracts. Qu Daokui, president of SIASUN, hosted the signing ceremony.

This action represented that SIASUN was to carry out a new stage of the "2+N+M" strategic layout! SIASUN planned and built an industrial park in Hangzhou, as its headquarters in South China. This project's timely completion determined whether or not SIASUN's "2+N+M" strategic layout would be completed on schedule.

In 2011, setting up a SIASUN base in Hangzhou was the first step in building its southern headquarters. Li Zhenggang was relocated to Hangzhou to be the general manager, taking charge of the start-up of Hangzhou Xiaoshan Linjiang Industrial Park's construction. On 16th September, a grand foundation-laying ceremony was held in the Xiaoshan Linjiang Development Zone. When the ceremony ended, Qu Daokui handed over to Li Zhengzhou: "All yours now, old boy. SIASUN always does the 'turnkey' projects for its clients. This time, you will also need to do a 'turnkey; project for SIASUN. In a year from now, I will 'collect the key'."

Looking at the wasteland by the Qiantang River, Li Zhenggang felt overwhelmed, not knowing what to do. Expecting this expert who grew up studying engineering technologies to be responsible for infrastructure was like forcing a crab to walk straight. Different professions, different worlds. It was such a conundrum for Li Zhenggang. But Qu Daokui relocated Li Zhenggang from Shanghai to Hangzhou for a reason.

Li Zhenggang is from Tai'an, Shandong. He was born in Shenyang in 1966 and returned to his hometown of Tai'an for elementary school. In 1987, he graduated from Zhejiang University with a precision instrument major and assigned to Shenyang No. 3 Machine Tool Factory. In 1992, he went to graduate school at the SIA and, after he graduated in 1995, started to engage in scientific research before joining SIASUN. Qu Daokui saw natural advantages in Li Zhenggang taking over Hangzhou, since Li was a student of Zhejiang University and was familiar with Hangzhou and had good connections there.

The functions designed for the southern headquarters focused on the research, development and production of standardized products, including brand robots, servo products, and the design and manufacture of system integration projects. SIASUN Robot Industrial Park is located in Hangzhou Xiaoshan Linjiang Industrial Park, including a research building, a product realization centre, an academic exchange and experiment centre, an exhibition and convention centre, a business incubation building group, a logistics centre and a comprehensive administration centre. The construction of the first phase of the industrial park was planned to cover 80,000 m^2.

SIASUN's southern headquarters complemented the new development opportunities with advanced equipment and sophisticated technology, realizing the "flying southwards" strategic plan. In the second half of 2011, Li Zhenggang came to Hangzhou from Shanghai, organizing a professional team, doing work and opening up a business in a rented office building, while starting the construction of Xiaoshan Linjiang Industrial Park at the same time.

"What was most unforgettable about the development process, or the most difficult in starting up the business, was building Hangzhou Robot Industrial Park. Infrastructure construction was a huge challenge for us" said Li Zhenggang. "I had been doing specialized technologies and was not familiar with infrastructure. The architecture area is also relatively complicated, as we all know."

SIASUN's infrastructure's bidding was won by Zhejiang Changcheng Construction Group Co., Ltd., a well-known company with tens of billions of annual output value. For some reason, the person in charge of the project was not local and the coordination didn't go so well. It caused Li Zhenggang great headaches. Even though SIASUN had money already in place, the project progressed very slowly and Li was burning with anxiety.

As the proprietor, SIASUN was to make payments in batches according to the project's progress, while the contractor would launch the construction with its own funds in advance. However, it turned out that the contractor wasn't able to do this. As a listed company, SIASUN could not break the rules. Yet the construction was delayed and the wages of migrant workers were unpaid. As a result, the migrant workers made their protests to Li Zhenggang instead. Li couldn't take it anymore and, filled with rage, called Qu Daokui: "I can't manage this project. I quit. I'd better go back to Shanghai."

"You are joking! How can someone from SIASUN say such things?" Qu said over the telephone.

"Too much shit. Too hard to deal with."

"That's why I sent you. You think I sent you to admire the view of the West Lake? Hangzhou is almost like your home turf. What's so difficult to crack? Behave yourself and do the work. Don't you play the whole 'Broken Bridge' thing with me." Qu unequivocally dismissed Li's thoughts of quitting.

Back then, Li was honestly thinking about giving up. The

contractor was definitely giving him a hard time. He said that, in all of his life to date, he had never undergone such enormous failure and that, in all of his working experience, he had never been faced with such an enormous setback.

The pressure that Li Zhenggang endured came from different angles: the construction project and the corporation. Even though people at the top didn't say anything, he knew it in his heart. The local government also put pressure on since the construction was delayed; Hangzhou had high expectations for SIASUN. In addition, as a listed company, SIASUN also faced pressure from the investors. By making such big investments, people expected to have outputs as soon as possible. Time is money. Delaying all the time solves nothing, as well as irritates the investors. The pressure put on Li Zhenggang was tremendous.

In June 2014, Hangzhou SIASUN Industrial Park officially opened. The research and design, administration and other departments all entered the park and all kinds of work went on smoothly. SIASUN in Hangzhou soon opened up the market. After a year of operation, a series of robot service centres was established in Ningbo, Wuhan and Chongqing.

A robot cyclone hit China in 2014, with 12 cities setting up robot industrial parks. From government subsidies to the parks' construction, industrial robots became popular all over China. The major manufacturing province of Zhejiang is involved out a "robots replacing humans" project at full speed. Zhejiang with its fierce ambition plans to deliver 5,000 "robots replacing humans" projects in the next five years, realizing a total investment of 500 billion yuan. The "2+N+M" strategic layout implemented by SIASUN coincided with the development rhythm of Zhejiang Province. Chinese robots can now surely embrace "paradise on earth".

In the meantime, China's market seems to be playing a strong note in the surging robot industry: with the development of informatization technology, such as the Internet, the disappearance of labour dividends, the onset of an ageing society, along with robot technologies making breakthroughs and the cost of robot continually falling, a robot age is around the corner.

Chapter X
Entering the Era of
Robotic Technology

The tiny vacuum robot became a "bottleneck" that hindered the development of China's integrated circuit (IC) industry. SIASUN elaborately developed the core robotic technologies (RTs) of China, challenging the foreign blockade on techniques once again.

There is one kind of wisdom, known as innovation. China has witnessed the new RT era.

I. Independent development of core technologies

During the 10th Five-year Plan period, the Ministry of Science and Technology organized research and development centred on the techniques and equipment for very-large-scale IC equipment. IC equipment is the most important part in electrical devices, serving the function of computation and storage. It is the definite "heart" of computers, digital household appliances and communication facilities.

Through the joint efforts of technology institutions, the main part of IC manufacturing equipment had been developed. However, the key vacuum (clean room) robots for manufacturing IC equipment needed to be imported from the US. At that time, all manufacturing giants had their ace, i.e., a chip, which was monopolized along with the vacuum (clean room) robot. Exporting to China required special permits with unannounced inspection articles. Vacuum (clean room) robots became a "bottleneck" that severely hindered China's manufacturing of semiconductor devices. If China wanted to make a breakthrough in large-scale ICs, it had to get rid of its dependence on imported key parts of semiconductor devices, i.e., vacuum (clean room) robots.

American manufacturers did not sell single vacuum (clean room) robot hands, only as a whole set. The little gadget required high technology and cost a lot. This monopoly generated high profits. Furthermore, according to America's export procedures, it took at least nine months from starting the application to completing the formalities. It took even longer to transport the goods to China. How could China's IC equipment develop, if obeying these procedures? We could do nothing but obey, even suffering injustice. Otherwise, China was not able to develop its IC industry equipment. This negotiation became a genuine "marathon". Between the 10th Five-year Plan and the 11th Five-year Plan, no results were delivered in those five years. A technological monopoly always leads to an unfair clause in business. Without advanced technology, one country does not have an equal say.

With its technology lagging behind, China was usually restrained by other countries.

Concerning vacuum (clean room) robot projects, American manufacturer was playing a game of "cat and mouse" with Chinese enterprises. They intended to drag China down in this industry. Apparently, they had no sincerity or real intention. Honestly speaking, a clean room robot was not mysterious at all. Chips in computers and mobile telephones had to be manufactured and assembled under vacuum conditions, which cannot be operated by people. A vacuum robot is specialized to perform this job.

After several struggles, the Chinese side felt quite "upset". The two sides had already made a deal through negotiation; however, the American side suddenly went back on its word and put on the brakes. The manufacturer said that the US had come up with new regulations. The buyer must accept the investigation of the State Council, the Federal Bureau of Investigation and the Department of Commerce, which had formulated very strict and unannounced inspection conditions. They would come to China to carry out an inspection every six months and the equipment would not be allowed to move out of its regulated location. The reason for this was to prevent China from applying the equipment to military projects.

This strike was fatal. They could always find reason to impose a technological blockade on China.

China could not accept this condition, which had no "sincerity". China was not spending money to buy equipment, but to buy humiliation and to sell dignity. One country could protect its technology and it was its right to impose a technique blockade; however, the country could not play tricks on or deceive others! What a humiliation this was!

This is how the US monopolizes its core technologies. Using it or not is your choice.

China would not allow the same humiliation to happen as that in the 1990s, when the supercomputer leased to the CNPC had been under 24 h supervision by the American staff. If China could not obtain the core technology of a vacuum robot, its IC equipment industry would be severely restrained. This technology had become a critical "bottleneck".

China's IC project needed Chinese technologies.

Experts from the Ministry of Science and Technology of China approached SIASUN: "You are the national robot research centre as well as the national 863 Programme robot industrialized base. Can you develop a vacuum robot?"

"Nothing is impossible. This is a mission entrusted by the nation, so it is our unshakable responsibility." Qu Daokui got to know about this project's background and accepted the task as decisively as Jiang Xinsong did when he was determined to develop AGVs to save the Jinbei auto project.

Qu Daokui entrusted the task to the SIASUN Central Research Institute. The director, Xu Fang, organized and led a group of technicians born after 1970 and 1980 to tackle the problem. This was another "story starting from zero".

"The vacuum clean room application was a completely new technology as well as a new field. At first, we felt at a loss and only had a few pictures for reference" Xu Fang, director of the SIASUN Central Research Institute, recalled. "Upon receiving the task, we went abroad to do our research. The Americans would definitely not show us the robot. Then when we went to Singapore but they only allowed us to observe a long distance away, while not letting us know the technical principles. We had nothing to refer to and had to start from scratch."

But we feared nothing! The SIASUN employees always bear a strong faith.

In 1984, Xu Fang graduated from Dalian Engineering College (now Dalian University of Technology) with a master's degree and stayed at the college to teach. His tutor was a robot expert who had just come back to the motherland after studying in Japan. A decent job did not make Xu give up his dream. He always wanted to carry out research and development work in an appropriate institution and apply his robot technology in practice, making useful and valuable products that served the public.

In 1995, Xu Fang came to the SIA as he wished and worked at the Robot Technology Engineering Development Department formed by Qu Daokui. When SIASUN was founded in 2000, someone persuaded Xu not to take risks. It was more stable to stay at the institute. This fragile scholar in his 40s was quite determined to "do business" and joined the SIASUN team. Xu Fang, with his solid theoretical foundation, was appointed director of the SIASUN Central Research Institute at that time and led several postgraduates in their work. During the process whereby SIASUN's products became marketized, the research and development team led by Xu Fang tackled a number of technical difficulties and provided customers with successful solutions, winning a batch of patent technologies for SIASUN.

This time, developing a vacuum (clean room) robot from scratch involved too many risks. This tiny gadget required great reliability. The IC production line could not pause for a single minute; otherwise, the loss would be great. Therefore, zero-mistake continuous work for every 10 million operations of equipment must be guaranteed. Moreover, the air quality in China was not as good as that in the US. The cleanliness and accuracy indicators required were also higher than those in the US.

SIASUN agreed that the clean room robot would be a key project of the 11th Five-year Plan and duly employed its "mystical powers". Xu Fang led his team to conduct a large number of experiments and attempted to tackle the problem over and over again. The preparatory work went on for more than one year. Investment worth tens of millions of yuan delivered no results. Xu Fang could not keep calm. He came to Qu Daokui and said, with a lingering fear, "I cannot estimate how much this project will cost..."

"You need not worry about the money issue. I will provide whatever you need." Qu interrupted Xu without letting him finish his sentence. "You need not consider that much. You just take charge and lead the team in finding the solutions. Leave all the rest to me. This is a nation-level project. We must accept it and give our country qualified products, whatever it takes. What's more, SIASUN never lacks money."

Back then, SIASUN was not only developing a robot product, but also shouldering national responsibility and dignity. This was something that could not be measured by money. SIASUN must help the country to create its own chips with the "SIASUN spirit".

Soon afterwards, a Chinese vacuum robot called "Jie Jie Jing Jing" (meaning very clean in Chinese) was created under immense difficulty and pressure. After two years of unremitting efforts, SIASUN had finally developed a high-standard vacuum (clean room) robot. Vacuum robots were quite fantastic. They could move rapidly and accurately in the spotlessly clean vacuum room, which amazed observer. They also "mysophobia", i.e., an elf keen on cleanliness.

On 21st June 2006, the vacuum (clean room) robot developed by SIASUN was approved by the relevant science and technology departments. This core technology not only filled China's gap in this area, its performance indicators were also higher than those of its foreign counterparts. The North Microelectronics Company, which intended to import vacuum robots from the US, immediately stopped marathon-like negotiations with the American side and chose to use the products domestically made by SIASUN.

The American manufacturer was unwilling to give up and tried to proceed with the North Microelectronics Company. Of course, the North Microelectronics Company was emboldened enough to turn down America's proposal as it had got what it needed from SIASUN. The American manufacturer almost begged: "Use ours, as long as the price is not lower than that of SIASUN." No extra condition was added.

The delegate from the North Microelectronics Company shook his head: no.

The Americans felt they had lost face but were unwilling to give up on the deal. They decreased the original price by more than 40%. The decreased price was even lower than that of SIASUN, which was dirt cheap anyway. Apparently, the American manufacturer broke its bottom line for the sale. This was the "bottom line-less" strategy of many American manufacturers: to squeeze competitors out of the market with a price lower than cost. What they wanted was to knock SIASUN's vacuum robot down when it had only just entered the market. This was a familiar trade war model based on the "law of the jungle" that Westerners believe in.

Chinese enterprises had seen this model many times and no one bought it. Chinese entrepreneurs had grown smarter and smarter.

SIASUN continued its triumphant pursuit and came up with a vacuum clean room coating film robot, a vacuum clean room carrying robot and vacuum clean room logistics automatic transportation equipment, providing a whole set of "turnkey" solutions.

The vacuum robots displayed their capacity in the IC industry, forming a new army for SIASUN.

In 2006, SIASUN invested nearly 300 million yuan to begin the second phase of construction of the Hunnan Robot Industrial Park, which would specialize in producing cleanroom robots and be officially put into use two years later. All of these vacuum robots have been applied in the automatic production of IC equipment. As the only domestic supplier of vacuum (clean room) robots, SIASUN has provided solutions in areas such as semiconductors, LED, photovoltaics, nuclear power, medicine and finance with Chinese intellectual property for the first time.

SIASUN not only broke the technological monopoly and blockade of Western countries, but also improved China's development level and innovative capacity in automation technology, thereby enhancing the country's competitiveness with its foreign counterparts and promoting the rapid development of China's information industry.

On 30th October 2010, the Taiwan Crystalwise Technology Company purchased vacuum (clean room) robots manufactured by SIASUN, which operated well with their main indicators and reached world-class standards. Taiwan was the most important semiconductor industry market worldwide. Being in Taiwan, the most important international market of IC manufacturing meant that SIASUN's vacuum (clean room) robots had reached an advanced level globally. Thanks to its excellent performance record, SIASUN flew the flag of "developed in China" at the peak of the international manufacturing industry.

In October 2015, SIASUN, along with the Shenyang Venture Capital Management Group Co., Ltd., the Shenyang Hunnan High and New Technology Venture Capital Co., Ltd., and the Shenyang Venture Capital Fund Co., Ltd., invested a total of 90 million yuan to set up the Shenyang SIASUN Intelligent Drive Co., Ltd.

SIASUN implemented the "dual-core" strategy in order to solve the problem of heavy dependence on imports of China's "core technologies" and "core parts". They would invest a great deal in research and development, spare no effort, unite to develop, turn "disadvantage" into advantage, and reinforce Chinese strength. This indicated that SIASUN was targeting the robot core components manufacturing field and planning a blueprint for the whole robot industry chain development. SIASUN's employees were determined to realize the "corner overtaking" of technologies through self-dependent innovation, completely breaking foreign monopolies.

II. "Waking up" foreign robots with a Chinese control unit

The SIASUN employees, with their innovative spirits and unique technologies, thoroughly broke up foreign monopolies and obtained new core technologies one by one. The company's rivals who used to be strict about the technology blockade were silenced.

Not only its foreign rivals, foreign robots also fell silent. More than a few foreign robots had "heart disease" and stopped working once they came to China. This made the foreigners upset. As a consequence, the fantasy that Chinese robots would waken up "sleeping" foreign robots by applying a Chinese core control unit became real.

The Ningbo Tuopu Group Company imported a whole set of foreign robots to install protective leather covers from renowned German suppliers. The German company called itself a top supplier worldwide and Ningbo Tuopu spent quite a lot of money.

However, these foreign robots slept in the factory and could not be woken up, leading to the failure of the whole project. The foreigners could do nothing and the managers of Ningbo Tuopu were upset and anxious.

Hearing that the welding robot from SIASUN was excellent, experts from Ningbo Tuopu went to see the company in Hangzhou and turned to Li Zhenggang for help, hoping to wake up the sleeping foreign robots.

Li Zhenggang handed this challenge over to "young marshal" Yang Yongshuai, so called because he was the youngest project manager.

Yang Yongshuai was born in Handan, Hebei Province, and graduating with a master's degree in 2011, after majoring mechatronics. SIASUN was holding a jobs fair at Zhejiang University of Technology at that time. After Yang Yongshuai handed in his CV, he soon became a member of SIASUN.

Having been trained at SIASUN headquarters in Shenyang for

several months, Yang went to the frontline of scientific research projects.

In May 2012, Yang went to work for SIASUN in Hangzhou as project manager. Within a year, he encountered the problem that foreign robots imported by Ningbo Tuopu had "fallen asleep" in the factory. Yang went to the Ningbo Tuopu workshop and found that there was indeed trouble. The procedure before the robots got involved was working well. As the robots could not help, workers had to set up a table to connect the preceding automatic equipment in order to replace the robots in installing protective leather covers in a hurry. The assembly line got stuck at this stage. An automatic assembly line turned into a semi-artificial line, increasing production costs and greatly decreasing production efficiency and product quality.

The engineer at Ningbo Tuopu said to Yang in embarrassment, "We did not know the robots well and blindly believed that foreign robots would be better. Now, we have encounter difficulties." Yang replied: "It is not that 'foreign robots' cannot adapt to our production environment. Actually, Chinese robots have out-competed foreign products in many technical aspects. The control unit of the Chinese robot is stronger than that of a foreign robot."

Although young in age, Yang Yongshuai was considerate when tackling problems. To solve this issue, he had meetings with the Technical Department and engineers again and again to adjust the solution. The first problem he encountered was whether to repair the foreign robots' control unit or to revitalize it with a "pacemaker", or whether to wake the foreign robots up by replacing their control unit with a domestic control system. He was faced with multiple choices. However, it was unknown which option would work. If the right choice was made, the project could be completed smoothly and delivered to customers on time. If not, with delays in time, customers would suffer great losses, which they would not be able to shoulder.

To meet the required deadline, the customer requested to sign the contract according to the terms of the "turnkey" project. However, there were many difficulties found with the project's topological swing-arm structure, including riveting techniques and installing protective leather covers. During this process, you might encounter unpredictable difficulties, even failures. Yang Yongshuai said, "This project was to design a set of welding robots to help Ningbo Tuopu's swing-arm robots install protective leather covers automatically. We have designed and supplied welding robots for Geely, Volvo and GM in Shanghai and Beijing Automotive. Now we are working at designing swing arms for Beijing Automotive. These companies have high demands in terms of delivery time. Their timetable for the whole production process is calculated in reverse according to the product's delivery time. So, the deadline is strict and rigid." The production process must be conducted strictly according to the timetable. Otherwise, the components cannot be assembled for the next procedure. If a component is completed behind schedule, customers might suffer a great loss.

Li Zhenggang said, "In Shanghai, if the automobile assembly line in GM pauses for 15 min, even the secretary of the Shanghai Municipal Committee will come to ask why. Generally speaking, once a new model is released, it must sell well. If one car can generate a profit of 20,000 yuan, what a large profit it will make after a whole day's selling! Like Geely's Buorui [a model of car], the ordering list was placed several months ago. Now, you may queue for a long time to order one Buorui. Delaying one day means a loss of several million yuan for the manufacturer. So, everybody will not allow a delay because they cannot afford a delay."

Usually, the deadline for product delivery was strictly established once a project was set up. Then, the project manager would divide the whole project into several units, with every unit being under the charge of a particular individual. To finish the project on schedule, the team led by Yang Yongshuai had worked overtime in the workshop for several months. The solution they adopted was to make their welding robots wake up the sleeping foreign robots by using a Chinese core control system. Once the foreign robots passed out completely, the welding robot could take on their job as backup and make sure the procedure was conducted smoothly. Why didn't they directly replace the foreign robots with domestic welding robots? The SIASUN team always considered their customers. Economically speaking, the structure and body of the foreign robots were still in good shape. The vehicles worked; only the control unit had broken down. So, they tried to wake the foreign robots up with welding robots, rather than completely abandoning them.

To fulfil a series of robot functions and meet the demands of the customer, the team had to break through the core controlling technique to ensure that every part worked in coordination to achieve a better effect. Yang Yongshuai considered solutions over and over again with other members and clearly listed all the technical risks of various degrees of uncertainty. "At the beginning, we set out several plans, but each plan contains certain risks. You cannot determine in advance which approach will work. As a result, we design at least three plans for each eventuality in parallel. If one solution does not work, we may turn to another one."

During that period of time, in order to tackle the problem and stick to the schedule, Yang led the team over three months of hard work, living up to people's expectation by waking up the foreign robots with a Chinese core control unit and successfully turning the "key" for Ningbo Tuopu. This was a breakthrough upgrade for the manufacturing and production arm of the Ningbo Tuopu Group.

SIASUN solved what the German company could not deal with, which made the customer very satisfied. This successful cooperation brought about subsequent orders. Then, Ningbo Tuopu purchased another three production lines from SIASUN in Hangzhou and invested more than four million yuan in each.

SIASUN established its reputation in the Yangtze River Delta area and its business expanded rapidly. The "ambition" to create Chinese robots was boosted in the most dynamic of coastal markets.

III. SIASUN's newness

There is a popular saying among the SIASUN employees: "If something has already been done by others, let them carry on. Do not eat buns chewed by others and do not follow the path paved by others. What we should do is open up new research fields, develop new products and create new value."

Innovation based on daily life is only one side of SIASUN's newness. It also has a secret team, namely, the "innovation team" of the Shanghai SIASUN Co., Ltd. It is the heart of the world of robots and the team holds up "innovation" as its constant pursuit.

One day in May 2016 when vice president Yang Luo passed by a conference room of the Innovation and Research Centre, he could overhear a heated debate inside Through floor-to-ceiling glass, he saw a group of young people sitting around, within which a male technician was bitterly quarrelling with a female technician.

This is a pretty common scenario for Yang; sometimes he also joins in. Yang gently pushed the glass door and jokingly said, "Hey guys! Arguing is okay but no fighting please". His words amused everyone. The young group got back to reality after indulging in their dreams of fantasy and continued their discussion. This is an innovation and research team consisting more than 100 people in SIASUN known as the "Stars of Innovation".

In April 2016, the "Stars of Innovation" were introduced to the Innovation and Research Centre, which had just opened in the Shanghai Jinqiao Development Zone. Most of them were young people of the post-1980 or 1990 generation. Some quit well-paying jobs in leading enterprises in foreign countries, while others had just got back from overseas studies, to join SIASUN. They had the same dream to build Chinese robots with oriental wisdom.

The scene described above concerns a quarrel about the technical control path of the dual-arm collaborative robot between engineers Chen Hongwei and Fan Liangliang, each refusing to give way and engaging in a heated argument. Most people might find it difficult to understand what they were doing. They are dream-filled zealots among the "Stars of Innovation" whose imagination knows no boundary. Is it necessary? Yes. It is exactly during such a collision of ideas that the spark of innovation is created. Who could foretell what they would come up with tomorrow? This is their rhapsody of innovation.

The dual-arm collaborative robot represents cutting-edge technology in the field of industrial robots. Each of its arms has seven axes or joints, fully performing the functions of human arms. At present, YuMi, as developed by the ABB Group, is the first of its kind in terms of dual-arm industrial robots used in human-machine collaboration and has been displayed in several exhibitions. Yet, it has a very low payload and can only fold paper airplanes.

The aim of the Innovation and Research Team of SIASUN is to equip the dual-arm collaborative robot with the arm strength of an adult. But this is not enough. They will also give eyes to the robot in order for it to decide its own moves according to the surroundings it sees. It is unique at home and second to none in the world. The dual-arm collaborative robot will surely have promising prospects.

In 2014, Shanghai Waigaoqiao Shipbuilding Co., Ltd., encountered a problem and asked SIASUN for help. Marine coating and cleaning were hard work. With complex and dangerous air operations, recruitment was getting tougher. Could robots do the work?

Waigaoqiao is the bellwether of the domestic shipbuilding sector and its shipwrights are bent on catching up with and overtaking their overseas counterparts to reach the advanced world level. However, the current working method has made it impossible, especially when human coating is faced with problems. With rising living standards, people are increasingly reluctant to undertake dirty, tiring and unhealthy work like ship coating. Besides, the coating needs air operations and, with such danger, recruitment is difficult. How to replace humans with robots and realize coating automation have become the problems to be solved by all shipbuilding companies.

The demand from Waigaoqiao and the desire of its shipwrights have motivated the Innovation and Research Team of SIASUN to innovate. They have conducted research on domestic and overseas shipbuilding industries and searched for the products needed. They found out a few years ago that the Japanese had come up with an approach but there were no products to show for it. Indeed, until now, no mature climbing robots for coating have ever appeared in the market. They foresaw a huge market for developing a "smart climbing and spraying robot" for coating and cleaning ships and large oil tankers.

The team put the idea into a project right away and got support from senior executives. The project was led by Liu Baojun, manager of the Research and Development Department. Liu, with his team of more than 10 young people, came to Waigaoqiao, communicated many times with its workers and identified a development path. After a year of tackling problems, Liu brought the "smart climbing and spraying robot" to the company for a trial. This fellow, the "climbing gecko", as it was known by the workers, was rather difficult to teach. It either swung in strong wind or was burned by the ship body at high temperature and scrambled all over the place in the burning sun.

Liu and his team had spent two years with the "climbing gecko". In the summer of 2015, because of the El Nino effect, Shanghai witnessed uncommonly high temperatures, up to 40°C in July and August. It was said that many Shanghai people went to Sanya to cool off. In the scorching sun, the temperature at the Waigaoqiao site reached 50°C and workers hit by sunstroke were sent to the hospital from time to time. Wearing safety helmets and overalls, Liu and his teammates stayed in their posts at the worksite. They could not wear sun helmets or hold sun umbrellas because they had to raise their heads to stare at the "climbing gecko" and debug the control system. Sweat salted their eyes and dizziness struck them within a short while; thus, they had to take turns to conduct trials. You could see how much effort was made judging from the dark bony faces of Liu and his teammates.

After two years of struggling and hard work, the team finally tamed the "climbing gecko" into a "worker with eyes and a mind". This fellow looks like a blue turtle, easily climbing the ship body's incline of 90° or even 100°. Without any cable or safety belt, it can still carry several spay guns, simultaneously and precisely coating ships. No matter how hostile the environment is, it is always meticulous and does a wonderful job. A "smart climbing and spraying robot" can replace four or five workers and work 24 h without stopping. All that is required is for one person to control the robot on the ground.

The dream of shipwrights has become a reality with the help of SIASUN's research team. It fills the gaps in the domestic and overseas market, especially in terms of coating and cleaning robots for large ships in China. China's shipbuilding industry has taken one step further towards automation and intelligence.

Innovation conjures up something from nothing. It represents a kind of power and confidence by which to realize dreams in the future. SIASUN takes innovation as its core and its staff always has the desire to seek something new in its hearts.

On the last night of 2014, the annual party of welcoming in the new year, while bidding farewell to the old one, culminated in the unique visual gala from CCTV. In the state broadcaster's No. 1 Studio, the Annual Awards Ceremony for Personal Scientific and Technological Innovation, jointly sponsored by the CAS, the Ministry of Science and Technology, the Ministry of Education and the Chinese Academy of Engineering, among others, took place in an atmosphere of grandeur and solemnity. This was a ceremonious gathering in the scientific and technological academic community.

Lin Huimin, an academician from the CAS, announced the first winner of the award: "The team under his leadership has created 108 innovations, all for the first time in the development of China's robotic history, and the robots developed by them are used in 15 countries around the world. He created, for the first time, the 40-ton heavy-load bi-moving robot in 2014 and then took a leading position worldwide for the development of the 20-kg large-load vacuum robot. With full confidence, he and his team are creating a new chapter in the development of China's robotics. He is Professor

Qu Daokui, president of SIASUN Robot & Automatic Co., Ltd., in Shenyang."

Qu Daokui and Xiao Zhi, the third-generation service robot recently developed by SIASUN, walked side by side onto the stage in a composed manner. With one asking questions and the other one responding on the stage, they communicated and interacted with each other. They even played an improvisational Chinese fan dance, which was rewarded with applause that brought the house down. Qu Daokui explained the high technology involved in Xiao Zhi's smooth dancing for guests attending the ceremony. He said, with full confidence, that against the background of transforming and upgrading human production and life, the era of intelligence has arrived, in which the robot will definitely play a significant role. Wang Tianran, the awards presenter and an academician of the Chinese Academy of Engineering, walked onto the stage with a smile and presented the award to Qu Daokui. When their two pairs of hands were held firmly together, it was within nobody's capabilities to know that, for this glorious moment, two generations of scientific researchers had made unremitting efforts in succession with the same spirit of development continued over previous decades.

The host asked academician Wang Tianran in a humorous

manner, "You and Professor Qu are scientists of different generations, so what are the differences in your respective research goal and the ideal you are pursuing?" Wang Tianran said, in a pleasant tone, "The goal and the ideal are the same, but our work is very different. What our generation did at that time was to carry out research in the field of application experiments, while Qu Daokui put Chinese robots on the market and kept this process growing. This is great progress, with which a new era has been created."

With the wisdom of the East, scientists of two generations have opened the door of opportunity. Furthermore, it is due to their desire to make a contribution to the nation through industrial development that they have made diligent efforts to pioneer and innovate. Seizing the initial opportunities offered by the market by means of core technology development, they have realized numerous leap-forward innovations in China's robot industry and higher pursuits in their mind, time and time again, thus making the flag of China's robots fly high atop the summit of the mountain of global high technology and adding brilliance to the ancient land of China.

Chapter XI
Aiming at 2025

Action plan: China's demographic dividend is gradually depleting while labour costs are increasing.

How can China maintain a strong driving force for development and grow from a big country living on manufacturing into a manufacturing power?

I. China's support for development

According to the IFR, China purchased one fifth of the robots in the world in 2013 and, for the first time, surpassed Japan to become the world's largest buyer of industrial robots. In 2014, a total of 56,000 industrial robots were sold on the Chinese market, accounting for about a quarter of the total worldwide.

For two consecutive years, China has become the world's largest market for industrial robots. Then, according to statistics recently released by the China Robot Industry Alliance, the number of industrial robots reached 800,000 in China. From 2009 to 2014, the sales of industrial robots on the Chinese market grew at an average annual rate of 58.9%. This year is destined to be a glorious year in the history of the development of industrial robotic manufacturing. The whole world has seen a wider and more in-depth application of robots in various sectors, as well as their invincible force in pushing labour-intensive industries to transform and upgrade at a rapid rate. In China, it is beyond all doubt that the robotic industry has indeed become a sunrise industry and a deep blue sea in the era of big data.

Against this background, Chinese scientific and technological elites gathered in Beijing to discuss and explore measures addressing this upcoming "revolutionary wave of robotics".

On 9th June 2014, the 17th Academician Conference of the CAS and the 12th Academician Conference of the Chinese Academy of Engineering were held in Beijing. Leaders of the core leadership in China spoke at the conference and the general secretary of CPC Central Committee Xi Jinping made a memorable speech.

Wang Tianran and Feng Xisheng, two academicians with the SIA, attended the conference and listened to the general secretary's speech. Wang Tianran said: "We knew that the general secretary would speak at the conference, but I did not expect that he would in particular mention robots. Indeed, he talked so much and so profoundly about robots that he seemed like a professional in this regard. We were all excited, inspired and proud at the conference."

The address of the general secretary was a long speech of over 8,000 words, of which more than 1,100 words were about tasks and directions in the face of current high-tech development, with 400 words dedicated to robotics.

The speech of the general secretary has given unprecedented priority to the robotics industry, that is, the national strategic emerging industry. This means that it is of increasingly strategic significance to carry out robot-driven upgrades in the manufacturing industry. The Ministry of Industry and Information Technology subsequently made it clear that it would organize and establish the development road map for China's robotics and the 13th Five-year Plan for the robotic industry.

This is a fight for the future, which is highly integrated with the national intention, while offering local benefits and meeting corporate demands.

China is moving towards an ageing society. With the demographic dividend depleted and the labour force on the wane, how can China maintain a strong impetus in manufacturing and become a manufacturing power? These issues have already affected the foundation for China's economic development and social stability. China's intelligent manufacturing, which deems robotics as a "priceless pearl", will become a sharp weapon to overcome the predicament.

China's manufacturing industry is faced with a difficult situation, in which it is beset by competitors from all directions. To ensure China's competitiveness as the world's factory and win initiatives to develop in the future, it is time for its robotic industry to take part in this rivalry and assume the attendant responsibilities.

In 2014, the "pearl in the crown" shone enough to shed light on the journey towards the development of China's manufacturing industry, as well as represented the bright hope that China would become a scientific and technological power. A trumpet was blown by the Zhongnanhai to welcome the robot revolution!

Premier Li Keqiang first put forward the ambitious Made in China 2025 Plan in the *Report on the Work of the Government (2015)*, in which a major direction was set to vigorously promote the deep integration of informatization and industrialization in the next 10 years. China is still in the process of industrialization and dependent on manufacturing as its most important pillar and foundation for the national economy. This is a reality that cannot be ignored.

After three years' preparation, the Made in China 2025 Plan was officially released by the State Council on 8th May 2015. It outlined the strategic planning formulated by the CAS, an official think tank in China, and is considered as "the first 10-year road map for China's three-step transformation from a big country dependent on manufacturing to a manufacturing power with each step consisting of 10 years".

The Made in China 2025 Plan and Industry 4.0 both target intelligent manufacturing. Amid the Industry 4.0 competition, many developed countries and regions, such as the US and Europe, consider the development of robotics as a national strategy, which has exacerbated the competition.

In response, SIASUN has established its digitalized intelligent factory for the Industry 4.0 era, which is credited by the domestic robotic community as "the authoritative research and development institution for complete set technology and robotic automation equipment in China". SIASUN's next step is to copy this kind of production line nationwide. As a national brand of China and the bellwether of the domestic robotic industry, SIASUN will help the Made in China 2025 Plan to extend beyond China and go global in a real sense by taking full advantages of its innovative technologies and scientific platform.

II. Dazzling skills of a "superman"

At the same time, when the 10-year road map for the Made in China Plan was being prepared, the national departments of science and technology were exploring related applications.

In 2012, in order to improve the localization of the automobile manufacturing industry, the Ministry of Industry and Information Technology was determined to establish a localized research and application programme for China FAW's automobile welding assembly line as the benchmark project for China's intelligent factory.

This was the first project in China in which a great number of domestic robots was applied in the production line for automobile welding. This means that the key technology was the "pearl in the crown", namely, the robot.

In the rivalry among many domestic competitors, Wan Jintao, the representative of SIASUN, won the project bid. Appointed as the head in charge of this key project, he assumed the research and development task for the project along with his team. Looking at this honest young man, an expert couldn't help saying with worry: "You are so bold, Jintao. How dare you take on a project with such high requirements? If you mess it up, not only will SIASUN's fame be ruined, but also the confidence of automobile factories in domestic robots."

As the high-end industry for the application of robots, the automobile market is almost cornered by foreign countries. China FAW's programme for a domestic welding assembly line required the six-axis robot, which was the superior version among China's welding robots: a "superman" of robots. People in the robotic industry were then well aware that no manufacturers in China were capable of producing such advanced robots, not to mention the manufacturing techniques that could be applied to the production line. Could SIASUN's researchers develop qualified six-axis advanced robots and establish China's intelligent factory? It's no wonder that experts were worried.

"Please don't worry, experts. We can finish the task satisfactorily" said Wang Jintao, the general manager of SIASUN, who was born in 1980s but prudently Confucian-looking with a demeanour of a general.

Though still young, Wang Jintao remains rather dashing in spite of his politeness. He became a member of the research and development team at SIASUN after acquiring a doctoral degree; he is now the general manager of the Robot Business Department in SIASUN. In addition to his outstanding performance in the research and development programme for new robots, he is brave enough to challenge authorities around the world.

He is one of the key forces on the research and development team in SIASUN. In terms of industrial robot in this context, the computing method for a new type of buffing and polishing robot must be determined according to the modelling established in line with the textbook definition of a surface algorithm. But there was always an error in the computing and the causes could not be identified. Was there a problem with the textbook definition of a surface algorithm? In many people's opinion, it was an impossible situation! This algorithm was created by the French mathematician DeBoer.

Through numerous tests and verification, time and time again, Wang finally came to the conclusion that the textbook definition of a surface algorithm is defective. When he made a decision to correct this defective mathematical definition and propose a correction as the research topic for his graduation thesis, he was highly praised and supported by his tutor Qu Daokui. "Innovation is in need of being overturned. It is only through overturning the predecessor and overturning the past that breakthroughs and development can be achieved in the sciences." Qu said as much to encourage Wang. After revising the textbook definition of a surface algorithm, Wang sent his new conclusion to De Boer. Two weeks later, Wang received a passionate letter of thanks from De Boer, in which he confirmed that his surface algorithm was indeed imperfect and that the former definition was not precise, while promising to address the mistake in subsequent textbooks.

It was due to Wang's courage to explore, challenge and innovate that a technological difficulty, which hadn't been solved for a long time, was finally wiped out in the process of SIASUN's development of vacuum (clean room) robots. Later, he became one of the technological pioneers in the development of industrial robots and has since worked as the general manager of the Robot Business

Department.

In the research and development work into and application programmes for China FAW's automobile welding production line, it was necessary to initially address difficulties in the development of the six-axis industrial robot, as a high-quality industrial robot involved high technologies and high inputs in China. Wang Jintao was confronted by two tremendous pressures: the failure of the programme due to the failure of the whole production line; and the replacement of SIASUN's robots by foreign robots due to their lack of competence in meet the desired requirements. Either of the two consequences would mean the failure of the localization programme in China.

In this robot application programme, in addition to the technological difficulties concerning the six-axis welding robot that had to be solved, it was also necessary for the robots to be compatible with the former Japanese welding assembly line, which had definitely complicated the programme in respect of technology. Did the SIASUN development team have the spirit of inclusiveness and the wisdom of a "superman"?

Wang made the reply inspired by a wisdom characterized by the SIASUN spirit. Faced with various pressures and technical difficulties, both he and deputy general manager Chen Weilian led the team in order to demonstrate that the SIASUN spirit is focused on unyielding efforts and courageous innovations.

This was the first robot project in China in which Chinese robots would work together with foreign robots on the same production line. As the Yaskawa robots from Japan had been applied at an early stage, the standards of those foreign robots had to be taken into consideration during the design stage of the Chinese robots, which would be applied in the context of cooperative production at a later time, no matter how advanced the design would be. At the same time, when Chinese robots were applied on a large scale, a high rate of production also had to be maintained for Chinese robots on the basis of their compatibility with foreign robots. This was tantamount to competition between the Chinese robot and the Yaskawa robot from Japan on the same welding production line.

Wang Jintao and his team were usually faced with many operational logic and communications mistakes during the process of design, installation and debugging. In order to ensure the normal operation of the production line, they had to watch the production on the day while further optimizing the "brain" or control system of the Chinese robot at night when their clients were at rest, so as to make

Chinese welding robots more intelligent than the Japanese robots. Six months later, they finally overcame numerous difficulties and completed the project as scheduled. Experts came in order to approve the robots. Standing in front of the automobile welding production line on which the Chinese robots had competed with the foreign robots, the experts were so happy to see that the super version of the Chinese welding robot worked so flexibly with threads in its hands, such that its welding performance was not inferior to that of a foreign robot. They offered praise with a relieved mind: "This is the hope expressed in the Made in China Plan."

China's first "intelligent factory" came into being right there. This Sinicized automobile welding assembly line was quite successful due to its sound operation. This represented a major breakthrough in the application of Chinese robots in the field of automobiles and has since been widely applied in the production lines of Brilliance Auto and those of DFAC. Later, China's super welding robots were invited into the factories of some international automobile manufacturers such as GM, BMW and Volkswagen for upgrading purposes and to replace foreign robots.

In 2014, an error occurred in the system of the excavator big-arm welding robot imported by Shandong Lingong Construction

Machinery Co., Ltd. It was in need of repair, but the quotation from the original foreign manufacturer was too high. As workpieces in need of welding by this kind of welding robot are both large and thick, welding must be repeated across many layers several times. So, the quality of the welding by the robot cannot be ensured as thermal deformation and the like can easily cause a problem.

For a long time, medium- and heavy-plate welding has always been a high-end application in the field of robot welding. Only a few foreign robot companies have mastered such technology. Therefore, companies overseas have raised their prices. The managers of Shandong Lingong were caught in a dilemma as they were reluctant to give this money to foreign companies on the one hand, while the excavator big-arm welding robot would lie there useless if it was not fixed on the other hand.

On hearing this news, Wang Jintao came to Shandong Lingong. After a check, he knew that it was the foreign robot's "brain" (core control unit) that had gone out of service. He promised Shandong Lingong that SIASUN would solve the problem in the foreign robot's "brain" by replacing it with the "brain" of a Chinese robot. Is it possible for a Chinese company to fix the problem of a foreign robot? Half believing in the promise, Shandong Lingong had just established a contract with SIASUN, in which it was stipulated that no money would be paid until the "illness" of the foreign robot had been "cured".

Another six months flew by with intense research and development. In the end, the team led by Wang Jintao fixed the problem by completely substituting the control system in the foreign robot with that of the Chinese robot. With the foreign robot controlled by the brain of the Chinese robot, the client carried out welding on large workpieces. Flaw detection was then applied to every workpiece and the result was perfect. The general manager of Shandong Lingong was very happy: "From now on, let's use our Chinese robots and say goodbye to the foreigners." He immediately entered into a purchase contract with SIASUN to purchase more than 10 sets of excavator big-arm welding robots. This is how Chinese robots developed towards the high end and grew into a major force in China's manufacturing.

III. Liang Liang's show in the Zhongnanhai

On 20th August 2015, Wang Jintao, general manager of the Robot Business Department of SIASUN, suddenly received a telephone call from Qu Daokui, asking him to go immediately to Beijing and bring with him SIASUN's robots. This was because SIASUN's robots had been invited to give a show in the Zhongnanhai.

SIASUN's two intelligent service robots, Yue Yue and Liang Liang, have been familiar faces at some grand occasions, serving respectively as Miss Etiquette and Mr Etiquette, who greet guests with their tender, childlike tones. Yue Yue is of course beautiful, but Liang Liang's muscular figure is more attractive. This pair of perfect partners have become superstars at large events and attracting the attention of many guests.

A couple of years ago, when the Shenyang Administrative Examination and Approval Centre was officially put into operation, Yue Yue and Liang Liang were invited to be Miss Etiquette and Mr Etiquette. They dutifully performed their jobs without any complaints or demanding any extra conditions for their work. Therefore, they earned the praises and love of the people. The centre kept them and handed over special positions to them. Since then, Yue Yue and Liang Liang have become famous.

This time, Liang Liang was invited to go to the Zhongnanhai. It was soon known that the State Council would host the first special lecture for this administration in the No.1 Conference Room in the Zhongnanhai on the following afternoon. The lecturer was the academician Lu Bingheng, a 70-year-old senior expert, while the audience included the premier and the vice premier of the State Council, as well as state councillors, ministers and major heads of state-owned enterprises and financial institutions. The number of VIPs attending such a lecture was unique.

The No.1 Conference Room is usually the place where the executive meetings of the State Council are convened for discussions on key policies. But, on that day, it hosted a special lecture with a fashionable topic: advanced manufacturing and 3D printing.

In fact, the arrangement of this lecture was quite innovative in itself. In addition to conventional staff, there was a special guest: an intelligent robot. Isn't that Liang Liang? People at the lecture sent pictures and videos to the author's smartphone. Standing at the entrance of the venue in politeness, Liang Liang was holding a silver tray and presenting drinks to participants in the lecture.

Premier Li Keqiang came over at that moment. His eyes sparkled with delight when he noticed that Liang Liang wore "a smile on his face". In a bright mood, Premier Li Keqiang said, "Isn't this SIASUN's robot?" Liang Liang's many little friends were also invited to attend this important activity, including SIASUN's vacuum (clean room) robot. They were arranged in a special area, each displaying their unique charm to the listeners with a different expression. Indeed, every one of them was a "representative" in the field of China's high technology.

Premier Li Keqiang hosted this special lecture. He made it crystal clear that today's technological revolution plays an extremely crucial role in promoting economic development and upgrading. We are encouraging popular entrepreneurship and innovation and it is also through means of innovation that opportunities for business start-ups are created. Premier Li said: "Leaders of the State Council, every minister, heads of SOEs and financial institutes are invited to attend this lecture, because this lecture can expand our knowledge and inspire us to think in an innovative way."

In order to motivate China's manufacturing industry to grow from big to strong, implementing actions related to the Made in China 2025 Plan and the Internet Plus Plan must be speeded up, while industrial and technological changes and reforms must be achieved through business start-ups and entrepreneurial innovation. China's manufacturing industry can foster new advantages through transformation in the development mode and reach for the medium- and high-end level. While learning new technologies in the lecture, nearly 100 listeners felt the charm of contemporary intelligent science and technology by watching the performance of these intelligent robots.

IV. The alliance between BMW and SIASUN

On 14th June 2016, German Chancellor Angela Merkel came to Shenyang and made a special visit to the BMW Brilliance Automotive Tiexi Plant, where she cut the ribbon at a ceremony away from the assembly line for the new BMW X1 plug-in hybrid model.

Somebody said that Shenyang is the best industrial base in China and that Germany is the best industrial country in the world. The alliance between them would be the best thing in the world's industrial history!

In 2013, BMW of Germany wanted to build a new engine plant in Shenyang. This was the first time that the BMW engine would leave its headquarters in Germany and be produced overseas. German people are renowned for their strictness in manufacturing. In terms of strategic measures, the Germans, by no means, make an easy decision.

The BMW engine is "an in-house treasure" in Germany, for which the Germans want to seek a "house" overseas. What German people value is not only the Chinese market, but also the city of Shenyang in China. They want to achieve a radiating expansion from here to cover the whole area of China and even Southeast Asia by exploiting the advantages in science, technology and location along the so-called Ruhr of China. This is a plan for technological expansion as well as the pursuit of strategic development.

But the "house" of BMW is by no means a conventional one; rather, it is aligned to the standards of Industry 4.0. The person in charge of the bidding for the BMW engine project was Ralph Hattler, a senior expert. He is so experienced that he knows all about the robotic technologies of various countries in the world like the palm of his own hand. In the field of industrial manufacturing, the Germans have a particular standard for foreign products.

After an initial round of verification, they at last decided to introduce German robots into Shenyang. Then, while no one knows where it came from, the Germans heard something about SIASUN Robot & Automatic Co., Ltd., in Shenyang and knew that its robots had been used in core plants of GM.

Half believing what he had heard, Ralph still came to 16 Jinhui Street in the Hunnan High-tech Development Zone, Shenyang, in other words, the address of SIASUN, and knocked on the door to pay SIASUN a visit.

Qu Daokui led Ralph to visit SIASUN's workshops at first, during which Ralph opened his blue eyes wide all the way. When Qu Daokui led him into SIASUN's production line shop, where the "artificial man is produced by an artificial man", Ralph couldn't help but exclaim a "wow". It was so startling that he couldn't believe what he was seeing. It was beyond his expectation that SIASUN was capable of producing robots with the help of robots. Ralph changed his mind; no more arrogance nor prejudice. He extended his hands toward Qu Daokui in enthusiasm.

Returning to headquarters in Germany, he firmly expressed: "Why should we seek a partner from afar while neglecting one that is within our reach. China's SIASUN is our best partner." The headquarters subsequently decided to choose SIASUN as its preferred partner. Soon afterwards, a delegation of experts sent by the BMW headquarters came to Shenyang and negotiated with the company. BMW of Germany decided to build an engine plant in Shenyang and SIASUN was completely qualified to participate in the open bidding for the automated storage and retrieval system.

This was the first time that SIASUN had to compete with international tycoons on an equal footing.

In the end, SIASUN won the bidding due to its AGVs involving an all-weather navigation system, which turned out to be the favourite of BMW.

SIASUN's success on the BMW programme has become the stuff of legends in the robotic industry. But that was just Qu Daokui's first trump.

In September 2015, the author went to Shenyang for an interview at the BMW Brilliance Automotive Tiexi Plant. Located in Shenyang Economic and Technological Development Zone, Liaoning Province, the Tiexi Plant covers an area of 2.07 km^2 and is the production base for the BMW X1 and BMW 3 series, albeit made in China. It is also the 25th latest plant belonging to the BMW Group in the world. It has a total investment of up to 1.5 billion euros and is designed under a unified plan with the construction consisting of several phases. According to the planning of world-class factories, this factory was to be provided with four major techniques regarding automotive manufacturing, namely, stamping, welding, painting and final assembly. In the assembly shop, there were as many as over 300 robots. It's the shop with the highest rate of automation in the whole Tiexi Plant.

In the engine manufacturing shop, the author saw SIASUN's intelligent compound robot, a kind of "porter" combining SIASUN's AGV and welding robot. Running merrily to and from in the automated warehouse, it flexibly placed the hot sand core on vertical racks one after another. A German expert at the scene told the author that they had intended to adopt conventional automatic charging technology, requiring the use of at least 10 robots. But SIASUN adopted exclusive technology for the purposes of automatic battery replacement. When the power of the "porter" is exhausted, it will replace the battery at the charging station, instead of queuing up for charging. Six sets of such robots are quite enough to meet the demands. It is cost-effective as well as resource-saving.

It is due to the continued penetration of Chinese high technologies in German projects that the Sino-German Industrial Park has been built in the Tiexi High-tech Development Zone in Shenyang.

Chapter XII
The Giant Continues
to Move Forward

When elites gather together, who can accept the "admission ticket" for the future in advance?

The action moment for the first phalanx of Chinese robots.

I. China supports the robot

On 23rd November 2015, that year's WRC was held ceremoniously at the National Convention Centre in Beijing! Technological authorities, experts and scholars from all over the world came to exchange views about robots, with different types of "elite" in robotics coming together.

With the dream ahead of the journey, we can follow it in reality. This was a grand gathering for an all-round display of academic results in robotics and industrial intelligence! This was a gala for robots as well as a world-class "grand gathering of intelligent technology".

As indicated by the theme of the 2015 WRC (Leading to an

Intelligent Society through Collaboration, Convergence and Win-Win, China will work with world-class research and development teams and institutions to build an innovative platform for international cooperation and collaborative development in the field of robotics.

Snow covered the whole of Beijing just a couple of days before. 2015 was somehow called by meteorologists as the year in which the fiercest El Nino phenomenon would occur in history. In late November, the north of the Yangtze River welcomed a heavy snow. It was a fine day after the snow. The whole world was wrapped up in white, with the cold wind blowing vehemently. During the time when the WRC was being held, the temperature in Beijing suddenly dropped to the record low in the same period. Despite the coldness, the entrance to the National Convention Centre was still crowded with enthusiastic delegates at 9 a.m. The fervency triggered by robots in the land of China swiftly swept away the coldness in recent days. This was a new scene in China thanks to the robots.

The conference was hosted by the China Association for Science and Technology, the Ministry of Industry and Information Technology and the Beijing Municipal People's Government. More than 100 domestic and foreign companies participated in the Robot

Expo to showcase leading robot products.

Due to careful planning by the organizers, the conference consisted of three parts, namely, the World Robot Forum 2015, the World Robot Expo 2015 and the World Adolescent Robot Contest 2015, in which discussions, exhibitions and competitions were held, and various marvellous talents and robots had gathered to show their amazing skills. The conference had immediately become a focus of the world's attention and attracted much concern among the public. This was the panoramic rehearsal for "a future created by intelligent technology" as well as an early admission to "a smart life".

Who can accept the "admission ticket" for the future in advance?

At the entrance of the exhibition hall, a row of big characters jumped into sight saying "The Future Created by Intelligent Technology and a Smart Life": that was SIASUN's theme for this conference. Exhibition Booth A001 facing the entrance of the exhibition hall was the area for SIASUN.

Visitors rushed around all at once.

"Hello! You are welcome to visit SIASUN." Yue Yue and Liang Liang, whirling merrily with a pair of sparkling, smiling eyes, kept greeting the visitors enthusiastically. On this day, Liang Liang was cool and Yue Yue was very beautiful. Both of them were in new costumes: there was a brooch on Yue Yue's chest, and a pink scarf around Liang Liang's neck, which spoke to beauty, warmth and joy.

Some curious visitors walked onto the exhibition stage, holding the hands of Yue Yue and Liang Liang, asking: "What are your names? Can you play with us?" Yue Yue and Liang Liang talked and interacted with the visitors. Some people asked Yue Yue and Liang Liang to dance. They invited a girl to dance together to the music. What a great improvement for Yue Yue and Liang Liang in just a short period of time!

But it is SIASUN that should be treated with increased respect. If you are a visitor with a pair of careful eyes, you would notice that all the elite robots from SIASUN's five production lines have been displayed on the exhibition platform for visitors, which includes the industrial robot, the AGV, the clean room robot, the service robot, and the special purpose robot. The three bluish-white single-armed seven-axis robots are, in particular, slim and flexible, breaking people's impression that the robot hand was originally rigid and awkward in appearance. The music played when the single-armed seven-axis robots were performing. A Taiji martial artist dressed in white went onto the platform and cooperated with the robots to deliver a Taiji performance.

The stunning skills of SIASUN's robots at Exhibition Booth A001 attracted the attention of all the people in the exhibition hall! It was the debut for Chinese robots on an international stage! SIASUN's gift for surprising the audience are the compound robot and the single-armed seven-axis robot: both of them were not only the most intelligent robots at the Expo, but also the first two intelligent robots launched by China. High intelligence had been displayed through various means at the Expo, which was a feast for the eye. Every visitor enjoyed the exhibition and was unwilling to resist every wonderful performance. However, compared with those dazzling robots with special skills, the opening ceremony in the main venue and the activities in the main forum were even more exciting.

Around this time, in the hall of the Robot Expo, which covered more than two million m^2, various cool high-tech robots became the most eye-catching attractions due to their different styles and marvellous skills. Like immortals with unique magic akin to the Eight Immortals in Chinese mythology, the industrial robots showed their "muscles" by moving their big arms, while the flexible and smart service robots and special robots demonstrated their capacity to carry out every conceivable mission, as witnessed by those gathered on-site, thus representing a consensus in the robotic industry that

China had welcomed in the era of robots.

Fabo, a junior robot among all the robots, came over towards the audience when they set foot in the exhibition hall. "Hello, I'm robot Fabo. I feel so excited to see so many visitors. Please forgive me if I say something improper. I'm only aged one year old after all." This childish sound came from the household robot Fabo. He resembled "Baymax" (a comic character) in appearance, wearing a glass mask on his round face, in which there was a pad. There were also many honeycomb-like holes in the bottom, containing built-in air purifiers. What could Fabo do for the average household? "I'm capable of many things like singing, dancing, watching movies, chatting with you, learning things, telling stories, controlling home appliances, and purifying air." Everybody would love this type of robot. Fabo was co-developed by Beijing Evolver Robot Technology Co., Ltd., and Beihang University. Engineer Liu Ping explained to the audience that the small-scale quantitative production of Fabo had cost under 10,000 yuan. It was no longer hard for ordinary households to purchase Fabo.

"Beep!" A whistle sounded. "Kick off!" In the robot football performance area, a robot football match had started. There were two teams, Red and Blue, each consisting of five cute Little Naos (AI robots for competitive performances). With their eyes flashing, they rushed toward the orange-red small football. In fact, they movements were not fast, but the competition was really heart-stirring. The two teams were as strong as two national football teams. The Blue team was the robot football team of the University of New South Wales in Australia and had already won the World Cup Championship. The Red team was the robot football team from the University of Science and Technology of China.

"Whoops, it fell. Can it stand up on its own?" A Little Nao on the Red side fell down and the audience began to worry about it. But the Little Nao got up off the ground, bent its legs and, with a swift movement like that of a bouncing fish, rose to its feet. It stood like a man. The audience exclaimed: "It stood up. It stood up!" At this moment, a Red Little Nao kicked off in the midfield and the ball went straight into the goal. The Blue goalkeeper fell voluntarily to the left like a general, blocking the ball outside the goal. The attack was neat, so was the defence. The audience awarded the adamant Little Naos with enthusiastic applause...

At the Expo, visitors totalled 12,000 on the first day, 15,000 on the second day, and was expected to exceed 10,000 on the third day. The exhibition hall was certainly crowded. At this conference, the Beijing Consensus and the concept of mutual harmony, mutual sharing, mutual creation and win-win were put in the spotlight, a sign of joint efforts for the development of human civilization.

The results of this conference can be summed up by the following four sentences: providing opportunities for innovators to learn, offering cooperative platforms for corporations, guiding the way for entrepreneurs, and inspiring adolescents to forge a spirit of innovation.

Chinese robots were welcoming in an exciting new era.

II. Necessary harmony between human and robot

At the beginning of July 2015, a report in the Western media about the "killing" of a man by a robot spread quickly, which caused people to panic for a while. It is due to this false news that scientists involved in robotic research in China have given serious and profound consideration to robots.

Four guests were invited to make speeches on strategy and development trends at the summit forum of the conference. Wang Tianran, director of the National Engineering Research Centre on Robotics, a researcher at the SIA and an academician of the Chinese Academy of Engineering, first gave a speech titled 'Robots

In Support of China's Intelligent Manufacturing', in which he mentioned that robots are indispensable to China's goal of intelligent manufacturing and that the next-generation robot should work harmoniously with humans, which will be an opportunity for China as well as provide the direction of development that should be prioritized.

Wan Tianran has worked on robots for over 30 years and is a respectable expert in the field of robotics. As far as he is concerned about this topic, the so-called harmony between human and robot refers to the capabilities of the robot in terms of working closely and cooperatively with humans in the same normal environment, improving their own skills independently and safely interacting with humans in a natural way.

Professor Zhao Jie is the director of the School of Robotics at the Harbin Institute of Technology and the team leader of intelligent robot research for the 12th Five-year Plan and the 863 Programme. He said: "The harmony between human and robot is indeed the focus of concern among the public at present. The relationship between human and robot will change, if harmony between human and robot is realized. It is a relation of friendship between the two sides. They can understand each other, know each other and help each other. It is against our intention and against the direction we want to pursue if the robot were to simply bring harm to people."

It was on that very day that the news of the death of a worker at the hands of a production line robot belonging to Volkswagen appeared in the Western media, prompting uproar among the public. Readers exclaimed that the science fiction of Hollywood movies was becoming a reality. Is it possible that the robot is a threat to humans? Professor Zhao Jie responded thus: "This is a misunderstanding about the robot. The report in the Western media is exaggerated, but it is also a warning for us. How to achieve human-robot harmony has become a prominent problem and it is worthy of close attention by the robotic industry."

In recent years, as technology has become more and more mature and sophisticated, the AI possessed by robots has also become more and more advanced. Therefore, some experts have put forward the theory of robot threat, claiming that scenes in novels could happen in reality. In fact, we are still unable to make a conclusion about whether robots with AI capabilities will harm humans.

However, the accident that happened in the Volkswagen factory around that time indeed concerned public, while those in favour of the theory of robot threat are becoming more and more firm in believing their opinions. It was reported that the tragic accident happened in a Volkswagen factory located near Kassel. A 21-year-old technician was suddenly caught by a robot and pressed onto an iron plate when he was installing the robot with his colleagues. He was severely hurt and died of serious injury. Qu Daokui said in a disapproving manner: "It is impossible for robots to launch active attacks against people. As of today, there is no such a thing as this. If this really happened, it must be a workplace accident caused by improper operation. The media has exaggerated the truth."

Two years ago, the Australian media reported an incident about a robot that had burnt itself. According to reports, this self-burning robot was an advanced sweeping robot. It had become fed up with family chores and burnt itself because it was so dissatisfied with reality. There was a fire but the firefighters only saw ashes when they arrived. The male owner of the robot insisted that it had been turned off before he left the house. He was preparing to sue the robot maker. Thus, the automatic turn-on and mysterious suicide of the robot have remained a case without answers. This robot was just an advanced automatic vacuum cleaner, not intelligent enough to kill itself. Such groundless news has no reason. But it is a piece of evidence confirming that people are asking themselves, "How should humans treat robots? And how should humans get along with robots?"

Mankind is faced with the issue of harmony between human and robot.

As soon as the turmoil triggered by the robot accident had subsided, people noticed that a huge warning sign had been erected in the most prominent place at the gate of the BMW Brilliance Tiexi Factory in Shenyang. Anybody who wanted to enter the factory had to receive safety training from the security personnel and wear helmets, goggles, working clothes and protective boots. Have these strict protective measures being taken because of the accident caused by the robot at Volkswagen? According to an engineering technician of SIASUN, Germans have always been rigorous and strict, as well as recently increased their safety standards. In the factory area as well as in the shops, a lot of safety warnings about the use of robot and mechanical arm can be seen. In an effort to prevent injuries caused by the mechanical arm, robots are either kept in special cages or in places where guardrails are installed to keep them away from people. It seems that Germans have become more careful in this regard since the accident.

German Volkswagen soon confirmed the news of the accident. The technician violated security regulations during his shift. He entered the safety cage to install the mechanical arm and an improper operation led to the accident. Terror is not the key to solving problems. It is through innovation that problems can be solved and terror expelled. Instead of rejecting the service of robots, it's better to embrace robots and make them serve humans for the better. We cannot always treat AI as a zero-sum game between human and robot. We should also spot the "multiple-sum" logic in all this. The robot functions to assist humans in finishing certain tasks.

Human-robot harmony has become an issue of common concern among scientists all over the world. Wang Tianran said that, in terms of the fulfilment of human-robot harmony, SIASUN has already achieved worthwhile results in exploration, as well as found a way to approach that goal step by step. In the exhibition hall of the Expo, SIASUN's first-ever single-armed seven-axis robot had a contest with a Taiji player. They interacted with each other in such a harmonious way that waves of applause from the audience were heard time and time again. This was truly a special way to present the harmony between human and robot.

However, although it is the ultimate goal of the people to produce robots that can understand the world like human beings, there is still a long way to go from a macro perspective.

III. Beijing Consensus

On the evening of 23rd November 2015, the "Night of Innovation" was ceremoniously held with a grand gathering of elites from all over the world, representing the culmination of the 2015 WRC in Beijing.

In a warm atmosphere, the academician Wang Tianran and the president of SIASUN Qu Daokuo invited Professor Tan Zizhong and Professor Xi Ning to sign the Beijing Consensus on Robotic Innovation and Cooperation together with more than 200 experts and scholars from home and abroad. They agreed to work together to strengthen international academic and industrial exchanges on robotics, establish an international cooperation and training mechanism for robot talents, popularize robotic knowledge and promote robotic applications, and extensively inspire a passion for the innovation of robots in society, thus accelerating the sound development of China's robotic industry.

Speaking of the feelings about this particular WRC, Professor Tan Zizhong said earnestly: "I feel quite happy and relieved to see the performances of the robots. This is a good start after all. But really good companies like SIASUN are still too few in number. Some companies seem pretty high-end, but they are quite weak in crucial technologies. The development of technology is a long journey. There's no shortcut except to go forward step by step. However, thanks to strong support from the Chinese government, it is the time for Chinese robots. For many years, we have been longing for Chinese robots to stand on the stage of the world."

Shortly after the 2015 WRC was concluded, SIASUN and the North-eastern University jointly established the Robot University. Its aim is to foster high-end talents in the field of robot development though cooperation between universities and enterprises.

In January 2016, it was again reported that SIASUN had successfully acquired 100% of the shareholder rights of the Tautlov Vocational Training School in Germany and that the Sino-German

SIASUN Education, Science and Technology Group, co-funded by SIASUN and Anxin Consulting Corporation, had been established, the first enterprise of its kind in China to acquire a German educational institute with 100% ownership. Making use of the practice and training bases of the "intelligent factories" in both China and Germany, SIASUN will make it a priority to support "Chinese craftsmanship" through cultivating and fostering highly qualified and capable technicians and engineers. This acquisition is of great significance for the introduction of Germany's dual educational system in a comprehensive and in-depth way, as well as for the implementation of the Made in China 2025 Plan.

Currently, SIASUN is once again planning to upgrade the company by carrying out the "4 Plus 2" Strategy in the future, namely, the strategy of four industrial sectors plus the strategy of two platforms. The four industrial sectors refer to Industry 4.0 intelligent manufacturing, the service robot, special purpose manufacturing for national defence and vocational education, while the two platforms are the innovation platform and the finance platform. With fresh planning and new dreams, SIASUN will launch a new high-speed expedition with high expectations.

On 16th June 2016, another piece of exciting news was

announced: the meeting to establish the China Robot Top 10 Summit, voluntarily initiated by the backbone enterprises in China's robotic industry, would be held at SIASUN in Shenyang.

Focusing on the strategic targets of the Made in China 2025 Plan and combining the development phase of the 13th Five-year Plan for the robotic industry, this summit integrated governmental, industrial and financial resources to create a sound ecological environment for the development of China's robotic industry and guide its healthy sustainable development. It is expected to help the top 10 enterprises to grow into brands with international influence and competitiveness and help realize China's great leap from a big country dependent on robotic technologies to a strong nation owning advanced robotic technologies.

Xin Guobin, the then Deputy Minister of Industry and Information Technology, delivered a warm speech at the conference and put forward four constructive proposals and requirements for the development of China's robotic industry, which are of profound significance given the high expectations for China's robotic industry.

First, China's robotic industry must go fast as well as far. At present, a tendency towards a "low level of a high-end industry" is manifested in China's robotic industry, with no hidden worries about overinvestment. Robotic companies should avoid blind expansion and low-level redundant development.

Second, it is imperative to focus on reality as well as on the future. Enterprises must look to the future, pay attention to weak links in the industry, be aware of the development trends ahead, identify their own market places and work unremittingly to reap results in the long run.

Third, both independent development and cooperation are necessary, as well as paying attention to the cooperation between corporations in order to achieve complementary advantages and win-win benefits. Meanwhile, there should be focus on innovation in the robotic industry for it to better integrate with other industries.

Fourth, be dependent on ourselves and take advantage of others. Besides achieving the development of enterprises by making full use of their strengths in capital and talent, entrepreneurs should also have an international perspective and be good at using and integrating global resources.

At the ceremony hosted by Qu Daokui, representatives from 10 corporations, showing their determination and purposes with proud emotion, as shown by the Chinese nation, expressed a common declaration: through openness, pragmatism, innovation and collaboration, we will forge world-class robotic enterprises by means of strengthening self-discipline in industry, promoting fair competition, improving industrial innovation, enhancing product quality, fostering the industry chain, and promoting demonstrations of applications!

The Top 10 enterprises are:

Shenyang SIASUN Robot & Automation Co., Ltd.

Harbin Boshi Automation Co., Ltd.

Ninebot (Tianjin) Technology Co., Ltd.

Anhui Efort Intelligent Equipment Co., Ltd.

Nanjing Estun Automation Co., Ltd.

GSK CNC Equipment Co., Ltd.

Jiangsu Huibo Robot Technology Co., Ltd.

Beijing CANBOT Robotic Technology Co., Ltd.

Guangzhou Start to Sail Industrial Robot Co., Ltd.

Beijing TINAVI Medical Technologies Co., Ltd.

Among these 10 outstanding companies, six of them produce industrial robots and the other four develop service robots.

The top 10 corporations have come together to form the first phalanx of China's robot industry and sing the strongest chorus for the Made in China Plan.

Shouldering the hope of the national industries, they advance in long strides towards 2025 as well as the era of intelligence.